holly HORROR ™

HOLLY HORROR ™

Michelle Jabès Corpora

Penguin Workshop

PENGUIN WORKSHOP
An imprint of Penguin Random House LLC, New York

First published in the United States of America by Penguin Workshop,
an imprint of Penguin Random House LLC, New York, 2023

Holly Horror™ and related trademarks © 2023 Those Characters
From Cleveland, LLC. Used under license by Penguin Young Readers.

Inspired by the characters of Holly Hobbie

Visit us online at penguinrandomhouse.com.

Library of Congress Cataloging-in-Publication Data is available.

Printed in the United States of America

ISBN 9780593386217

1st Printing

LSCC

To my mother.
Who always came when I called,
Even in the darkest hour,
To chase the nightmares away.

The boundaries which divide Life from Death are at best shadowy and vague. Who shall say where the one ends, and where the other begins?

—Edgar Allan Poe

The little silver car darted down the country roads like a minnow, cresting the hills and dipping low into the valleys, carrying three new souls into western Massachusetts. Evie Archer sat in the passenger seat, watching the first few rust- and honey-colored leaves begin to fall. Beyond, the sun was low on the horizon, setting the mountaintops ablaze with golden light. Evie knew she should have appreciated the sight of a sky unbroken by apartment buildings and skyscrapers, but all it did was make her feel small.

She fingered the cream-colored lace of her favorite shirt—an old maroon cotton tee that she'd found thrifting and upcycled into something more fashionable. She'd cut off the sleeves and snipped the bottom into a wavy asymmetrical line, then sewed about a foot of vintage lace to the bottom to create a dramatic hem. A bit more lace around the neckline completed the look. She'd laid it out on her bed with a pair of comfortable jeans last night as her traveling outfit.

"So listen," her mother, Lynne, was saying as she took another tight turn. "You guys know that Hobbie House needs a lot of work, and I can't afford to have the whole place professionally cleaned right now, so we should start by fixing up the rooms we'll need right away."

"Sure, Mom," Evie said, wondering what her friends back home in New York were doing right now. Were they thinking about her? She checked her phone for messages, but there were none. She reasoned that it was still a school day; they were probably just busy. She put the phone facedown on her lap and tried not to think about it.

In the back seat, huddled among the duffel bags and suitcases, her younger brother, Stan, said nothing. Evie glanced back to see him hidden deep inside his black hoodie, playing some stupid game on his phone.

"Stan, honey, are you listening?" Mom said.

Stan grunted, just loud enough to be audible by human ears.

"Anyway," her mother continued as they approached another hairpin curve, "we'll tackle the bedrooms first, then the kitchen— oh, probably a bathroom we can all share, and—"

There was something in the road. Some lumbering, dark thing. Mom didn't see it because she was too busy talking about the house, but Evie saw it.

"Mom! Watch out!" Evie shouted.

"What?" her mother gasped, wrenching the steering wheel and slamming on the brakes. The little silver car swerved wildly, skidding to the side of the road. Evie shrieked as a rock was thrown up and hit the windshield like a bullet. The car came to a stop, and for a moment there was no sound inside except ragged breaths.

"What's wrong?" Mom exclaimed.

Evie turned to look behind them, certain she would see a small, bloodied corpse.

But there was nothing.

"I saw an animal in the road," Evie said, suddenly uncertain. "Like a small dog, or a cat or something. I thought we were going to hit it."

Mom eyed the tiny crack in the windshield where the rock had hit and sighed heavily. Evie noticed that despite the hours of packing, loading, traffic, and nearly crashing the car just now, her mother's wavy, caramel-colored hair still looked perfect. "Evie, I was *watching* the road. I didn't see any animal. You're lucky we didn't hit a tree or something. That wouldn't be a great way to start our new life here, now, would it?" She put the car back into gear and started driving again without another word.

"Sorry," Evie said after a moment. She ran her fingers through her hair. It was a little greasy.

"It's fine," Mom replied, in a tone that clearly said it wasn't. "Look! We're almost there." She pointed to a green road sign that read RAVENGLASS, 2 MILES. "Are you excited?"

Evie nodded, pasting on a smile. In the back seat, Stan hadn't moved. *Incredible . . .* she thought.

"Sometimes your eyes can play tricks on you, you know," Mom said, her voice softer now. "Sometimes we think we see things that aren't really there. Like a mirage in the desert."

"I guess so," Evie said, not wanting an argument.

But I did see it, she thought. She had seen it walk, seen its fur, seen its flashing eyes as it looked up at the car speeding toward it.

Didn't I?

Her mouth was dry, so she grabbed the Big Gulp of Coke that they'd picked up at a gas station and took a long drink. Something was stuck to the sweaty bottom of the plastic cup. Evie peeled it off and peered at it. A small yellow sticky note with four words written in pen: KEYS, CELL PHONE, WALLET. It was her father's handwriting. It must have been inside the cup holder when she'd set the Big Gulp down. He was always forgetting things—his lunch, his wallet, his children's birthdays—so he'd often write them down to remind himself. Artists were forgetful like that, he'd always said. Like that made up for everything.

Evie stared at the note for a moment before crumpling it up in her hand, opening the window, and throwing it out.

As they crested the next hill, an old wooden sign with gold letters came into view.

WELCOME TO RAVENGLASS, MASSACHUSETTS
EST. 1856

The local road they were on dropped them right at the center of Main Street, in the middle of a town that looked like the cover of an old *Saturday Evening Post* come to life—pure Americana, stars and stripes, and apple pie. A neat line of colonial-style buildings—cream and pale yellow with shutters painted in red and green—nestled under the far-reaching boughs of black oak trees, resplendent in their autumn colors. There were a few little shops and cafés, a redbrick church with a real bell in its belfry, an inn, a fancy restaurant, and a little place right at the edge of town called Birdie's Diner.

Evie sniffed the air, which smelled like a combination of fried chicken and something spicy. Her stomach growled. They hadn't eaten since leaving the city. "I'm hungry," she said.

"Have a granola bar," her mother said. "We'll pick something up after we get everything inside and settle in. Isn't the town lovely? It's just so . . ."

Evie went ahead and supplied the correct word. "Quaint."

She pulled a couple of bars from their snack bag and tossed one into the back seat, feeling a little bit satisfied when it bounced off Stan's head. It must have momentarily roused him from his phone coma, because a moment later, she could hear him munching.

"We're going to live *here*?" Stan asked, pressing his face against the window. "In the Land That Time Forgot? If they don't have Wi-Fi, I'm hitching a ride back home. Seriously."

"They have Wi-Fi, Stan," Mom replied smoothly. "And you can't hitchhike back home. This is our home now."

Evie swallowed a lump of granola and chocolate as the full impact of those words hit her. Everything she knew—her entire loud, crowded, messy life back in New York—was gone. Divorce had snuck up on her life last year and swallowed it whole, like a snake, leaving nothing behind but pain and memory.

After the settlement, her mother realized that they had a big problem. Mom's old job at the Hyatt didn't pay anywhere near enough for their three-bedroom apartment, not even with the child support payments, and especially not after all the legal fees. She had about two months' rent left in her savings, and then they were going to be living hand-to-mouth. Things looked grim until the night Evie overheard Mom call her sister, Martha Hobbie, and ask her a question that changed everything.

"Martha, do you think we could move to Hobbie House?"

Hobbie House.

Those words had been spoken in hushed tones throughout Evie's life, like a curse. The house, a place that had been in her mother's family for about fifty years, was up in a small town in the Berkshires called Ravenglass. Aunt Martha lived in an apartment in town there—and was the official caretaker for the house. Evie always wondered why her aunt didn't just live at Hobbie House. After having spent her whole life in cramped apartments, Evie could hardly imagine what it would be like to have all that *space.* Why would anyone choose some tiny apartment over an entire *house?*

Then again, Aunt Martha was a superstitious sort of person, and Hobbie House did have a certain . . . reputation.

Evie shivered, the breeze suddenly chilling her. She closed the window and pulled her dusky pink cardigan close around her shoulders. Regardless of the house's history, her mother saw it as their salvation. "A fresh start, a big bedroom for each of us, and best of all: *It's free!*" Mom had announced this to Evie and Stan after hanging up with Aunt Martha. Stan had immediately made it clear how much he hated this idea by going on a hunger strike and slamming doors, but Evie had just nodded and smiled. "That's great, Mom," she'd said.

"Isn't it?" Mom had replied. "Just what we needed. Some good news."

That night was the first time Evie let herself cry.

But now, surrounded by the stunning beauty and tranquility of Ravenglass, a tiny ray of hope pierced through her inner gloom.

Maybe life will be good here, she allowed herself to think. *Maybe it will be okay.*

The GPS on her mother's phone started to act funny once they left the town behind and went in search of Hobbie House. Because it was nearly two hundred years old, the house wasn't on Main Street, and it wasn't part of either of the two planned communities built in Ravenglass over the past sixty years. They followed the GPS down a one-lane street called Knickerbocker Road that dead-ended at an overgrown field, where a single, tumbledown shack stood, its broken windows glinting in the setting sun like jagged teeth.

"Well," Mom said, putting the car in reverse. "It's been forty years since I've been here, but I'm pretty sure that isn't the house."

"God, I hope not," Stan said, peeking through the space between the front seats to stare at the shack.

"We passed a mailbox a little while back," Evie said. "It was kind of hidden by some bushes. Maybe that was it?"

Once Mom turned the car around, she went along the little road slowly, and all three of them peered through the thick trees on both sides, looking for an opening.

"There!" Evie exclaimed, pointing. Sure enough, there was a rusty white mailbox, almost completely engulfed by creeper vines, next to a clearing in the trees and a narrow lane, leading up.

Mom rolled the car to a stop next to the mailbox, and Evie stuck her head out of the window to study it. Along the side, written in cracked black paint, were the letters *HH*. There was something else, too, something scribbled in faded red ink above the two letters. It looked like someone had tried to wash it off, with little success. Evie squinted. What did it say? After a moment, the words became clear.

HORROR HOUSE.

"This is it," she said, her voice dry. "We're here."

Her mother pulled the car into the narrow, winding lane and started to climb. A row of elm trees stood like sentinels alongside them, and once or twice Evie could have sworn she saw the flash of a white-tailed deer darting away at the sound of their approach. It wasn't until they'd reached the top of the hill that the trees cleared and they got their first glimpse of the house.

The house had two faces. One faced them, and the other looked away, as if staring into the distance back toward town. It had been white once, but time had erased all that, leaving most of it gray and rutted. Burgundy shutters framed the windows, which covered both faces and all sides of the octagonal tower that made up the left part of the house. Both sides boasted a wide porch, leading to doors painted blue. The place looked untouched by any living thing, aside from the bittersweet vines that grew everywhere, strangling porch posts and creeping like spiderwebs up as far as the two brickwork chimneys. Next to the house, a large apple tree stood alone, its trunk thick and twisted, its branches heavy with fruit.

"Look at that," Mom breathed. She glanced over at Evie. "What do you think?"

Evie stared at the house. For some reason, she was reminded of the scene where Pinocchio went deep into the ocean to save his father and was swallowed by the whale. A huge, ancient thing that had lived for centuries past, and would live on centuries more.

"Everything comes in," said Geppetto. *"Nothing goes out."*

"Evie?"

She was being ridiculous. It was just an old house that needed a few coats of paint and some pruning shears. Nothing more.

"It's amazing," she finally said. "I wonder what it looks like inside."

"Probably wall-to-wall rats," Stan said. "Black mold, *definitely* ghosts—"

"Shut *up*, Stan," Evie muttered, elbowing him in the chest.

"Ow! Mommm, she's hurting me!" He poked Evie in the ribs.

"Stan, stop annoying your sister. Oh! Look, there's Martha."

Up ahead, in a circular paved area in front of the house, a woman in a deep purple shawl stood watching them pull in. Next to her, a rickety hatchback sat idling, its engine burbling with effort.

Mom parked the car in front of the house and jumped out. "Sis," she said, opening her arms. "It's good to see you."

Evie hadn't seen her aunt in years, not since the last time she'd come to visit them in New York. She was like a Wonderland version of her mother. Instead of Mom's neat, wavy bob, Aunt Martha wore her hair long and silver gray. They were both thin, but Aunt Martha was gaunt, whereas Mom was slender. Next to her mother in her tan capris and tasteful turquoise blouse, Aunt Martha looked like a fairy-tale witch in her shawl, long black skirt, and tall leather boots. Mom wore only simple silver hoop earrings, but Aunt Martha looked as if she were wearing every piece of jewelry she owned. Gold bangles jingled on both wrists, rings studded with semiprecious stones adorned every finger, and around her neck hung a glass blue amulet of the evil eye. Despite the past year of trouble, Mom still looked vibrant, whereas Aunt Martha looked as if she had seen things she would rather not repeat. She had a certain feral wildness about her that was as different from her mother as Evie could imagine.

Aunt Martha smiled and embraced Mom, but Evie noticed that the smile did not reach her eyes. "Have a good trip?" she asked.

"Getting out of the city was a nightmare, obviously—but other than that, smooth sailing," Mom replied.

Aunt Martha turned her eyes to Evie and Stan, who had gotten out of the car and stood a little distance away. "Hey, kids," she said. Stan offered an awkward, one-armed hug. Evie, on the other hand, wrapped both her arms around her aunt and squeezed. She smelled like a smoky mixture of sandalwood and clove, and when she pulled away, Aunt Martha looked at her with a mixture of affection and something else that Evie couldn't decipher. "Well, I'm sure you're all tired from your journey and have a lot to do," she said, pulling away. She rummaged in the brown leather purse at her side and handed Mom a set of keys she found there. "Here you go. Those should open both front doors and the shed in the back. If you need anything, you can just—"

Mom blinked down at the keys that Aunt Martha had given her. She laughed. "You—you're not thinking of *leaving*, are you?"

Aunt Martha stood as rigid as the elm trees that surrounded them. She took one step back toward her rumbling car. "Well, yes. I have some clients coming in this afternoon, and I thought you'd want your space—"

Mom's nostrils flared. "Oh, I see. You have *clients*."

"Yes, I do."

Evie looked away. She knew that her mother's relationship with Aunt Martha was tense, at best, but Evie had hoped that things would be different now that they were moving to Ravenglass.

"I thought you'd at least come inside, catch up—"

Aunt Martha's face turned to stone. "I don't go inside, Lynne."

Mom stared at her. "What do you mean, you don't go inside? You've been the caretaker for this place for years."

"I hire people to keep up the place, just basic stuff. I don't go in there."

"But—why?" Mom sputtered.

"You know why."

Mom laughed, a harsh, humorless laugh. "Are you serious?"

Aunt Martha said nothing.

Mom shook her head. "You are unbelievable. You know that?"

Aunt Martha turned back to her car and stopped with her hand on the door. "I'm sorry, kids," she said to Evie and Stan. "Come and visit me in town after you get settled, okay? My door is always open."

Evie nodded and raised a hand in farewell as the old hatchback struggled back down the narrow lane.

"Unbelievable," Mom muttered, shaking her head with a sigh as she walked back to the car and popped the trunk open.

"Which way is the front?" Stan asked, staring at the two faces.

"I don't think it matters," Mom replied. "Looks like the movers used the north entrance, so we will, too. Here, honey." She tossed the keys to Evie. "Go ahead and open the door. Stan and I will start bringing things in."

Evie nodded and turned to the house. The western face was bright with sunlight, while the north face that she approached was in deep shadow. The porch groaned under her feet as she tried a couple of keys until one slid into the lock smoothly.

When she opened the door, the house seemed to exhale, as if it had been holding its breath, waiting for them to come.

Evie stepped into the gloom of a large farmhouse kitchen. A heavy wooden table dominated the middle of the room, which was lined with open shelving weighed down with piles of plates and bowls. A large, old-fashioned stove skulked in the corner, and everything in view was covered in a thick layer of dust. Against one wall, and trailing out into the hallway beyond, were neat piles of moving boxes, left behind along with a pink invoice by the moving company. A yellowing plastic telephone sat on the countertop next to her, its coiled cord sagging limply by its side like a sleeping snake.

"Hey!" Evie looked up to see her mother stumbling through the door, carrying two bulging duffel bags. "What are you doing standing around? Come outside and help!"

Nodding, Evie went back out to the car to grab whatever was left in the trunk. After three more trips, they had brought everything into the house. Mom stood in the center of the kitchen, hands on hips, surveying her new home. "Well," she said crisply. "The place needs a lot of work, but it's got good bones. Don't you think?"

"It sure is big enough," Stan said, pulling off his hoodie to look around. His dark hair was messy and hung over his eyes. "Our entire apartment could fit in this kitchen." He glanced down the hallway. "Looks like the other door leads into a living room. There's stairs over here going up."

Evie had an odd sense that the house had gotten stuck in time—not once, but twice. Remnants of the 1980s—thick yellow phone books, copies of the *TV Guide*, and a grimy radio-cassette player with a bent antenna—were strewn throughout a room that looked like it had been designed in the 1800s. In one corner, hanging over a wooden butter churn, Evie saw a framed needlework sampler dated 1851. Colorful flowers and trees surrounded a quote stitched in careful lettering:

The year rolls round, and steals away
The breath that first it gave;
What e'er we do, where e'er we be,
We're trav'ling to the grave.

Evie felt her mother behind her, also reading. "Not exactly my taste," she said. "But it is very *authentic*." She coughed. "Whoo! I'd better start airing this place out and cleaning up so we can unpack. Why don't you kids go up and pick your rooms?"

Stan was pounding up the stairs before Evie could even pick up her duffel. "I call first dibs!" he shouted.

"Stan! Wait!" Evie shouted back, grinding her teeth in annoyance. She shouldered her bag and went through the hallway into the living room. Rays of sunlight pouring through the windows illuminated legions of dust motes floating through the air in Stan's wake. With only a cursory glance at the squashy armchairs and fireplace that dominated the room, Evie climbed the staircase to reach the second-floor landing. Stan poked his head out of one of the doorways to look at her.

"This one's mine," he said. "It's the biggest. Mom's going to want the one at the end of the hall that has its own bathroom."

"And why do you get—?"

"Bye now," he said, and slammed the door in her face.

Evie stifled the hot rush of irritation rising inside her. "Fine," she said through gritted teeth. She continued down the hallway to the last door and pushed it open.

If Stan got the biggest bedroom, it must be huge, Evie thought. Because the room she was looking at was anything but small. Two large windows dominated the back wall, and a double bed with a delicate gold frame sat between them. The floor, like the rest of the house, was hardwood, except for a dingy Oriental rug that must once have been green. The furniture was painted cream, with gold scalloped edges. A few pictures in tiny frames hung on the walls, but mostly they were papered over with pages from *Seventeen* magazine and *Tiger Beat*. Advertisements for Maybelline Kissing Potions, and photos of teenaged heartthrobs with mop haircuts, so sun faded that their faces were ghostly white.

Evie touched the bloom of a mummified rose on the dresser, felt it crumble under her fingertips. Next to it lay an old photograph, its corners brown and curling. It was a picture of a girl she'd seen many times before, with a serious face and long, ginger hair. She was sitting in this very room, gazing out one of the windows to the woods beyond.

Evie felt a strange tingling in her stomach as she realized:

This was Holly's room.

The bedroom of a lost girl.

*H*olly Hobbie. *The Lost Girl of Ravenglass.*

Evie had first heard the story when she was a little girl, just old enough to be curious about the things her mother talked about behind closed doors. Holly was Mom's and Aunt Martha's cousin—her mother, Elizabeth Hobbie, was their aunt, and Holly her only child. When they were young, Martha and Lynne had sometimes come to Ravenglass for Christmas. Aunt Martha was older by five years, but Lynne and Holly had been close in age.

But that all ended forty years ago, when Holly was just fifteen years old.

Since then, Mom had never returned to this place. Not once.

Eventually, after Great-Aunt Elizabeth and Great-Uncle Dan moved away, Aunt Martha came and never left.

Evie looked at the room with new eyes.

In all the years of her life, the few times Holly had come up in conversation between Aunt Martha and her mother, or anyone else, no one ever referred to Holly in the past tense. Since she was never found, and a body never recovered, Holly seemed to exist in a nebulous place between life and death.

Like Schrödinger's cat, she thought. It was something that her science teacher had told her about once—a thought experiment about a cat inside a box that is simultaneously alive and dead.

She set her duffel down on the bed and was about to head back downstairs when she heard something.

A soft, rhythmic sound.

It was coming from the closet.

Evie's heart thrummed, but she moved toward the door. It was already ajar. She pulled it open with a jerk and stepped back. A pair of flashing eyes looked out at her from the darkness within.

Evie sighed with relief. It was just a cat. "Hello, you. Come on out now. Oh, what have you got there?"

After a moment, the cat padded out of the closet. It was an orange tabby, its long fur matted in parts, a notch missing from one ear. When it saw Evie, it dropped something small and wet at her feet.

It was a dead mole, eyeless and torn almost in two. The cat, its mouth covered in blood, sat with its tail curled primly, and began to bathe itself with its neat pink tongue.

Evie drew back, repulsed. But the cat only purred, winding around her ankles. "Gross," she said, looking around for something to pick up the bloody bundle. But all the cleaning supplies were still packed. "Don't go anywhere," she told the cat.

Downstairs, Mom had finished wiping down the table and countertops and had started to separate the boxes into piles for each room. "These are yours," she told Evie, pointing to a small mountain. "You can start taking them up."

Evie opened her mouth to say that there was a stray cat living in her room but decided against it. Her mother had never let them have pets in New York, and Evie wasn't about to let her kick this one out on day one. "Okay," Evie said, reaching for a roll of paper towels. "I just need to—"

"On second thought, don't worry about the boxes right now. The sun's going down and none of us have eaten dinner yet. Can you pick something up for us from that little place down the street? I think it's only, like, half a mile away or so."

Evie shrugged. "Sure," she said. The best thing about growing up in New York was that parents got used to the idea of sending their kids out into the world without supervision. Evie had started riding the subway alone when she was only twelve. Walking down the street in a small town was nothing compared with downtown Manhattan during rush hour.

"Take your phone with you," her mother said, pressing two twenty-dollar bills into her hand. "And don't get me anything spicy."

The neon sign for Birdie's Diner glowed like a beacon at the edge of town. Above the name, written in curling red letters, the outline of a yellow bird flicked back and forth—first at rest, and then with its wings outstretched, ready to fly.

The diner reminded Evie of a boxcar, abandoned by some old freight train, left to sink its wheels into the earth and never move again. The golden stripes above and below its windows were freshly painted, but its silver roof was tarnished like an old spoon. Half a dozen cars were parked in front, and Evie was greeted by a wave of heat and friendly noise as she walked inside.

Above the red vinyl booths brimming with customers, a froth of multicolored paper lanterns hung, illuminating the diner with a warm, muted light. A long white counter dominated the place, with little silver-and-red stools lined up in front of it. Alongside the chatter, an oldies radio station played on unseen speakers, adding to the sense of bygone nostalgia. Behind the counter, a stout, pink-cheeked woman in a sauce-spattered apron bustled about, calling out orders to the cooks in the kitchen and the waitresses flitting from table to table in canary-yellow uniforms. Her raven-black hair was pulled into a bun at the nape of her neck with a pencil stuck in it. The little name tag pinned to her apron said BIRDIE.

"Order up!" Birdie called, slinging two bowls of steaming food onto a tray. "Two kimchi bokkeumbap for table four!"

The savory, spicy smell that wafted past Evie's nose as the waitress carried it away made her mouth water. She walked up to the woman a little timidly, and said, "Excuse me."

Birdie turned her dark eyes on Evie and cocked her head to the side. "You're new," she said. It wasn't a question.

"Oh, yes. I'm Evelyn Archer—Evie. My family just moved into Hobbie House this afternoon. We're starved, so we thought—"

"Hobbie House?" Birdie said, her eyebrows rising. She turned toward the end of the counter, where Evie realized an elderly woman was sitting at a small table next to the kitchen. She wore a floral housedress and cardigan, and looked like a smaller, older version of Birdie herself. "Umma!" Birdie shouted, followed by a string of Korean that Evie didn't understand.

The elderly woman glanced over somewhat vaguely and nodded before turning back to stare out the window in front of her.

"Mama Bird used to know the people who lived there," Birdie said to Evie. "They would come here to eat back when she ran this place." A pained look passed over her face. "She won't remember that, though. Dementia." The clatter of a plate landing behind her on the pass broke her out of her thoughts. "So, you want to eat? How many people?"

"Three . . ."

"Ten minutes," Birdie said. She scribbled something on a little notepad and slapped it on the pass between her and the kitchen.

"B-but don't I have to order?" Evie stammered. "Isn't there a menu?"

"No menu," Birdie said, waving her hand as if swatting a fly. "I'll give you something, you'll like it. Okay?" Before Evie could reply, Birdie had already turned away to grab takeout bags for another customer who had just walked in.

"Um . . . okay," Evie said to no one in particular, and moved over to lean against one of the stools at the counter. She looked around. Most of the customers were couples or families, all except for one girl who sat in a booth by herself, typing furiously on her laptop. She looked about Evie's age and was the kind of girl she expected to see back in New York, not here. She wore a black knitted cap, and the short, curly hair that spilled out from under it was seafoam green. She seemed to be oblivious to everything around her. After a moment, she stopped and turned her face until she was looking straight at Evie with large, round eyes.

Evie looked away quickly—she'd been staring. She was studying some interesting-looking wooden masks on the wall when she felt someone slip next to her.

"Hey," a voice said. "Farmgirl."

Evie turned to see the girl standing next to her, sipping at a glass of some kind of pink milkshake from a straw. "What?" Evie said.

"New here, huh?" the girl said.

Evie rolled her eyes. "I know this is a small town, but you've got to have some random people show up sometimes, don't you?"

The girl shook her head. "Not in the fall. Summer people, yes. But they stop coming after Labor Day."

"Well, I'm not a farmgirl, anyway. We just moved here from New York City."

"Nah," the girl replied. "You look like you should be holding a newborn lamb or standing in a field of wheat."

Evie glanced down at her chunky brown sweater and floral blouse and sighed. "It's the freckles, isn't it?"

"Hey, it's not a bad thing. Who doesn't love lambs?" She took a long sip from her drink.

"What are you drinking?"

"It's Korean strawberry milk. Want some?" She held it out for Evie.

Evie laughed awkwardly. "You don't even know me."

The girl shrugged and stuck out her hand. "Tina Sànchez, and you?"

Evie shook it. "Evie Archer. Nice to meet you."

Tina pointed the drink toward her again. "How about now?"

Who is this girl? Evie thought, but she couldn't help but smile. She leaned forward and took a sip of the drink. It was sweet and creamy, touched with the tartness of fresh strawberries. "Wow, it's really good," she said.

"I'm addicted to them," Tina said, staring into the glass. "Be careful or you will be, too. So, where's your new place? Edgewood? The Glade?"

"No," Evie said, still relishing the taste in her mouth. "We just moved into Hobbie House."

Tina froze midsip. She set the glass down on the counter and stared at Evie in a way that made her squirm. "No way," she breathed. "You moved into Horror House?"

Evie winced.

"Wait—the psychic, right? Madame Martha. Are you her niece?"

"I am," Evie said warily. "You know Aunt Martha?"

Tina raised an eyebrow. "I'm the police chief's daughter. I know *everybody*. And all their skeletons." She took Evie by the wrist and pulled her back to the empty booth.

"But, I have to—" Evie protested.

"Sit," Tina commanded.

Evie sat.

"You know about that house, right?" Tina asked in a low voice.

"About Holly? Yeah, I mean, I know what my mom told me, which isn't much. Just that Holly disappeared from her bedroom back in the eighties and was never found."

Tina's jaw dropped. "Are you seriously telling me you never did a deep internet search on this? You *are* a farmgirl." She pulled her laptop toward her.

What if I don't want to know? Evie thought, but she said nothing.

A minute later, Tina turned the laptop to face Evie. "There, it was right in the *Boston Globe* archives."

Warily, Evie lowered her eyes to the screen and began to read. It was a scanned copy of the front page of the paper from December 19, 1982. A single headline dominated the front page: "Hope Fades as Months Pass since Teen's Mysterious Disappearance."

Ravenglass, Mass. It has been more than eight weeks since fifteen-year-old Holly Hobbie—known by many as the Lost Girl of Ravenglass—vanished from inside her home, a story that has captivated the nation ever since. What could have been a standard missing-person case quickly garnered national attention when details of Holly's disappearance and the history surrounding her house were revealed.

Holly's parents, Elizabeth and Daniel Hobbie, who had reported a disturbance in their home that evening, told authorities that their daughter had been in her bedroom when she screamed. When they reached the bedroom, they added, Holly was not there, nor was she anywhere in the house. Despite claims from Mr. and Mrs. Hobbie that Holly could not have left the house without their knowledge, Ravenglass police chief Richard Dixon told reporters at the time that they were exploring all possible avenues, including the possibility that Holly ran away from home. Many expected her to reappear within twenty-four hours. However, those hopes faded quickly as days passed with no sign of the missing girl.

Holly's parents were under investigation for a brief time, dragging the two into the national spotlight, but without evidence, the investigation was dropped.

. Holly Hobbie's disappearance raised suspicions, and a touch of fear, for some residents of Ravenglass who are familiar with the local legend tied to that very house. First built in the mid-nineteenth century, the house is a historic landmark that had a story of its own long before the Hobbies lived there.

According to legend, the original occupant of the home in the 1850s was discovered inside the home, dead from a shotgun wound. His murder was never solved, and his only child—a young girl colloquially called the Patchwork Girl for the dress she had always worn—disappeared the same day, never to be found.

There has been no further investigation into Holly's whereabouts. She is remembered by her family and friends as an Honor Roll student who loved animals and considered herself an amateur local historian . . .

"Order up for Evie Archer!" Birdie called from the counter.

"I've got to go," Evie said to Tina, standing. "My mom is waiting."

Tina sighed. "Fine, but you're not getting away from me that easily. Will you be going to RHS on Monday?"

"Yeah, sophomore year." Evie wasn't thrilled to be starting at Ravenglass High nearly a month after the school year had started—being the "new girl" was hard enough without it being so obvious.

"Oh, awesome!" Tina replied. "I'll see you there. We have a lot to talk about."

Evie turned away, her happiness at already having a friend in Ravenglass tempered by what she'd read about Hobbie House. *Does it really matter what happened there forty years ago?* she wondered. Evie didn't think so. The past was dead and gone. Evie had no interest in looking back.

She was making her way to the counter when a hand grabbed her by the arm. Evie turned to see Birdie's elderly mother looking up at her from her chair, her eyes cloudy with cataracts.

"Holly," she said, her voice a harsh rasp. "I haven't seen you in so long." Her grip was remarkably strong.

Evie blinked down at her. "What? No, I'm not—"

"Come closer," Mama Bird said, motioning.

Evie swallowed and bent down until her ear was next to the old woman's lips. "I want to tell you a secret, Holly. Can you keep a secret?"

Suddenly the air inside the diner felt hot and close, the friendly chatter too loud. "Yes," Evie whispered, despite herself.

"Evie Archer!" Birdie's voice cut through the moment, and Evie stood up straight, her heart pounding.

"I'm sorry," Evie said to the older woman, pulling away. But Mama Bird would not let go. Her gnarled fingers dug into the meat of Evie's arm.

"Oh, Umma . . . ," Birdie said when she caught sight of them. She hurried out from behind the counter and laid a smooth white hand over her mother's wizened one, whispering in Mama Bird's ear until the grip on Evie's arm relaxed. "She doesn't mean any harm," Birdie said, patting her mother on the shoulder. "Just gets confused sometimes." She walked back to the front counter and grabbed a bulging yellow plastic bag. "Better take your food before it gets cold. Gamja hot dogs are best piping hot!"

"Gamja—?" Evie started to say.

"Hot dogs on sticks covered in French fries." She handed the bag to Evie. "I dare you to eat just one."

Evie took the bag with a smile. The smell coming from it was making her mouth water. "Thanks," she said, paying the bill. "I can't wait to try it."

"Hurry home now," Birdie said. "I don't know what it's like where you came from, but here in Ravenglass, when night falls— it falls fast."

Outside, the day was dying. The last few rays of light burned like embers on the horizon, and a chill wind blew through the trees, making Evie quickly regret leaving the warmth of the diner. She walked briskly back up the street toward the narrow lane to Hobbie House, the heavy bag of food bouncing against her leg.

Her phone buzzed in her pocket, and she pulled it out quickly, hoping it was a message from one of her friends. But it was just her mother, texting to ask if Evie was on her way home. Evie replied, stuck the phone back in her pocket, and sighed.

She could hardly believe that just this morning, she had been saying goodbye to her home in New York, her voice echoing in the once cluttered apartment that was now empty. It was as if a knife had come down and severed her old life, leaving her to stumble into this new one.

Tina's reaction to the fact that she'd moved into Hobbie House worried her. She'd thought that after forty years, no one would care about the checkered history of the house, but clearly at least some people still did.

More than anything, Evie wanted to be anonymous. To dive under the surface of the world, let the waves pass over her and crash against someone else's shore. She didn't want to be *that girl*.

The girl who lives in the Horror House.

The wind picked up, rushing through the trees like a roll of thunder, sending a maelstrom of leaves across her path, along with the heavy smell of flowers and rot. The night had deepened so softly that Evie hadn't noticed how dark it had become. In New York, it was never dark or quiet. There were always the sounds of cars passing, of people in the street, and the low rumble of the subway passing deep beneath the earth. But here, the darkness was so thick she could almost touch it, the shadows so impenetrable that they could hide almost anything within them. Here, she could hear her every breath, and every snapping twig made her wonder what might be out there, watching her.

She started to walk a little faster.

Finally, she reached the end of the lane and saw Hobbie House, lights blazing in every window. It looked so different lit up in the night, like some ancient creature awoken after a century of slumber.

I'm home, she thought, and the word was strange, like an ill-fitting coat. Her mother opened the kitchen door, and light spilled out from inside to meet her.

3

"**W**hat's wrong with you?"

His voice was bigger than the world. It echoed, the words repeating again and again and again as everything shattered and rained down in a million tiny pieces, each one sharp enough to cut.

Evie woke up to the sound of her alarm. She reached for it, knocking her phone off the nightstand in the process, and scrabbled on the hardwood floor until she was able to turn the thing off. She lay on her back in the tangle of blankets, staring at the spiderweb cracks in the ceiling. The residue of the dream clung to her like a cold veil. She'd had it many times before, each time the same.

I don't have time for that today, she thought, rubbing her eyes and the images from her mind.

It was her first day of school at Ravenglass High, and she didn't want to be late.

The walk from Hobbie House to RHS was about a mile, although Evie believed there was probably a shortcut through the woods. She made a mental note to herself to do some exploring one day soon and find it.

She didn't mind the walking. In fact, the idea of not walking for miles every day was totally alien to her after growing up in the city. It gave her time to think, and to calm her nerves.

Just blend in, she told herself, brushing a leaf from the hem of her long olive skirt. Another one of her handmade pieces—this one a reimagining of an A-line Victorian walking skirt. *Blend in, and everything will be fine.*

Evie joined the steady stream of students flowing into the redbrick high-school building with fifteen minutes to spare. On the walls of the hallway inside, the words HOME OF THE FIGHTING MINERS! were painted in blue lettering, along with a logo of a man wearing a headlamp over two crossed pickaxes. After checking in with the front office and receiving her schedule and locker assignment, Evie made her way to her first class: Family Consumer Science.

"Do you really need to take this class?" her mother had said when she'd seen Evie's choice of electives. "Wouldn't you be better off with languages or programming or something? *I* can teach you how to cook."

But it wasn't cooking Evie was interested in. And when she stepped into the classroom and saw the neat, white sewing machines lined up on tables, she knew she'd made the right decision. She sat down at one of the machines, letting her bag slip from her shoulder to the floor. They were all Singer machines, which was all right—but nothing like her vintage Brother 151. These were plasticky, with only a few basic stitches, unlike her machine, which was built like a World War II tank and could stitch circles around anything in that room. She'd found it at a Brooklyn flea market a few years ago and used her entire savings to buy it. She liked to say it was the only Brother in her house that she enjoyed spending time with.

Evie could feel eyes on her as she sat, her fingers exploring the new machine. She tried to ignore the glances and the whispers as the room filled up and the teacher stood, ready to start class as soon as the bell rang. Just before it did, one last student came through the doorway.

"Hurry up, Mr. King, you're dangerously close to being late," the teacher said.

He was tall and broad shouldered, the light pink of his fitted T-shirt a stark contrast to his deep brown skin. He gave the teacher an easy, disarming smile. "Yes, ma'am," he said, and slipped into the room with such speed and elegance that it took Evie a second to realize that he had sat right next to her.

She risked a sidelong glance at him as the teacher took attendance. In profile, his face reminded her of the ancient Egyptian statues she'd seen at the Met—his high cheekbones, his full lips. After a moment, she saw his eyes flit over to her, and she quickly looked away. She could feel a flush creeping up her neck as she studied the teacher's tight black curls intently, trying desperately not to look again. But she couldn't help it. When her eyes flicked back to him, he had his eyes crossed, and the very tip of his pink tongue poking out the side of his mouth.

She snorted, covering her smile, and the teacher's face turned to her. "Ah! Yes, our new student. Please stand up, Miss Archer."

Kill me now, she thought as she stood, digging her fingernails into her palms when all eyes turned to her.

"Okay, students, this is your new classmate, Evelyn Archer— she just moved to Ravenglass from New York City. Please make her feel welcome."

"Hi," Evie said, scanning their faces—some curious, others bored—before abruptly sitting back down.

"Today we'll be continuing our sewing unit," the teacher said. "I expect you all to finish up your practice stitching today or tomorrow at the latest. You'll need to get moving on the patterns for your final project if you're going to have it finished by the end of the quarter." As the rest of the class broke into busy chatter, the teacher walked over to Evie's table. "Now, Desmond," she said, leaning in and giving the boy a pointed look. "If you can get our new student caught up on what we've learned over the past two weeks, that would go a long way in improving your grade in this class . . ."

"Of course, Ms. Jackson," Desmond replied smoothly. "I'd be happy to."

When she'd walked away, Desmond sighed. "Here's the thing, Evelyn," he started to say.

"Evie," she corrected.

"Here's the thing, Evie," he went on, leaning close. He smelled like the woods. "I am good at a lot of things, but sewing isn't one of them."

Evie chuckled, and picked up a spool of red thread from the table. Within a minute, she had switched the Singer on, filled the bobbin, and threaded the machine. "That's okay," she whispered back. "Because I am good at it."

"Oh, thank god," he said with a grin. "So, you're going to tell Ms. Jackson what an excellent teacher I am, right?"

"Right," she said.

Evie picked up the practice fabric and started sewing, following the looping patterns with a straight stitch, then adjusting the machine to do a zigzag stitch and an overlook on the hem. Just when she was starting to get into the zone, she heard a *crunch* from the machine next to her.

"Ugh, not again." Desmond was hunched over his machine, staring at a nest of blue thread in the middle of his fabric.

"Jammed up?" Evie asked.

Desmond sighed as she scooched over to untangle his machine. "You know, I only took this class because I thought it would be an easy credit. I got football season, Honors Chemistry, *and* AP Anatomy and Physiology—I don't have time for this."

"Sewing isn't easy," Evie said. "I mean, nothing is easy if you want to do it well."

"You make it look easy," he said, watching her.

Evie smiled, fumbling with the thread. "I've just had a lot of practice. I make a lot of my clothes myself."

"Did you make what you're wearing now?" he asked.

"The skirt, yeah." She paused and then said, "I like the way it makes me feel, wearing the things I make. Like I'm . . . more myself." She looked down shyly.

He didn't say anything for a moment, and she could feel his gaze on her. She felt it as clearly as a touch. "So, what's it like living in the Horror House? Little different from city life in New York, I bet."

Evie looked at him. "How did you know?" she asked.

Desmond shrugged. "Word travels fast around here. Especially when it has to do with that place."

Now it was her turn to sigh. "I don't know. It's a house. What else is there to say?"

He held his hands up in surrender. "Hey, you can't blame me for asking. You'd have to be dead not to be curious."

"I don't blame you," she said. "I mean, it's big and filthy, although a lot cleaner now that my mom has had a few days to tackle it. Other than that, it's kind of like living in a museum. There's all these, like, artifacts lying around, untouched for all these years. It feels . . . unfinished somehow."

"Unfinished," Desmond echoed.

"Yes," she said, suddenly feeling like she'd said too much. "Your machine should work now, let me just test it out." She slipped his practice fabric under the presser foot and softly pushed on the foot pedal to get the machine going. It hummed gently under her fingertips, stitching a line of blue across the rough muslin.

Then, a flash of movement caught her eye from the window in front of her. It looked out onto a wide lawn where a single hemlock stood. Tall grass gone to seed waved lazily in the breeze. And although the sun was shining brightly that morning, something dark and formless was walking there, like a shadow.

As Evie watched, it stopped next to the tree, and as if feeling her gaze upon it, began to turn to look toward her. "Hey, what's that?" Evie said softly.

"What's what?" Desmond asked, glancing out the window where she was looking.

"You don't see that?" Evie said. She stared at the shadow, transfixed, until a lightning bolt of pain brought her back.

"Oh god," she said, looking down to see blood fountaining from the tip of her pointer finger, spreading across the white fabric with frightening speed.

"The needle went straight through your fingernail," Desmond said, pulling her hand from the machine.

"I—I got distracted by . . . ," she stammered, glancing back out the window. There was nothing but the grass and the hemlock tree. "Nothing. I guess it was nothing."

"No worries," Desmond said smoothly. He was wrapping a tissue around her finger and holding it firmly. Within moments the tissue was soaked through with blood.

"Oh," Evie said, feeling dizzy, finger throbbing.

Desmond wrapped another tissue around the last one and held her hand up at eye level, almost as if they were about to step out onto the dance floor in some fairy-tale ballroom. His hand was warm. "Holding it above your heart will help stop the bleeding," he said. "Just breathe."

She breathed. Around her, some of the other students had noticed the commotion and watched them with interest.

So much for blending in, Evie thought.

"What's going on here?" Now Ms. Jackson had noticed, too. Her eyes widened when she saw the bloody tissues. "Evelyn, what happened?"

"It's my fault," Evie said quickly. "I wasn't looking, and the needle just—"

"Desmond, please accompany her to the nurse's office immediately." She shot him a look that said, *You can say goodbye to
that extra credit, young man.*

Evie couldn't look at Desmond as they walked down the long hallway toward the nurse. "I'm so sorry," she finally said.

"Sorry? For what?" he asked. "You're the one with the open
wound, not me."

"I just—I made a scene, and made you look bad . . ."

"Girl," he said, leveling a look at her. "You're going to have
to work a lot harder to make *me* look bad, you know what I'm
saying?"

She smiled. He was trying to put her at ease, and she was surprised to find that it was working. "Well, anyway, I feel pretty
stupid, considering I told you how good I was at sewing and then
immediately put a hole in my finger."

"You can make it up to me by making sure I get at least a B in
that class, how about that?"

Evie nodded. "Deal." She looked down at her finger, swaddled
in tissue. It still hurt, but it seemed like the bleeding had stopped.
"You may not know how to sew, but it seems like you know your
way around minor injuries."

Desmond gave a little shrug. "I'm looking at nursing schools.
Maybe Duke or UNC—if they give me some football money."

They'd arrived at the door to the nurse's office. Evie put her
hand on the doorknob and hesitated. "You know," she said. "If

you're going to be sewing people up one day, you should really know your way around a needle and thread. Maybe this class is worth your time after all."

"Yeah," Desmond said. His brown eyes wandered over her hair, her face. "Maybe it is."

Inside, the nurse carefully peeled off the bloody tissues and then washed the neat little hole with rubbing alcohol. It should have stung like crazy, but Evie didn't feel a thing.

The rest of the day passed without incident, a blur of textbooks and assignments and teachers announcing her name. Evie was standing at her locker after the final bell when Tina passed by, chatting with another girl. When her gaze fell on Evie, she stopped.

"I'll catch you later, Kitty, okay?" Tina said to the girl.

Kitty glanced up at Evie, her eyes curious behind a pair of oversize tortoiseshell glasses. She was short—even shorter than she looked, given the size of her wedge heels. She brushed the thick, dark brown fringe from her face and nodded.

"Text me," she said to Tina, and walked on.

Evie slammed her locker shut and slung her bag over her shoulder.

"So," Tina said as they joined the stream of students heading home, "how was your first day?"

"I wish I could say I made it out in one piece, but that would be a lie," Evie replied, and held up her bandaged finger.

Tina's eyebrows shot up. "Oh my god, what happened?"

As they made their way outside, Evie filled her in on the events of the morning. She could see that Tina was doing her best to appear sympathetic but failing miserably at concealing her glee.

"Oh, just go ahead and laugh," Evie said with a wave. "I can see you want to."

"I'm sorry!" Tina said, giggling. "It's just the most gruesome meet-cute I've ever heard, that's all."

"It wasn't a meet-cute," Evie said in the most unconvincing way possible. Tina leveled a sidelong glance at her as they reached Main Street. "So . . . what's he like, anyway? Desmond, I mean. He's probably dated half the girls in school."

"Nah," Tina said. "Desmond is heir to the throne of King Quarry, so he's always been pretty careful to keep his nose clean. His parents keep him on a tight leash."

"King Quarry?" Evie asked.

"His family's business, just up the mountain. Been around since the late fifties. The quarry probably single-handedly kept Ravenglass afloat for decades before the tourists found this place. Still does. Lot of folks who live here work for King Quarry in some way. And when Mr. King retires, it will all pass to Desmond."

"I thought he wanted to be a nurse," Evie muttered to herself.

"What's that?" Tina asked.

"Oh, nothing. Well, I've got to go." Evie pointed up the lonely road that led to Hobbie House.

"You know, I'd love it if you showed me around one day—the house, I mean," Tina said. Her voice was hopeful.

Evie swallowed, and made her voice bright. "Sure, maybe once we get things unpacked. The place is still a mess, and it will probably take a few weeks before things are cleaned up and all."

"A few weeks," Tina repeated. She nodded and looked away. "Yeah, okay. I'll see you tomorrow, then."

"See you!" Evie said, and hurried up the road.

The wind pushed Evie's copper hair across her face as she made her way up the narrow lane alone. As she passed the mailbox, she noticed that her mother had already gone over the words *Horror House* with a coat of fresh white paint. *She doesn't waste a minute, does she?* Evie thought. She reached up to tuck the loose locks behind her ear and pressed forward up the hill.

She felt bad turning Tina down, but Evie still wasn't convinced the girl's friendliness was genuine, and not just curiosity about Hobbie House. Evie just wasn't quite ready to let her—or anyone—inside.

"Oh, great! You're home," Mom said when she saw Evie walk in. She looked smart in a mint-colored blouse and blazer, and was finishing off leftovers from Birdie's. "God, this is even good cold," she said through a mouthful of food.

The house was virtually transformed. All the dust and old bits of things had been taken away, and there were only half a dozen boxes still waiting to be unpacked. Everything shone and smelled a little of oranges from the cleaning spray her mother loved.

"Wow," Evie said. "You've been busy."

"Very," Mom said, dumping the empty food containers in the trash. She walked over to one of the remaining boxes and set it on the table. "I only have a few things left to put out—just knick-knacks, mostly." She rummaged around inside the box and pulled out a newspaper-wrapped parcel. Nested inside was a small glass bluebird. Evie saw her mother's face tighten as she held it in her hand. "Here," she said, handing it to Evie as if it were a hot potato. "Put it wherever you like."

Evie cradled it in her palm, like she would a real baby bird. It felt cool, and heavier than it looked. "Okay," she said. She ran her fingertips along the base of it, feeling the initials engraved there. RA.

Mom took out the other items from the box and set them on the table in neat rows. A set of votive candleholders, a couple of stone lion bookends, some framed photographs of the family. "Your father is in Paris for the rest of the month," Mom said, not looking up, "but if you want to text him, he'll be able to receive it. I think he's got some international plan or something."

"I don't really want to text him," Evie said, picking up one of the framed pictures. Her parents at Coney Island, grinning at the camera. Evie in pigtails, barely six, holding a dripping ice-cream cone, and Stan just a babe in her mother's arms. The image was taken at an angle, making it look like the whole world behind them was off-balance, like they were already on a carnival ride. Evie went over to the baker's rack in the corner of the kitchen and set both the bluebird and the picture down on one of the shelves.

"Up to you," Mom replied. Then she looked up and smiled, effectively banishing the seriousness from the moment. "Well! Stan texted to say he's staying after school with some new friends, and I have to be at the Blue River Inn in fifteen minutes for a job interview," she went on. "It's that pretty place on Main Street we saw on the drive, remember? I found out the owner is looking for an assistant manager, and I just thought, *How perfect*. Right?" She didn't wait for Evie to answer. "I'll be back for dinner, but if you could take these boxes up to the attic while I'm gone, that would be very helpful. It's just stuff from the storage unit we don't need right now. I'd rather not put anything in the cellar until I'm able to get someone down there to check for mold. Great-Aunt Liz always kept the door shut—something about 'bad air.' It's old. Older than the house—maybe even the town itself, so who knows if there's any ventilation down there. Anyway, better safe than sorry. The attic's dusty, but at least it's dry."

"Okay, Mom," Evie said.

Mom plopped the empty box in the trash, grabbed her purse, and was out the door. "Bye, honey!" she called.

Evie dropped her bookbag to the ground and sat in one of the old wooden chairs. "My day was fine, Mom, thanks for asking," she said to the empty kitchen. "I met a boy, got a new hole in my finger . . ." She grabbed an apple from a bowl on the table and took a few bites. Pulling her phone from her bag, she glanced through it. Her heart leaped when she saw that one of her friends from the city had sent her a picture of herself with a few other people from their group. Miss u! the text read, along with three hug emojis.

A lump rose in her throat. She had thought a message from her friends would make her feel good, but it was having the opposite effect. Instead, seeing the picture made her feel painfully alone. She considered how she might reply, thought about telling her friend about sewing class, about Desmond, about shadows, and secrets—

Mama Bird's wizened face appeared in her mind. *I want to tell you a secret, Holly,* the old woman had said. *Can you keep a secret?*

Evie deleted the picture, put the phone down on the table, and took another bite of apple. There was no time for texting now, she had things to do. Hoisting one of the cardboard boxes into her arms, she slowly made her way up the creaky stairway to the second floor.

The entrance to the attic was at the end of the hall, accessible by a thin rope hanging down from the panel in the ceiling. She put down the box and pulled the rope, causing a cascade of dust to rain down on her when it opened. After unfolding the ladder, Evie tucked the box under one arm and slowly made her way up.

Definitely a mistake not bringing my phone up here, she thought as she blinked into the darkness. *A flashlight would have come in handy right about now . . .* She placed the box on the floor and then stood up, groping for a light. Her hand finally struck a swinging string, and when she pulled it, a single bare bulb stuttered to life above her.

The attic was large and airy, with the exposed rafters of the roof high enough above her that she could stand at her full height without stooping. The front window had been boarded up—Evie wondered if it had been broken at some point and blocked to prevent wildlife from coming in.

Like that cat . . . she remembered. She hadn't seen it again since that first day, and wondered where it had gotten to.

There was a surprising amount of *stuff* in the attic—things had been left behind downstairs here and there, but it was nothing like this. There were more than a dozen boxes of various sizes piled up, along with at least two dozen bolts of old fabric wrapped in plastic.

"No way," Evie whispered. She pulled off the plastic to get a closer look. Other than smelling faintly of mothballs, the fabric was in perfect condition. Soft cottons and linens in white ditsy prints, brown gingham, and blue paisley. Evie felt a thrill just touching them. A treasure trove of authentic vintage fabric! And so much of it! Maybe she could even use it for her final project in sewing class.

Is there more? she wondered. She began peeking into boxes, but only found some old crockery wrapped in newspaper and boxes of moldy-smelling books. Behind a pile of boxes, tucked into the corner of the attic, she found an old steamer trunk sitting next to a white full-length mirror that seemed to match the furniture in her bedroom. She kneeled in front of the trunk and unlatched the clasp to push it open.

A face peered out at her from inside, its eyes unblinking.

Evie shrieked and recoiled from the trunk, nearly toppling the pile of boxes onto her head.

Then she looked closer and sighed. "Idiot," she scolded herself, her heart still hammering.

A doll sat upright inside the trunk. A hunk of its auburn hair was missing, and there were little tears all along its red, white, and blue sailor suit. It was just one of the dozens of items inside the trunk—old cassette tapes and a silver Walkman, piles of teen magazines, and two other dolls, one a Raggedy Ann whose innards were spilling out of a broken seam, and the other a doll with a porcelain face, dressed in lace and velvet.

This is all Holly's stuff, Evie realized.

She thought about Holly's parents, Evie's great-aunt Elizabeth and great-uncle Dan. Her mother had told her years ago that they'd moved to California the year after Holly disappeared and hadn't had much contact with the family ever since. The last time her mother had spoken to Great-Uncle Dan was last year when he called to say that Elizabeth had died. "The cancer is what took her," Mom had told Evie the day it happened. "But she'd been gone for a long, long time."

Evie imagined being surrounded by all the things that reminded you of someone you had lost. Someone who was there one moment and gone the next, like a cruel magic trick. To walk through life in a house and a town where every detail made fresh the pain of that person's absence.

Some memories were too painful to keep. Some needed to be packed away in the dark and forgotten. Evie could understand that.

She reached into the trunk and lifted the doll. It was nearly two feet long and heavier than she expected. Instead of the blank smiles that Evie was used to seeing on lifelike dolls, this one had a crafty grin, and a sidelong glance that made it seem like the doll was looking at something over Evie's shoulder. Evie turned it around and saw that it had a drawstring in its back.

It must be one of those old talking dolls. No way it still works . . . But she pulled the string, anyway.

A small voice dragged to life from inside the doll, slow and distorted as if the mechanism wasn't quite right.

"I feel so very, very sick," the doll said.

Evie felt a prickle at the back of her neck. She pulled the string again.

"I'm always cross when I'm sick," the voice slurred.

Again.

"I hope I get some flowers."

Again.

"Will you take care of me?"

It must be for some kind of doctor game, Evie thought. She remembered seeing another old doll once where you could change out the little record inside for different games. But when she pulled it again, the doll began to sing in a slow, toneless voice.

Playmate, come out and play with me,
and bring your dollies three.
Climb up my apple tree,
look down my rain barrel,
slide down my cellar door,
and we'll be jolly friends forevermore.

Evie swallowed. Odd . . . The song had nothing to do with doctors. She turned the doll over and tried the string again, but it had stopped working altogether.

"Huh," she said, and set the doll down beside her. She rummaged through the rest of the trunk, seeing what else she might find. Beneath the magazines she found a little diary clasped with a tiny silver lock. *Holly's diary*, she thought, her curiosity piqued. She'd told herself she didn't want to know anything about what had happened in this house all those years ago. But a diary . . . How could she resist?

She couldn't find the key anywhere in the trunk, but figured she'd be able to break the lock if she wanted to. She set the diary next to the dolls and kept pulling more items out of the trunk. At the bottom she found some clothes, a stained white scarf edged with lace, a dress with pearl buttons, and a blue bonnet that looked almost as old as the house itself.

Evie brushed the dust off the bonnet and held it up to the light. Could it have been something that Holly had found in the house when her family moved in? The bonnet certainly looked like it could be more than a hundred years old—although it was in surprisingly good shape if it was.

On a whim, she turned to the mirror and pulled the bonnet onto her head, tying the ribbons in a loose bow at her throat. She studied her reflection. Her long copper hair that flowed down in waves under the bonnet, and the freckles sprinkled over her nose and cheeks. *With this on I definitely look like a farmgirl*, she thought, remembering what Tina had said in the diner.

A long, eerie sound came from the talking doll, like a sigh.

Evie's eyes flicked toward it, but it was silent now. *The drawstring must not have fully retracted the last time I pulled it.* When she looked back at her reflection in the mirror, she froze.

Had her hair been exactly that color before? It looked more red than copper, but perhaps that was an illusion of the dim light. But then, there were other things, too. Her eyes were a darker shade of green, and her face seemed thinner, her cheekbones more pronounced.

Her lips in the mirror began to move, mouthing something.

Four words.

Staring at her reflection, having not moved at all, terror bloomed in Evie's chest like a flower, wrapping its tendrils around her heart and turning her blood to ice.

She scrambled to her feet, and the bonnet slipped off her head as she backed out of the attic and nearly fell down the rungs of the ladder, folding it up and slamming the ceiling panel closed. She knew she had left the light on up there, but Evie didn't care. She ran into her bedroom, slamming the door behind her, and sat on the bed, her whole body trembling and slick with sweat. She gasped, taking in great lungfuls of air as she remembered to breathe.

She knew exactly what the reflection had said. It was her own lips saying them, after all. Or at least, she thought they were. Four innocent little words.

Come play with me.

5

When Evie was little and Stan was just a baby, she used to love listening to her nanny read from *Alice's Adventures in Wonderland*. She would sit on the blue shag rug in their apartment and listen to Miss Olive read about falling down the rabbit hole and meeting the Cheshire Cat. Miss Olive thought the story was silly, but Evie always took it quite seriously, as if Alice's adventures were parables she needed to memorize for later.

When they finally got through the book, Miss Olive brought *Through the Looking-Glass* home from the library, thinking that little Evie would want to hear more stories about Alice. But they'd gotten through only the first few pages before Evie had begged her to stop reading.

It was the opening scene in the drawing room, where Alice is talking to her kitten and imagining what it would be like to live in Looking-glass House, the house within the mirror over the fireplace. And as she imagines what it would be like to pass through the gauzy veil between her world and the other, suddenly she finds herself up on the mantel, pressing through the mirror. And just like that, she's in the Looking-glass world, which is just like her own, except completely different.

"Oh, what fun it will be," Alice says with delight, "when they see me through the glass in here, and can't get at me!"

It was at this point that Evie started to sob. And when Miss Olive, bewildered, asked what was wrong, six-year-old Evie had cried, "Alice thinks it's fun, but it's not! They'll see her, but they can't help her when she's in Looking-glass House!" She'd been inconsolable that entire afternoon—her mother had even checked her for fever when she got home and found Evie in bed, exhausted from crying. Miss Olive had never read from the book again.

Even as she grew up, the idea still haunted her. She thought about it sometimes and was never quite sure which part of it scared her more. Was it that Alice made something so frightening happen, just by imagining it? Or was it the idea that even after Alice came back through the Looking-glass, she could never really be sure which side of the mirror she was on?

After that first day of school, Evie made sure she was always busy. Luckily for her, between catching up on her assignments and helping her mother with the house, it was easy. She was so tired by the end of every day that she fell asleep the moment her head hit the pillow. She had no dreams.

At least, none that she remembered.

She'd texted her friends back in New York a few pictures of the house and her room, a few scenic shots of the mountain, the way it looked in the morning on her way to school. They always replied promptly, with exclamations of "Amazing!" and "So cool!" and an assortment of emojis, but never more than that. She was losing them, she knew. The more time that passed, the more she would fade from their minds, like an old photograph left in the sun.

She was scrolling through her old texts from her friend Hannah on Thursday evening when Stan came in with a glass jar full of buttons. "I found these at the bottom of my closet," he said, tossing it onto the bed next to her. "They're lame, so I thought you'd like them."

"Gee, thanks," Evie said. She picked up the jar and gazed at the kaleidoscope of multicolored plastic, wood, and metal buttons inside. "I actually really do."

"Duh, because you're lame, obviously."

"Obviously," she agreed.

She expected Stan to leave the room as soon as his errand was complete, but instead he lingered—his hands in the front pocket of his hoodie, looking at things. He clearly wanted company but was too "cool" to say so.

"So, um . . . ," Evie said after a minute or two, "what do you think of the house?"

Stan shrugged. "I dunno. It's weird. Old and weird. Makes weird sounds at night—did you notice?"

Evie thought about the skritching sounds she'd heard coming from the vent the night before. "Yeah, it's probably mice in the air ducts." She thought about the small, dead creature the cat had given her as a present. "Or moles."

"Ugh, gross," Stan said, his lip curling. He shook his head and sat on the edge of her bed, just close enough so that her feet brushed up against his back. "I don't know exactly what this place feels like, but it doesn't feel like home."

"I know," Evie said softly. They sat together like that until it was time for bed.

Evie was in the girls' bathroom on Friday morning before school started when they came in. Four girls, laughing and chattering like a flock of starlings. Evie glanced at them through the mirror. She'd seen a couple of them before in her classes, but didn't know them by name. One of them, a bottle blonde who reminded Evie of an Instagram filter come to life, stopped midsentence when she locked eyes with Evie. After a moment, the other girls noticed and fell silent, too. The girl was holding a takeout cup of coffee, and took a slow sip from the lipstick-stained rim.

Evie turned off the faucet and dried her hands on a paper towel, their gaze prickling across the back of her neck.

"Lock the door," the blonde muttered to the girl behind her. *Click*.

Evie clenched her hands into fists to keep them from trembling and turned around. "Do I know you?" she asked, trying to keep her voice even.

"Not yet," said the blonde. "But I know you. The new girl, right? Evie Archer. The one living in that murder house."

Evie clenched her teeth, but said nothing.

"Well, New Girl," she said, her voice sugar sweet. "My name is Kimber Sullivan. I'm here to help you! New school, new people—I'm sure it's all *very* confusing. So let me give you a hot tip." She walked right up to Evie and leaned in close. "Stay away from Desmond King, if you know what's good for you. Or maybe you don't! You did move into that house, after all. Maybe you just have a death wish. Right, girls?"

The other three tittered nervously.

"I didn't—" Evie started to say.

"Oops!" Kimber said, pretending to stumble forward. Her cup tipped and spilled coffee all over the front of Evie's white blouse.

Evie gasped, the hot coffee scalding her skin.

"Oh!" Kimber exclaimed, feigning dismay. "That just ruined your poor shirt, didn't it? You know, Evie, you should really be more careful." With one final glare, she dropped the empty paper cup on the floor, unlocked the bathroom door, and stalked out—her cronies following at her heels.

Evie stood alone, dripping. The coffee was saturating her blouse in a growing brown stain, and little droplets of it were all over her arms and face. She pulled fistfuls of paper towels from the dispenser and furiously rubbed at the stain, making it much worse.

She bent over the sink, washing her face and then drying it with more paper towels. Her face was flushed, her eyes red.

Don't you dare cry.

Don't you dare.

She imagined grabbing a fistful of the girl's bottle-blond hair, dragging her toward that mirror, and smashing her head into it. She imagined the sharp pop of sound as the mirror shattered,

Kimber's thin scream, and the tinkling of broken glass as her head hit it again and again—

"Hey, are you okay?"

Evie jumped back from the sink like she'd been stung. Tina was standing in the doorway, her eyes wide. Her green hair was extra curly today, making her look like some sort of woodland fairy creature. "I'm fine," Evie replied, quickly wiping the emotion from her face.

"You don't look fine. You look like a hot mess. I saw Kimber and her crew walk out of here a minute ago laughing and had a feeling something was up. What happened?"

Evie dropped the sopping wad of paper towels into the trash can and sighed. "She warned me to stay away from her boyfriend. And decided to make the point extra clear by throwing her coffee at me."

"Her boyfriend?"

"Yeah. Desmond King."

Tina snorted. "He's not her boyfriend. Not anymore, at least."

"What do you mean?"

"Well, they'd been dating for a while, but something must have happened, because they were on the outs at the beginning of the school year. Desmond's too polite to talk about it with anyone, but Kimber's been going around saying that they're just 'on a break.' Sure doesn't seem that way to me, though. Sounds like she's just trying to save face by going all alpha on you." Tina took off her backpack and got out a sweatshirt, handing it to Evie. "Here. It doesn't really match the whole arcadian milkmaid thing you've got going, but it's better than nothing."

"Thanks," Evie said, and pulled the army-green sweatshirt over her head. Fortunately, it was long enough to cover the stains.

"So, you and Desmond, huh?" Tina said, raising an eyebrow. "After you told me that story about him bandaging you up like Florence Nightingale, I knew something was afoot. I just hope you didn't leave behind any broken hearts in New York."

Evie considered the brief relationships she'd had during freshman year. Boys who were either so nervous just being around her that they could barely hold a conversation, or whose only goal was a make-out session they could tell their friends about. They'd bored Evie to tears. "No broken hearts," she said. "Seriously, though, everyone is blowing this whole thing out of proportion. Desmond is just being friendly. That's all." She eyed Tina suspiciously. "Are you going to quote me on that?"

Tina's eyes narrowed. "What do you mean?"

"My first day, everyone already seemed to know who I was." She looked at the floor. "And where I was living. And I hadn't told anyone that but you. The way you ask questions, and the way you were writing on that laptop at Birdie's, I just thought—"

"What, that I run the local rumor mill?"

Evie swallowed, suddenly wanting nothing more than to take it all back. Tina had come to her rescue, and here she was making accusations. *Stupid.* Tina was looking at her steadily, hands on her hips, waiting for an answer.

"I guess I was just worried that you were only interested in me because of the house," Evie finally said.

There was a pause as Tina took that in.

Oh god, she's mad. Evie had a strong desire to take off the sweatshirt, hand it back to Tina, walk home, crawl into bed, and try this whole "life" thing again tomorrow. It wasn't even 8:00 a.m. How could the day have already gone so wrong?

"Well, you're right," Tina said.

Evie wasn't sure she'd heard her correctly. "I'm *right*?"

"Yes, when I met you at Birdie's on Saturday, my first thought was just to get as much information out of you about that house as I could. Look, Ravenglass is no New York—interesting things don't happen here very often. And you were interesting. I'm not the town rumor mill, but I do like to know what's going on. I'm going to be a journalist one day, so I know the value of a juicy story." She looked at Evie then, and her face was serious. "But I also know the value of trust. I didn't tell anyone about you, Evie. I swear. Thing is, I didn't have to. News travels fast around here, with or without my help."

Evie nodded. She believed her.

"So yes, I admit to pumping you for information about Hobbie House at first. But that's not it anymore. I like you, Evie. You're different from a lot of the fakes and poseurs around here. Real. In a quiet, Jane Eyre kind of way."

Evie smirked. "That sounds . . . not great."

"What do you mean? She *is* great! Jane Eyre is a *strong, modern woman.*"

The first bell began to ring. Evie bent to pick up her bookbag from the floor. "Okay, well, us strong, modern women had better get to class," she said.

Tina put a hand on her shoulder as Evie moved past. "What I'm trying to say is, you can trust me. Okay?"

Evie sighed. "Okay."

"Good. Then trust me when I say this: Be careful with Kimber. She's the mayor's daughter, and she takes full advantage of that fact. Always has. Her and her little brother, Dylan. No matter what kind of trouble they've gotten into, Daddy always comes to the rescue and makes it go away."

"Don't worry," Evie replied as they walked out of the bathroom and into the crowded hallway. "I plan on staying as far away from her as possible. And from Desmond, too, I guess."

Tina gave her a sidelong glance. "Really? But I thought—"

"I told you, there's nothing between us," Evie said firmly. "Listen, all I wanted to do when I moved here was just have a normal, quiet life. And if I have to steer clear of one boy to have that, then fine."

"All right then," Tina said, sounding unconvinced. She smiled a smile that seemed to reach her earlobes. "Good luck with that."

All the students in FCS had finally finished their practice stitching, so Ms. Jackson spent the first fifteen minutes of class showing them how to pin and cut sewing patterns. Evie sat at a table in the back, half listening. She tried to put the morning's unpleasantness out of her mind, but every time she moved, the stiff, sticky fabric of her stained blouse kept reminding her again of Kimber's sneering face, of her cronies giggling along, of the sound Evie had imagined her head would make smashing into the glass—

"Miss Archer," Ms. Jackson was saying.

Evie blinked and sat up straight in her chair. "Yes?"

"Are you clear with all of this? I know it's a lot to catch up on in just a few days."

"I've got it," Evie said, nodding.

From the front of the class, Desmond had turned around to look at her, a question in his eyes. Evie looked away.

"Good," Ms. Jackson said. "If you haven't chosen a pattern yet, today's the day. After that, you can go in the back room and choose your fabrics. For your first project, I'd stick to the cotton, shirting, chambray, or ponte shelves, all right?"

While most of the students piled into the back room, Evie went to flip through the boxes of sewing patterns. She still hadn't decided what she wanted to make for her final project. The thought of using some of those vintage fabrics from the house thrilled her, but she hadn't gone back in the attic since—

A cold chill ran through her, and she shivered.

She refocused on the patterns. There were button-down shirts, stuffed animals, tote bags, pajama pants . . .

"Hey," a deep voice said.

Evie glanced up. Desmond was leaning against the table, carelessly handsome in his T-shirt and jeans. Morning light shone on his face, making it look like polished stone. "I thought we had a deal," he said, his voice playful but also a little hurt.

"You've been doing a lot better with the machine the past few days," Evie said, unable to meet his eyes. She stared at a pattern for a jumpsuit that looked like the 1990s had thrown up on it. It was probably the ugliest thing she'd ever seen, but at least it kept her from looking at him. The weight of his gaze pressed on her until she was breathless. "I'm sure you'll be fine on your own now," she finished. The words tasted bitter in her mouth.

There was a beat when she thought he was going to walk away, but instead he took a step closer. "Was it something I said?" he asked.

She continued to flip through the box. "No, not at all. I just—"

"Do you not like me anymore?"

Evie paused. His closeness had a pull like gravity, and though she fought to escape it, she found that she neither wanted to nor could. "No," she said, looking at him.

"No, you don't like me anymore?" he said, and the corner of his lip twitched in a little grin.

"No, no," she stammered. "I mean—yes, I still like you." She said it before she really realized what she was saying, but by then it was too late. The little grin blossomed.

"Why are you sitting all the way back here, then?" he asked.

With her plan in shambles, Evie groped for an answer. Telling him about her run-in with Kimber was the last thing she wanted to do—talk about making a bad situation worse! "I'm just worried about keeping my grades up," she lied. "My mom is pretty strict about that stuff, and she wants to make sure I focus on my work and stay away from any . . ." She faltered.

"Distractions?" he finished.

She swallowed, and prayed for a hole to open in the earth and swallow her.

Desmond laughed.

"What?" she said. *Why is it so hard to be normal?*

"Your face— It's just—" He was still laughing.

"It's not funny," she said, crossing her arms. But it was. Her lip curled, betraying her with a smile.

"I'm sorry, I'm sorry," he said, wiping at the corner of his eye. "I'll stop." He looked down at the jumpsuit sewing pattern she was holding and grimaced. "Is that what you're going to make? It's . . . um . . . interesting."

Evie scoffed. "No, it isn't. It's terrible. It's an affront to all clothing everywhere. This pattern and every other one like it should be thrown into a fire so that no one can ever bring this evil into the world again."

"All right, dang, okay," Desmond replied with a chuckle. "Tell me how you really feel. I was just trying to be nice."

Evie put the pattern back into the box. "I'd rather you be honest than nice."

Desmond nodded. "All right. Honesty it is, then. For both of us."

Evie glanced out the window to the field, to the hemlock tree and the tall grass. There were no shadows today.

But there could be. Would you tell him about them if there were? Would you tell anyone?

"Absolutely," she said, and closed the box.

What about Kimber? What's going to happen when she finds out?

But somehow those thoughts couldn't penetrate her mind. She was having fun. She would worry about Kimber later. She would worry about everything later.

They stood together and looked through more boxes of patterns, their hips almost touching. "How about this one?" she asked, holding up a pattern for a football jersey. "It's not too difficult, and you can even put your number on it if you want to be fancy."

"You know I want to be fancy," he said, squinting at the pattern. "This looks good to me. But what are you going to make?"

"Oh, I don't know," she said. She thought about the old fabric, the soft blue gingham, the rich goldenrod with the tiny green flowers, all of it guarded by her fear of the attic. They would be so perfect for—

"A dress," she said suddenly. The air smelled like flowers.

Desmond looked over. "Did you find a pattern you like?"

In an instant, an image had materialized in Evie's mind. Ever since she'd started sewing, she'd often be struck by inspiration and have to stop whatever she was doing and sketch out a new piece. But this was different. This felt like something outside her finding a way in—as sudden and shocking as a lightning strike. She knew every piece she'd have to cut for this dress, every curve and stitch. She knew it as if it were already made.

"I don't need one," she said. She felt peculiar, as if she had stepped over an invisible border and found herself in a strange country. She would make a prairie dress—long and billowy, with voluminous sleeves and ruffles on the skirt, and a modern neckline and bodice that married the vintage design of the past with the present. It would be feminine, elegant, one of a kind. It would be her greatest creation yet.

"Show-off," Desmond replied. "Do you want to go look at some fabric then?"

She smiled slowly, as if she'd just woken up from a wonderful dream. "No, I'm going to bring some things from home." Suddenly her fear of the attic seemed absurd, childish. Whatever she'd seen up there couldn't hurt her. She'd go up there this afternoon, while the sun was shining, and pull out all that old fabric. A new project was just what she needed to get her mind off her troubles.

Yes, just what she needed.

6

The Ravenglass General Store took up the bottom floor of a three-story colonial building right in the center of Main Street, cream with forest-green double doors, and red, white, and blue bunting hanging over the windows. It was where most of the town's residents got their groceries and supplies—if they wanted anything beyond what the General had in stock, they had to drive ten miles out of town to the nearest supermarket.

Evie stood in front of the big display windows after school, which were decorated for the season. FALL INTO SAVINGS! a painted sign read, surrounded by cozy products like apple cider, breakfast teas and coffees, and pumpkin spice everything. There were also socks, mittens, autumn wreaths, and child-size scarecrows slumped blithely in a row. The door tinkled as she walked inside—the whole place smelled like cinnamon, and the sounds of Motown played faintly from unseen speakers. She picked up the few items her mother had asked her to buy—bread, butter, some canned soups—and checked out. After FCS, she'd been eager to go home for the fabric, but as the day wore on, her resolve to go back to the attic faded, and the fear returned. It was silly, she knew that, but she was still relieved when Mom texted at the end of the day to ask her to run errands.

Unfortunately, it didn't take very long to buy those few items, and she still had a few hours to kill before dinnertime. Her mother had been called back for a second interview at the inn and wouldn't be at home, and knowing Stan, he was probably out roaming the town with those boys again. The last thing Evie wanted was to be at Hobbie House alone.

She wandered down Main Street, peeking into the store windows as she went. A block down from the General she stopped at a sandwich board sign on the sidewalk. TAROT AND PALM READINGS, it read. UPSTAIRS TO THE LEFT—NO APPOINTMENT NECESSARY. Evie craned her neck to study the narrow, redbrick building squeezed between a bookshop and the All That Glitters restaurant. A dry cleaner clearly occupied the first floor, but Evie couldn't see inside the second-floor window. All she could see was a wall of thick purple curtains and a neon sign of an open hand and the words PSYCHIC READER glowing beneath.

"Aunt Martha," Evie whispered to herself. In the flurry of her first week in Ravenglass, Evie hadn't given her eccentric aunt's invitation to come visit a second thought. But here she was, on her doorstep, looking to kill time.

The side door next to the dry cleaner opened to a dim, airless stairwell littered with dry leaves. Evie climbed to the second-floor landing, where a tall vessel blooming with umbrellas and walking sticks stood next to a peeling metal door. Evie tapped with the metal knocker, and within moments, she could hear footsteps approaching from inside.

Aunt Martha was clearly expecting a customer when she opened the door. She was dressed in a crimson blouse and a long skirt covered in complex patterns of red and indigo and gold. Her silver hair flowed freely down her back, and half a dozen gold bangles encircled each of her wrists, making a gentle ringing sound as she moved. She seemed almost like a stranger—Evie had always known Aunt Martha was a professional psychic, but she'd never seen her in action. The expression on her face was noble and grave, but all that melted away the moment she saw Evie on the landing. "What a wonderful surprise!" she said, smiling. "Come on in, girly. I'll put the kettle on."

The apartment was just as Evie had imagined—and hoped—it would be. Ornate tapestries and abstract paintings hung on the deep blue walls, and in the corner, a heavy wooden shelf held all manner of books, crystals, and other unnamable, mystical-looking things. A low table covered in a silken cloth stood in the middle of the room, with overstuffed chairs on each side of it. The thick purple curtains blocked out the sun so that the hooded lamps and scattered candlelight were able to create a comforting gloom even in the middle of the day. "This is my reading room," Aunt Martha explained. "My actual apartment is through here." She led Evie through a door to another space—an open kitchen with a sitting room, leading to a single small bed and bath. The place was much more conventional than the reading room, but still had Aunt Martha's signature style of clutter and oddments.

Aunt Martha went straight into the little kitchen and clattered around in her cabinets after turning the fire on under the teakettle. She pulled out two brown mugs and measured tea out of a silver tin while Evie settled herself on the squashy green couch. "Chamomile okay for you? It's very relaxing. I'll add a little lavender and rose petal to it, too. After the week you've had . . ." She didn't finish the sentence.

How would she know the kind of week I've had? Evie wondered.

Mom had always scoffed at her sister's psychic claims—she'd always figured Martha just had good instincts or, less generously, that she was a good liar. Evie was a little more willing to believe there might be something to it. Life seemed more interesting that way. Then again, it wasn't too far of a leap to assume that Evie's first week in Ravenglass would be stressful.

"How's the House?" Aunt Martha asked. Evie could hear the capital *H* just in the way she spoke the word.

"It's okay," Evie said. "It's so *big*. I thought it would be such a relief after the cramped closets we lived in in New York, but . . . I don't know. Somehow I don't love that feeling of so much emptiness all around me." She paused, contemplative, and then turned to her aunt, who was busy spooning honey into the mugs. "Is that why you never lived there?" *Or why you won't go inside?* Evie thought that last part but didn't say it. Something about the question felt dangerous.

Aunt Martha hesitated. After two false starts, she finally said, "This place is my home. I just wouldn't feel comfortable anywhere else."

She's lying, Evie realized. *Or at least, she's not telling the whole truth.* Evie should know. She did it all the time.

"How about school?" Aunt Martha asked, changing the subject.

Evie shrugged. "It's okay. I've made a couple of friends, but some enemies, too. I don't get it. I'm just this random, quiet person, and yet somehow I'm surrounded by all this drama."

Aunt Martha chuckled. "I don't think you draw a very accurate image of yourself, Evie." Her aunt's eyes met hers, sharp and intense. "Your voice may be quiet, but your spirit is loud. And loud spirits tend to attract attention. Sometimes good, sometimes not so good."

Evie nodded, suddenly chilled.

Come play with me.

At that moment, the teakettle began to scream.

Evie gasped at the sound, and Aunt Martha looked over at her, the steaming kettle in her hand. "Are you all right?" she asked. "You look pale."

"Yes, the kettle just scared me, that's all."

Aunt Martha poured the water and brought the mugs over to the couch. She put one into Evie's hands. Its warm heaviness soothed her. Aunt Martha perched on the arm of the love seat and regarded her. "Is there something going on, Evie?" she asked. "I'm delighted you came to visit, but I get the feeling that there's something you're not telling me."

I should never have come, Evie thought. She took a sip of the tea, even though it was still too hot, and tried to figure out what to say. However good Evie was at detecting lies, her aunt was ten times better.

As if sensing Evie's discomfort, Aunt Martha put a hand on her shoulder and said, "How about this. If you don't want to talk about it, why not ask the cards for advice?"

Evie looked up, her unease replaced by curiosity. She'd never had a tarot reading done before, though she'd always wanted one. Not only that, but it would get her right out of this awkward conversation. "Sure," she said. "I'd like that."

Aunt Martha led her back to the reading room and closed the door behind her. "Sit," her aunt said, and she gestured to one of the overstuffed chairs. Once Evie settled in, her tea warming her hands, Aunt Martha went to the bookshelf to light a stick of incense and turn on some low, soft music. She paused at a line of small boxes on the shelf before picking one and bringing it to the table. "For you, I think we go with the classic Rider-Waite deck. It is your first time, after all." She placed the wooden box on the table between them and opened it. Inside, Evie saw the light blue checkered back of a worn deck of cards. Aunt Martha lifted them out with reverence and handed them to Evie. "Shuffle the deck—however you like. Do it until it feels right. It's okay if you don't want to tell me what you want to ask the cards, but I want you to think about that question while you mix them."

Evie nodded, and began awkwardly shuffling the oversize cards. They felt good in her hands, smooth and heavy, their edges soft with age. As the smoky aroma of sandalwood filled her senses, she relaxed and closed her eyes.

A question for the cards. She tried to think of normal things.
How do I deal with my annoying brother?
Will I make new friends in Ravenglass?

Will I get good grades in school?

But something else kept creeping in at the edges of her mind. A skulking darkness that she could not understand but refused to be ignored.

What's wrong with you? it whispered.

Evie opened her eyes and set the cards down on the table. She had a sudden desire to throw them across the room, to watch them scatter, unable to reveal whatever they had seen when she let them peer inside.

Aunt Martha was looking at her, expectant. "Finished?" she asked.

It's just a game, Evie told herself. *It's just for fun*. She gave a small smile. "Yes," she said. "All done."

Aunt Martha took up the cards in her long, elegant fingers and weighed them in her hands. For some reason, Evie was reminded of something she'd seen during that visit to the ancient Egyptian exhibit at the Met—the illustrated scene of "The Judgment of the Dead." In it, the heart of the dead is weighed against a feather plucked from the goddess of truth. If the heart does not balance the scales, then the dead soul will be condemned to be devoured by a great beast who stands by, watchful and hungry. Evie found that she was holding her breath, and finally let it out in a shuddering exhale.

Aunt Martha glanced up at her. "Are you all right?"

"Totally fine, please go ahead."

Aunt Martha nodded. "I'm going to do a Celtic Cross reading. It's a ten-card pattern, a cross on the left, a tower on the right. The six cards of the cross tell us about your situation as it is, and the four of the tower represent what the cards would like to tell you." She began to lay out the cards one by one.

The High Priestess.

The Moon.

The pictures on the cards looked ancient and mysterious, with dark lines and bright, primary colors. Evie saw a man on a boat, rowing a lonely mother and child out to sea surrounded by six swords. She saw a man mourning over three spilled cups, and another man sitting upright in his bed, head in hands, nine swords hanging on the wall behind him. And there were more.

The Devil.

The Eight of Cups.

The Lovers.

There was a blindfolded woman standing on uneven ground, her body bound, surrounded by eight swords. And then, the tenth card.

Death.

When Aunt Martha saw the expression on Evie's face, she chuckled and said, "Don't look so worried. The cards aren't meant to be taken literally." But Evie could see fear in her eyes.

"What does it mean then?" Evie asked in a low voice.

Aunt Martha cleared her throat and was silent as she studied the cards. "This is you," she finally said, pointing to the card in the center of the cross. "The High Priestess is the divine feminine, a figure that exists between darkness and light, between the seen and the unseen. The Moon card crossing the High Priestess represents the conflict before you." She stopped, a slight shake of her head. "The Moon is a very strange card—I don't see it come up in readings very often. It's a card of illusion. Of dreams. It warns us that things are not always what they seem. If we dig deeper, sometimes we discover that beneath the surface, everything is connected."

She pointed at the four cards surrounding the center of the cross. "These cards represent the past and the present, your conscious and subconscious. They tell me that you dwell on events of the past, events that keep you up at night. A lonely journey brought you to where you are today, and if you do not face these things"— her eyes drifted to the Devil card—"then you are at risk of succumbing to the shadows within yourself."

The tea had gone cold in Evie's hands. She set it down on the table, suddenly feeling as if she could not breathe. The heady scent of the incense that had been soothing before was choking and thick and close.

I feel so very, very sick.

"I have to go," Evie said, standing up.

Aunt Martha looked stunned, and put up a hand to stop her. "But—I'm not finished. Don't you want to hear the advice the cards have for you?"

But Evie was already picking up her bags weighed down with cans of soup. "I'm sorry, I didn't realize what time it's gotten to be. My mom's expecting me," she lied.

Her aunt must have sensed the excuse, and pleaded for her to stay. "Evie, please don't be upset. I know the tarot can be a little unsettling, but if you'd just sit down—"

Evie was almost crying now, which made her feel stupid and angry. She bade the tears not to fall. "I'm sorry," she said again.

She turned away to fiddle with the clasp on her bag, giving herself a moment to regain control. When she turned back to face Aunt Martha, she'd wiped her face clean. "I really do want to hear the rest of it," she said evenly. "Maybe I can come back later this week? What day is good for you?"

Aunt Martha made as if to say something, but stopped before she could. "Any afternoon is fine," she said instead. "I'm always here."

"Great," Evie said. "I'll see you soon, then."

"Do you have my number?" Aunt Martha asked, getting up to walk her to the door. "In case, you know, you ever want to talk."

"I'm sure I can ask Mom for it," Evie said.

"Well, take this, anyway." She reached into a little glass bowl on a table by the door and picked up a thick business card. It read MARTHA HOBBIE, PSYCHIC READER, and listed her phone number and email address below. She handed it to Evie.

"Thanks," Evie said. She gave her aunt a quick hug goodbye, turning away before Aunt Martha could say anything further.

Evie burst out of the door of the building, the brightness of the afternoon nearly blinding her. But she hardly noticed. She took in long gulps of fresh, cool air and stood there on the sidewalk until her heart stopped hammering. A woman pushing a baby carriage cast a concerned look her way as she passed by.

Evie hurried on, pulling up her coat collar as she went. The movement caused Aunt Martha's business card to slip from her pocket and begin to blow end over end in the breeze. Evie chased it down, picking it up off the sidewalk and dusting off the dirt. On the back of the card, making it look almost like a miniature tarot card itself, was an image of the High Priestess. The choice made sense, given Martha's profession as a kind of modern priestess herself, but Evie couldn't help but feel that it was an odd coincidence.

She said this card represented me.

In her blue robe and horned crown, the High Priestess gazed straight out at her, seated between a white column and a black one, a crescent moon at her feet. Behind her, a veil decorated with pomegranates hung. Evie remembered buying pomegranates from the local grocer near her apartment in the city, round and red and bursting with juice. They always reminded her of the myth of Hades and Persephone she'd read as a child from her illustrated book of Greek myths.

"He gave her a honey-sweet pomegranate to eat, bringing her to the hidden places, deep in the earth . . ."

She shoved the card into her pocket.

Evie told herself all kinds of pretty little lies on her walk home.

It was all nonsense. Mom thinks her sister is a kook for a reason. You've seen those shows about psychics, they just say the same vague things to everybody and then let people find their own meaning in it. It's a parlor trick.

She made her way up the narrow lane, its edges blurred with fallen leaves. Above in the trees, a single bird sang into the silence. "Whip-poor-will?" it trilled.

All these wild stories about Hobbie House are messing with your head. You've got to get it together before someone—

Evie stopped twenty feet before the door to the house. The big ginger cat was sitting on the porch railing, watching her come. His tail waved slowly below him, back and forth like a pendulum. Nearby, on the doorstep, was the small, bloody mess of another dead mole.

She bent down to look closer at it. Its throat was torn apart, and bits of dirt still clung to its small, still paws. Evie remembered her father telling her once why cats bring gifts like that to people. "They're showing you that you're part of their pack," he'd said. "And because you're part of their pack, they want to teach you what you need to know to survive."

In the woods, the bird continued its lonely song. "Whip-poor-will?" it asked. But no one answered.

7

Mom got home too late to cook dinner that night, so they sat around the kitchen table and ate canned soup and buttered toast. Dark clouds had blown in with the coming of night, and just as they settled in with their steaming bowls, a steady rain began to patter on the galvanized tin roof.

"I have great news," Mom said, dropping oyster crackers into her Manhattan clam chowder. "I got the job at the Blue River Inn! That's where I was all afternoon. Fiona—she's the manager—had called to let me know and asked if I could do some training so I could start right away. Oh, it's a *wonderful* place. So *cozy.* They make all their breakfasts in-house from scratch, with locally roasted coffee, of course, and even have a greenhouse in the back where they grow tropical flowers for the guest rooms. She gets kids from the high school to volunteer to keep it up, for some kind of class credit, I think."

Stan gave her a thumbs-up, his mouth full of chicken noodle.

"Now, this means that I'm going to have some late nights at the front desk," she went on, "but I know I can count on you two to take care of yourselves while I'm gone—right?"

"Sure, Mom," Evie replied. "We'll be fine."

"Good, good," her mother said. "How about you two? Stan, how's school?"

Stan shrugged, slathering his toast so thickly that it was more butter than bread. "It's okay."

"Make any new friends?"

"I've been hanging out with a few guys from the Glade."

"Oh! The Glade," Mom almost purred.

Evie had to physically restrain herself from rolling her eyes. During her time at school, she'd pieced together that of the two communities in Ravenglass, the Glade was the newer and wealthier one. A lot of longtime residents lived in older homes in Edgewood, but all the New York transplants and their families lived in the pristine, palatial houses in the Glade. Naturally, her mother would prefer they rub elbows with the rich kids. She never saw a ladder she didn't want to climb.

"So, Evie—have you given any thought to your plans for homecoming?" She raised her eyebrows meaningfully.

"I have not," Evie said, and it was the truth. And yet, just at the mention of the word, Evie imagined herself on Desmond's arm, looking up into the deep pools of his eyes. "I'm a little too busy at school to be thinking about stuff like that."

"Well, the dance is only a couple of weeks away, you know. It's a good opportunity for you to introduce yourself to the community and make connections. You can't just hole up in your tower with that sewing machine like some girl in a Grimms' fairy tale."

Stan snorted.

Evie felt her face redden. "Okay, Mom," she said. She shoved the last of her toast into her mouth and brought her empty bowl to the sink. "I have homework," she added, and went upstairs.

Evie closed her bedroom door behind her and leaned against it, just breathing. She tried to push the image of walking into the dance with Desmond from her mind, but it was stubbornly tenacious. She remembered the feel of her hand in his that first day—

Holding it above your heart will help stop the bleeding.

And she imagined that same press of his hand on the dance floor, raising hers as the music played—

No. It was impossible. Keeping up a secret friendship with Desmond was one thing, but going with him to homecoming was quite another. Kimber would know. *Everyone* would know. And then Kimber would make it her mission to make Evie's life miserable.

The pain of knowing it could never happen only made her want it more.

She sighed and had started to make her way into the room when something on the bed made her stop. A little white book with a silver lock.

Holly's diary.

A twinge of fear bloomed in her chest. *Didn't I leave the diary up in the attic?* But after a moment, the panic faded. Mom had been going through the entire house all week, organizing and throwing things away—she must have made her way to the attic and discovered Holly's trunk. She probably thought Evie would be interested in learning more about her famous family member and brought it down for her.

"She was fifteen when she disappeared," she imagined her mother saying. "Just like you."

There was only the small problem of the lock. Evie took the diary over to her desk and fished out a pair of scissors from her sewing kit. Sticking the tip of the scissors into the keyhole, she thumped on the handle with her fist until the lock gave way. It didn't take much. The diary looked like one a girl would pick up at the mall in one of those stores that sold cheap jewelry and pencils with decorative erasers.

She removed the lock and unfastened the clasp. As soon as she opened the front cover, a cascade of flower petals spilled out onto the desk—pale pink and as delicate as tissue paper. She brushed them aside and turned to the first page of the diary.

"January 1, 1982," it read in neat, looping handwriting. "Since I got this diary for Christmas, I figured the first day of the year would be a good time to start writing in it. Mom made her New Year's pancakes this morning, of course. Thank goodness we didn't run out of syrup because there's about three feet of snow outside, and if Dad had had to run to the General for more, he would have thrown a fit. Heather wanted to hang out, but there's no way Mom's going to let me go all the way to Edgewood on foot."

Just a normal girl living an ordinary life, Evie thought. But just ten months after she wrote those words, she was gone.

Evie went to turn the page and hesitated. She'd intended to avoid sticking her nose into the past. Hadn't she just told Tina the last thing she wanted was to be known as the girl who lived in "that house"? And yet, and yet . . .

With the diary right there in her hands, she simply could not resist climbing down into the rabbit hole and seeing what was inside.

She became excited, and decided to take a bath and bring the diary with her. Her mother had always hated her habit of reading in the bath—"you'll *ruin* your books!"—but it was something she'd always been fond of. And it would give her a chance to try out the big claw-foot tub.

She grabbed her fuzzy blue bathrobe and slipped down the hallway to the bathroom. Groping in the dark for the switch, she finally found it and flicked it on. An old brass fixture buzzed to life, flooding the bathroom with a sickly yellow glow. The cracked white tiles were cold against her bare feet as she padded to the claw-foot tub and wrenched at the green-tinged metal faucets until water rushed out. She twisted them until the water was hot, and then pushed the pull-chain plug home. She disrobed as the tub filled, and then slipped into the steaming hot water.

When the water level was high enough, Evie turned off the faucets and lay back. She sighed with pleasure as she pulled herself under, until only her face was above the surface. Her long hair floated all around her, Medusa-like. She closed her eyes for a moment, listening to the thick underwater silence. Back in New York, she always loved retreating to the bath after dinner and spending long evenings in that same silence. Down there, the sounds of the city and her parents fighting in the kitchen were muted, replaced by deep quiet and the gentle slosh of her body moving in the water.

Soon, though, her curiosity about the diary took over, and she sat up in the water, dried her hands and arms with a hand towel, and reached for the little white book. Flipping to the page where she'd left off, Evie began to read.

The first few pages were quite dull, the entries merely recounting the daily minutiae of Holly's life. Her life at school, her friends, her parents, her interest in local history. Evie got a kick out of reading about familiar things—buying sodas and candy from the General, classes at Ravenglass High, and eating at Birdie's Diner. Mama Bird ran the place back then. Holly called her Mrs. Kim, and seemed to spend a lot of time there, talking to her after school.

"I got a B on my Pre-Calc test," Holly wrote one day in April. "When Mom found out, boy, was she mad! Now she says I can't go to Heather's house after school until I prove I can do better. I got pretty upset, but Mom says crying never makes anything better. She is letting me do my studying over at Birdie's, though, so that made me happy. Mrs. Kim asked what was wrong when I went over, and I told her what happened. After that, she made me refill all the salt and pepper shakers. I kept asking her why, but she just told me to do it. When it was all done, she said that I couldn't do anything about my mom and dad, but I could do something about the salt and pepper shakers. I actually felt a little better after that!"

A saccharine cheerfulness seemed to permeate every entry in the diary, so that no matter what was happening, Holly took it in stride. Even when her mother ruled over her with an iron fist, punishing her every imaginable error, and her father sat by doing nothing, Holly simply found some good in it, or wrote about feeding the feral cats in the woods, or the sounds of birds. It all made her sound oddly childlike, even though she'd been Evie's age at the time.

And then, sometime during the height of summer—things began to change.

"I made a new friend today," Holly wrote on July 17. "She's not like anyone I've ever met before. She's a few years younger than me, but she seems so much older! I see her after school sometimes. We sit together under the apple tree, and she tells me these amazing stories. She likes for me to tell her stories about me, too, but mine are always boring compared to hers. She says she likes them, though, and asks all about Mom, and Dad, and even J. In fact, she might be the only person I've ever told about J! But she says she's really good at keeping secrets, so I'm not worried. We made a promise to each other that she wouldn't tell anyone my secrets and I wouldn't tell anyone about her."

Evie sat up in the water, her interest piqued. *Now this is getting interesting*, she thought. Who was this nameless new friend? And who was J? She read on.

On September 3, she wrote, "I've been sneaking out to Heather's house after school and telling Mom that I was at Birdie's instead. Today Mom found out. She yelled and stomped around the kitchen, and threatened to ground me for a month. I felt like crying. But then I remembered what my secret friend told me, so instead I just told Mom, very quietly, that she should stop talking before she says something she'll regret. I might as well have slapped her, that's how shocked she looked. She always liked to see me break. But I wasn't going to. Not anymore."

Not only had Holly's tone changed, but her handwriting had, too. The neat letters with the hearts over the *I*s were slowly replaced by a messier script. At times, the pen pressed so hard that ghosts of the words could be seen on the pages beneath.

And then, in the middle of September, Holly started writing about J.

"I just know I'm going to fail English this semester because J's in that class. We haven't been in class together since middle school, and now he sits right next to me. I think he did it on purpose, because he looks over at me sometimes. I can't always see him doing it, but I can feel it. Sometimes he passes notes to me folded into little triangles. I tuck them into my jeans pocket and read them at lunch when I'm alone. Today Mrs. Murphy called on me to answer a question about *The Scarlet Letter* and I couldn't because I wasn't listening. I was just thinking about him. Tricia laughed but I don't care because she's an idiot. I've always thought so, but I was too nice to even write it down. Why is that? It's not like anyone is going to read this. I don't want to be like that anymore. My secret friend keeps telling me that I should be myself. That there are gifts I have forsaken. She says, *What use are wings if not to fly? What use are teeth if not to bite? It feels so good to let go.*"

There was a break in the writing—several lines left blank as if to demonstrate Holly sitting deep in thought. And then,

"I think I'm in love with him."

Evie lost track of time as she read, the bathwater cooling around her. Holly's writing filled every inch of the pages that followed, the words spilling into the margins and climbing up the edges like little spiders. Here and there, the words blurred into each other, as if Holly had been scribbling so quickly that the ink had had no time to dry before the side of her hand smeared them. At the beginning of October, Holly began to write about the upcoming homecoming dance. With the prospect of going as J's date, some of Holly's old cheerfulness seemed to return.

"He's going to ask me, I just know it. I've been telling Heather every day how incredible it's going to be, but she only wants to talk about how I've been acting different lately. Isn't that a good thing? My secret friend thinks it is. She loves talking about the dance. She even said she knows exactly what I should wear! She's keeping it safe in a special place just for me. I can't wait!"

There was a sick feeling in Evie's stomach as she looked at the date of the next entry. October 30, 1982. The day of Holly's disappearance. She suddenly felt a desperation to stop reading. Put the diary down, pack it away, and never open it again. It was an unreasoning feeling that if she continued, she would be passing into a place from which there was no return.

But before she could choose, before a decision had been made in her mind, it was already too late. She was already reading the words. She was already on the other side.

"Mom grounded me on homecoming night she grounded me she's keeping me away from him and I don't know what to do," Holly wrote in a barely legible scrawl. "She's a blackhearted monster she's jealous and just wants to control me and Dad doesn't care he doesn't even bother getting up from the TV he is so worthless. But my secret friend told me that she's going to help me she's going to take me to her special place so that I can go to the dance and she says I'll look so beautiful that J will take me into his arms and everything else will go away and it will be so perfect she says. So perfect and so beautiful just like a dream come true."

All the rest of the pages were blank.

Evie was shaken, the excitement she'd felt earlier about reading the diary having given way to horror. People had always assumed that Holly had run away, or perhaps been abducted and never found—even though there was no real evidence to support either theory. But this diary seemed to suggest something else, something ghastly. Why had the newspapers never mentioned any of this? Had the police somehow overlooked the diary? Evie had never heard anything about Holly experiencing any psychological distress, and yet the diary made it crystal clear that she had, and that people back then knew about it. But why would they keep something so important a secret?

You should leave this alone, she told herself. *Nothing good will come of it. You've been losing your grip ever since you got here—and you think* this *is going to help? Forget about this and focus on what you can control.* She set the diary gently on the tile floor and took a deep breath. The thing was, it was more than just the questions about Holly's disappearance that upset her.

It was just how much Holly reminded her of herself.

The bathwater was cold and had receded slightly, but Evie wasn't quite ready to get out. Maybe if she refilled the tub and relaxed for a while, she'd be able to reclaim some of her earlier good feelings before going to bed.

She leaned forward to grasp the hot water faucet and gave it a twist. The faucet squealed in protest, but soon water started filling up the bath once more. Evie lay back and closed her eyes with a sigh. After a moment, however, she felt a chill reach her toes and pulled them back, alarmed. Was something wrong with the old plumbing? she wondered. Evie opened her eyes to check.

A torrent of sludge, thick and black, was being regurgitated out of the faucet. It had gathered in a heaving mass at the end of the bath, churning like a storm cloud, its tendrils creeping farther toward her as more of it poured in.

In seconds half the bath was filled with it, and it shone like an oil slick, opaque and black. She recoiled, but not before it could reach her, creeping up and around her toes, knees, and legs—cold as ice. And then, from somewhere beneath the surface, something touched her. Icy fingers that closed around her ankle and held it in an unbreakable grip.

F ear choked her like a hand around her throat. *Move! Move!*

But she couldn't. Like a hunted animal she knew the danger and yet couldn't run from it. Time slowed, and her every sense was heightened. The rush of water was thunderous, and an odd smell permeated everything. At first it was sweet and fragrant, but quickly it became cloying—the smell of rot.

The black water had filled the whole bathtub, complete, like a hole in the world. Her skin felt like tiny spiders were crawling all over it, searching, biting with a cold so complete that it felt like death. Blood thundered in Evie's ears—or was that the water, still rushing in? It was spilling over the edges. Her body was somewhere underneath the surface, unseen, and soon her head would go under, too. She gasped and tried to move, but her body didn't respond. Was it even there anymore? She couldn't feel anything but cold, couldn't see anything but the black water, couldn't smell anything but sweet decay.

The grip around her ankle pulled her down.

The water was up over her ears now. But instead of that tranquil underwater silence, Evie heard something else. A dissonant whispering, echoing through the water as if across a wide sea.

Look down, it said.

Look down.

The water was almost in her mouth.

Look down.

And then, from what seemed like a thousand miles away, she heard her mother's voice calling.

"Evie! Are you still in the bathroom? I need to ask you something."

Evie clung to the sound like a life preserver. Suddenly she felt she could move, could feel her body under the water. She reached out to grip the sides of the bath and pulled herself up out of the water with a violent jerk. The fingers held on for a moment, but then let go. She fell out of the tub onto the floor in her haste to escape it, her feet slipping on the wet tiles as she pushed herself against the far wall, sobbing. She curled up into a ball and buried her head in her arms, rocking, unable to bring herself to look at the bath, imagining that whatever had held her would surely come climbing out.

She heard the door open. "Evie, you can't run the water all night," her mother started to say, and then stopped short. "*Evie? What . . . What is going on?*" The faucet squealed once more, and the thunder of water stopped. There was silence, and then the wet sounds of her mother's bare feet on the puddled floor. A moment later, a hand on her shoulder. "God, you're freezing!" Mom said, recoiling. A warm, soft towel was wrapped about her body, and she sensed her mother squatting beside her. "Evie. Look at me."

"No," Evie managed to say, though it was more like a moan. "No, no, no."

"Look at me!"

Evie raised her head, fully expecting to see some dark, dripping specter looming over her mother's shoulder. But there was nothing. Even the water, which was still spilling over the lip of the bathtub, was clear.

Her terror, so sharp and focused a moment ago, scattered first into confusion and then, an instant later, into embarrassment. She pulled the towel around herself more tightly and cast a glance at her mother, who looked at her in exactly the way she knew she would. The same way people look at wounded animals. With pity. And caution.

"Now, tell me what happened," Mom said.

Evie hardly knew what to say. "I . . . I saw something," she stammered. "In the water."

Mom craned her neck to glance at the bathwater. She looked pained. "I don't see anything, honey," she said.

Evie's composure began to slip. *Not again*, she thought. Mom was here, touching her, looking at her, and yet it was like they were on different sides of an invisible veil. Evie's world was crooked, knocked off its axis and spinning out of control. It felt like a funhouse, where illusions and odd angles made you feel as if you were falling even when you were standing still. It was a familiar sensation, although she'd kept it at bay for a long, long time.

Pull yourself together! she commanded.

Evie sat up, tucking wet strands of hair behind her ears and wiping her face with the towel. "I must have been dreaming," she said. "I must have fallen asleep."

Mom looked alarmed. "Fell asleep in the bathtub? With the water running? Evie, you could have drowned!"

"I'm sorry," Evie muttered, because there was nothing else to say.

Mom sighed with such deep exasperation that Evie wanted to run away. "C'mon, let's get you up off the floor. Can you walk?"

With her mother's help, Evie clambered to her feet. As she dried herself and got dressed, Mom went about mopping up the floor with a towel and pulling the plug to let the bathwater out. Evie watched the water spin in a whirlpool down the drain until the very last of it glugged away with a sucking gasp.

"Come on, let's get you into bed," Mom said. She laid a hand over Evie's forehead, considering. "You don't feel warm, but then again you were stone cold just a minute ago. It's been a very busy week, and between the change of location and change of season, you could easily be coming down with something. You need rest. Can't have you missing school when you've only just started!" Already the cheer had crept back into her voice.

Evie knew she should have been comforted by it, but instead it irritated her. She slipped out from under her mother's touch and turned back toward the bathroom. "Wait, I have to get the diary." Somehow, the little book had avoided being soaked by the dripping water and was lying just under the head of the claw-foot tub.

"Diary?" Mom asked, looking at the book curiously.

"Yeah, Holly's diary. You brought it down from the attic for me, remember?"

Mom's eyes flicked to Evie's, cautious again. "No," she said. "I didn't bring anything down. It's Holly's diary? Are you sure?"

"I think so," Evie said after a moment, her mouth dry. "I don't know." Her mind was racing. *If Mom didn't leave the diary on my bed, who did?*

Mom cleared her throat. Her face was maddeningly sympathetic. "Evie," she said, "I can always call Dr. Mears, you know, if you feel like you need to—"

"No."

The word was a clean cut. Mom nodded once, and that was all. "Fine," she said. "Whatever you want."

Evie got up and pulled on her bathrobe, tucking the diary into one of the big front pockets. She twisted her hair into the towel and piled it on top of her head. "I'll be in my room," she said, and walked out.

Stan was loitering by his bedroom door, his narrow shoulders hunched inside his ever-present black hoodie. He watched her passage down the hallway with interest, his head cocked like a crow's. All his baby fat had vanished over the past year, replaced with a long leanness that made him look too old for Evie's liking. He used to look at her just like that when he was little—whenever something went wrong, he would check to see how Evie reacted, to make sure everything was going to be okay. But after everything fell apart, he stopped. Maybe he just didn't trust Evie to know if things would be all right anymore.

But as she passed him, he looked at her with that same old questioning stare. Had he heard what had happened in the bathroom? "What?" she said, stopping in front of him.

"What was it?" he asked, a glint of fear in his eyes. Despite how old he might act, he was still only ten. "What did you see?"

Evie licked her lips. "Nothing," she said. "It was nothing."

It was only nine o'clock, so Evie changed into sweatpants and a T-shirt, piled up the pillows at the head of her bed, and slipped under her quilt with the diary in her hand. She felt drained, but as the numb terror faded from her mind, she felt something else, too. When they'd first arrived at Hobbie House, Evie had been determined to avoid delving into the history of the house and Holly's disappearance. But now she was possessed with an equal determination to do the exact opposite. Something was haunting her; she couldn't deny it any longer. And somehow, she felt that unless she understood what it was, it wouldn't stop. It would only try harder to get her attention. She had to take control of the situation. If she did that, if she just figured out what was going on, everything would be okay.

She ran her fingers across the smooth white cover of the diary. *I didn't really fall asleep in there, did I?*

No, no—it was *real*, this thing. Whatever it was. It had to be.

Once, back in New York, Evie and three of her friends had sneaked into an old, vacant brownstone near her apartment. Hannah had brought a Ouija board, and they'd all sat down on the splintery hardwood floor and tried to talk to the spirits. Once they'd all stopped giggling, the planchette seemed to move, hovering over letters one by one. Each of them swore they weren't moving it, swore that their fingers were barely even touching the thing as it swung smoothly from one side of the board to the other. They'd watched, rapt, as it spelled out three words, pausing for a long moment between each.

I'm. So. Cold.

The girls had leaped to their feet, screaming, and hadn't stopped running until there was an entire city block between them and the old building. They'd stood there, panting, terrified and thrilled that their little experiment with the occult had worked so spectacularly well.

They never did it again, though. Hannah's Ouija board was probably still sitting where they'd left it, gathering dust.

They'd retold the story at least a dozen times ever since—it was great for parties. But where Hannah and the others remembered the experience as great fun, Evie always remembered it differently, if she chose to remember it at all. Most of the time, she tried not to.

It was the day she realized the possibility that the world was not as orderly as she'd been brought up to believe. That there were wild things, things that didn't follow the rules, things that most people liked to dismiss because taking them seriously opened a door that was better kept shut and locked tight.

Something changed inside Evie that day. Something that had never, ever changed back.

Evie had seen one of those things in the bathroom that night. She knew that. She'd opened that door, and now she was the only one who could close it again.

With that in mind, she flipped through the diary. She wanted to check that she hadn't missed anything after the last entry, but there was nothing. She was about to set it down on her nightstand when she noticed that it didn't quite close all the way. She opened the book to the back cover and saw that the diary included a small white pocket, probably meant to store notes or keepsakes. Turning the book sideways, she shook it until a gold locket fell out onto the quilt.

Evie picked it up. It was round and tarnished, and the chain that it hung from had a hook-and-eye clasp that looked old. The front of the locket was monogrammed, the two letters written in an intertwining, spidery script. Evie squinted, moving it closer to the light. "*S . . . F,*" she muttered. Sliding her fingernail in the crease, she eased it open and looked inside. A tiny photograph was pressed inside the back, so dark and ancient that Evie thought it must have been entombed in the locket for a century or more. She could hardly make out the image at all—but it seemed to be the head of a young girl, her dark hair plaited underneath a bonnet. She sat sideways before a murky background, her head turned toward the camera. But her face . . . her face was a ghostly blur, hazy and indistinct, as if she had moved just at the moment the picture was taken.

Evie closed the locket with a gentle snap and hung it before her eyes. It swung like a pendulum, back and forth. *It must have been Holly's,* she thought. *It was in her diary, after all.* But the initials and the simple age of the thing led her to believe that it had belonged to someone else before Holly got her hands on it.

Had Holly lain in this bed, holding this locket and wondering the very same thing?

Before long, Evie's eyes began to feel heavy. It was still early, but she was exhausted. She placed the locket on the nightstand with the diary, switched off the light, and pulled the quilt high up to her chin. Only moments later she was asleep.

In the dream, Evie stood out on the front lawn. The world was dark and murky, stained with the color of old things, and the big apple tree was smaller than she remembered. Apples littered the grass all around, soft and bursting with wormholes. Beyond the clearing, the woods loomed but did not move. The air was as still as glass.

Two girls sat under the shadow of the apple tree, one small and one tall, one dark and one fair. Their faces were both downcast, looking at something on the grass between them. They wore long, voluminous dresses and bonnets, and looked for all the world like two little dolls set up for play. The small one was humming a song that felt familiar, but Evie could not remember why. Evie did not want to go any closer, but she did, nonetheless.

The tall girl gathered some objects into her right hand and tossed them into the air like a bunch of jacks. They were tiny, ill-shaped things, and they hung there for an instant before soundlessly falling back to earth. The girl caught a few of them on the back of her hand, and then with a quick movement threw them up again to catch one in her palm. And still the small one hummed.

Evie was only a few feet away from them now. On the grass between the two girls, she could see a dozen little bones, artifacts from some long-dead creature. The tall girl opened her fingers to reveal the object inside, a tiny, perfect skull. "This will be my taw," she said. Her voice was scratchy, as if it were playing through an old record player.

"I don't want to play Scatters, let's play Friends," the small one replied sweetly.

"Are you sure you don't want to do Through the Arch?" the tall one asked.

"Oh! Yes! Through the Arch!"

The small girl made a little arch on the grass with her index fingers and thumbs. As she resumed her song, the tall girl tossed the skull into the air and swept one of the bones through the arch, catching the skull again before it hit the ground. "One," she counted. "Two . . ."

On the third try, the tall girl threw the skull wild, and it fell at Evie's feet. She bent to pick it up. It was the size of her pinkie finger, long and thin and resplendent with razor-sharp teeth. Instead of holes where its eyes would be, there was only smooth bone. It barely weighed anything at all.

The two girls stopped, and the small one looked up at Evie. Her face was blurred, her features shifting as if under a silk veil. "Holly likes this game," she said, her mouth a dark, unfocused void. "You're going to like it, too."

And then the tall girl turned toward her, but her face was not even blurry, it was nothing at all. It was a blackness that grew and swallowed everything—the bones, the apple tree, the woods, and Evie, too—

Evie woke up with a start, her bedclothes soaked with sweat. The clock on the nightstand read 3:09 a.m. Although the streetlights of Ravenglass could not reach Hobbie House, her bedroom was illuminated by the pale moonlight. Shadows pooled in the corners, while the house creaked and settled in itself like a great old beast trying to find a comfortable position to sleep.

But the house didn't sleep. And for the rest of that night, neither did Evie.

9

The final bell rang just as Evie made it to the classroom door. She had an enormous blue Ikea bag hitched over one shoulder and her bookbag over the other, so she had to turn sideways to fit through.

"Unlike you to be late, Miss Archer," the teacher said with a pointed look.

"Sorry, Ms. Jackson," Evie murmured, and hurried over to her table.

"What have you got there?"

"Oh, this?" Evie adjusted her fingers around the nylon handle of the bag. "It's something for my final project."

The stern expression on the teacher's face melted in an instant. "Is it?" she said with a smile. "How ambitious. Go on, now, and get started. I'm looking forward to seeing what you come up with. You made that dress you're wearing, didn't you?"

Evie glanced down at her honey-colored dress, the one with the empire waist, ruched bodice, and bishop sleeves. She'd made it last year out of a gorgeous cotton-poly blend she'd found at a remnant shop downtown. She called it her fairy dress.

"I did make it," Evie said, blushing slightly. "Is it that obvious?"

"Not to anyone but me," Ms. Jackson went on. She fingered the gathered cuff of her sleeve with the studied touch of a professional. "Handmade items have a certain spirit to them—an individuality. When you look at them, you know right away there is no other like it." She glanced up at Evie over the frames of her glasses. "I know that look. It's the look of an artist possessed with an idea . . . Don't let me keep you from it."

Evie nodded, and made her way to her table, doing her best to ignore the glances and whispers that erupted in her wake. She'd pretty much kept to herself since she'd arrived in Ravenglass, but that didn't stop the rumor mill from churning. And her friendship with Desmond was just the kind of grist everyone loved to throw onto the millstone.

He looked up from his Singer when she approached, his frustration turning to relief. "Thank god," he said. "I think I just sewed the sleeve onto the collar. I was about to call nine-one-one."

Evie laughed, and it made her feel human again. "Here, let me grab a seam ripper from my bag," she said, setting down her burdens. "We'll have to take out the stitches one by one."

"I'm about to rip a lot more than just the seam of this thing . . . ," he muttered, staring at the pile of black-and-gold fabric before him.

"Oh, calm down, we'll fix it," she said, and sat down on the stool next to him.

While Evie repaired the damage, Desmond eyeballed the blue Ikea bag on the floor. "Is that the fabric for your dress?" he asked.

Evie swallowed, her eyes following his to the bag. She heaved it onto the table beside the sewing machines and opened it. Inside were the white ditsy print, the brown gingham, the blue paisley. Some of the old, beautiful bolts from the attic. "Yes," she breathed. "It is."

As she had lain awake the night before, the memory of that dream alive in her mind, she'd tried to distract herself with thoughts of the dress she would make. The lovely dress that had come to her like a lightning bolt that day, fully formed. She'd thought about how much fabric she would need, the order and pattern of it. Normally that line of thinking calmed her when things in her life were stressful, but thoughts of the dress only wakened her further, and seized her with a desire to have the fabric in her hands that very moment.

She'd waited until the sun rose to brave the attic. Given everything else that had happened, she feared it somewhat less than before, but still Evie wanted to spend as little time there as possible. Quietly, so as not to wake her mother or Stan, she'd pulled down the ladder, scrambled up into the dimness, gathered the fabric in her arms, and dropped back down to the landing without pause. The whole thing had taken less than two minutes. Evie had carried the bolts to her bedroom and waited in the thin morning light, staring at the pile of fabric, until it was time to get dressed for school.

Desmond reached out to touch the white ditsy print, which was covered in tiny blue flowers and bright green leaves. He rubbed it between his fingers thoughtfully. "This stuff is nothing like what they've got in the back room. Real soft. Where'd you get it?"

"I found it in the attic. In Hobbie House," Evie said.

Desmond's nostrils flared, and he pulled his fingers away. She could see him resisting the urge to wipe his hand on his pants. "But it looks brand new," he said.

Evie shrugged. "I know. It's strange, isn't it? They were stored in plastic, though, so I guess that must have preserved them." She laid the bolts next to each other in a row, creating an earthy rainbow of pattern and color.

"So which one are you going to use for your dress?" Desmond asked.

Evie ran her hands across the silky softness, eager to lay them out and start measuring patterns, eager to fold and cut and pin, to take the image from her mind and make it real. "All of them," she replied.

"Three different patterns?" Desmond said, sounding confused.

"They may look like they don't go together, but they will," Evie said, pulling out a blue pencil and her special shears from her bag. "You'll see."

"I guess I will," Desmond repeated. "It sounds complicated. But then, you're a complicated girl."

Evie deliberately didn't stop what she was doing, didn't look at him. Was he mocking her? She couldn't tell. "Am I?" she said vaguely.

"Yes," he said as she rolled out the blue paisley. "But I like a challenge. You should see me with a Rubik's Cube." He snapped his fingers. "Solve it like *that*."

Evie sneaked a look at him and couldn't stop herself from grinning. "I'm not a Rubik's Cube. It's not that easy."

"That's what you think," he said. "I've already got the top face worked out, you just don't realize it yet. Mm-hmm. All clicking into place now. Watch out." He mimed the twists and turns of the Rubik's Cube until she had to laugh.

Evie could feel her resolve slipping. She wanted desperately to open up to him, to really be herself—but no, that was impossible. It was too dangerous, especially now. She had to keep him at arm's length, at least until she'd gotten everything under control. "You've got me all wrong, Desmond. I'm just a simple farmgirl who's new to this town and likes to sew. Just ask Tina Sànchez."

"Tina lies," Desmond said simply. "When it suits her, of course. She knows you're not simple, she probably just told you that to make you comfortable enough to spill some beans. Anyway, speaking of your being new—will you meet me after school? There's something I want to show you."

"What is it?" Evie asked.

"The crown jewel of Ravenglass, of course. King Quarry. My birthright." He said the last word with a hint of bitterness that surprised her. "It's a nice walk up the mountain to get there, and since it's going to start getting colder soon, I thought it would be a good day for it. What do you think?"

Evie thought about the homework she'd need to do, as well as the list of chores Mom had left for her on the kitchen table that morning. *It can wait,* some excited part of her urged. But what would her mother think about her going off into the woods with a boy she'd never met? *She doesn't have to know. And anyway, Desmond is the golden boy in this town. If anything, Mom will give me brownie points for expert social climbing.*

"Okay," Evie said. "Meet you out front then?"

Desmond smiled. "It's a date," he said.

As he moved away to try to work on his jersey project, Evie settled down to draw out her dress pattern and think. Did he mean like a *date* date? She'd told Tina she was going to stay away from Desmond and now here she was, doing the exact opposite.

At this point, it wasn't a matter of *if* Kimber would find out, but *when*. What was she thinking?

She suddenly remembered Holly's excitement as she wrote about talking back to her mother and spending time with the mysterious J.

"It feels so good to let go."

After everything, Evie wanted so desperately to feel good. Whatever the price.

Evie went back to the FSC classroom after school for a few minutes to cut a couple more patterns for the dress, and to wait until most of the students had already gone. When she finally ventured out, the flow of students had slowed to a trickle. She could see Desmond waiting for her through the window, earbuds plugged in, his lips moving to the words of a song. After putting away her project, she slung her bookbag over her shoulder and went out into the hall. But before she made it to the front doors, she heard Tina calling out to her. "Evie! Wait up!"

Not now, Evie thought, but there was nothing to be done. She stopped and waited until Tina caught up with her.

"Hey," Tina said, and they walked together to the exit. "You want to go to Birdie's? We could grab a snack and I could tell you more about the house . . . You know, if you want."

"Um," Evie hesitated. "I would love to, really. But I kind of have plans—" The moment they pushed through the front doors, Desmond turned around, looked at Evie, and smiled.

It took Tina approximately five seconds to size up the situation and understand what was going on. She leaned over to Evie as they walked down the concrete steps and whispered, "I thought you were going to avoid that particular situation."

"He's just giving me a tour of the quarry," Evie said. "It's no big deal."

Tina nodded slowly, her lips pressed together as if to keep any further argument from escaping. "Sure," she said.

"How about tomorrow?" Evie asked. "Birdie's?"

"Tomorrow," Tina agreed, and walked toward town, casting a curious glance at them as she went.

Evie walked up to Desmond, and he pulled the earbuds from his ears. She could hear the bass beats still pouring out as he shoved them into his jacket pocket. "Ready?" he asked.

She hitched her bookbag higher up on her shoulder and nodded. "I'm ready."

Instead of going back down to Main Street, Desmond led her across the north part of town, through streets that cut across Edgewood and the Glade. The Glade was pure suburbia, right down to the manicured yards and the white picket fences, but even Edgewood, with its elderly bungalows tucked into clearings between dense thickets of oak, seemed perfectly ordinary compared with Hobbie House. The houses in these neighborhoods stood together, in neat little lines or clustered in cul-de-sacs. Hobbie House stood alone. After living her whole life with neighbors on the other side of every floor and ceiling, Evie wondered if she'd ever get used to it.

Once they passed the last house in Edgewood, Desmond pointed up a winding road and said, "We're going up here, to the mountain pass. There's a pretty wide shoulder, and no traffic comes this way other than trucks heading to and from the quarry, so don't worry."

"I'm not worried," she said, and followed him under the dark canopy of trees.

It wasn't long before she'd worked up a sweat—the road maintained a steep incline as it climbed up the mountain, and it was rough going in some spots that had become slippery with mud. At one point Evie nearly took a fall, but Desmond reached out to steady her, his warm hand clasping her elbow until she regained her footing. The air grew cooler as they climbed, and it was quiet except for the dry rush of fallen leaves blowing in whirligigs across the road.

Cresting the hill, they reached a clearing, and Evie could see Ravenglass laid out beneath them in miniature. The neat pattern of homes on the north end, the school campus to the east, and Main Street underlining it below, buildings huddled on either side like animals around a watering hole. The tree cover surrounding Ravenglass was broken only by the serpentine shape of the river, which encircled almost the entire town—the western mountains where they stood finished the job.

She and Desmond stood together, studying the view while she caught her breath. "It's really beautiful up here," she said, feeling the need to break the silence.

After a moment, he said, "Even a beautiful prison is still a prison."

She glanced at him. "What do you mean?"

Desmond shrugged. "I was born here, have lived here all my life, and my parents expect me to die here like a good boy. It's a nice town. But life's too short to live and die in a nice town." He looked down at his hands. "Sometimes I think I'd rather monumentally fail at something different somewhere else than be a complete success here. At least I'd have a story to tell."

"A nurse."

Desmond gave a lopsided grin and nodded. "No matter where you go, people need two things: teachers and nurses. I picked one."

Evie held up her finger, which only had a Band-Aid on it now. "Well, my finger didn't fall off yet, so you're off to a great start."

They kept walking, and eventually came to a fork in the road. The left-hand side was still paved and new, and the right-hand road quickly turned to gravel. In the distance, Evie could see a wall of the scrub-covered mountain rise from the end of the gravel road, where piles of gray rocks littered the ground below. Set into the mountain wall was an open mouth, framed by old timber and adorned with a rusting sign that read NO TRESPASSING.

"What's that?" Evie asked.

"Oh, that's the entrance to the old gold mines. No one's gone down there in, like, a hundred years except safety inspectors from the county. They sniff around every once in a while to check for dead tourists, but that's about it. You know, city folks who wander in there, thinking they'll find something shiny, and fall down a mine shaft."

Evie laughed. "Wait, gold mines? Is that why we're 'The Home of the Fighting Miners' and all that?"

Desmond nodded. "There hasn't been any gold mining here in a long, long time—but it's still what Ravenglass prides itself on. Back in the early 1800s, Ravenglass was just a little collection of homes and a general store—not really a town at all. But around 1855 the gold rush hit right north of here in Vermont, around Stowe and Plymouth. So when a man showed up to announce that there was gold in these hills, people were eager to believe him. His name was Wallace Brand, and he was some prospector type from California. He said he'd found gold flake in the river and knew it was flowing down from a vein in the mountain. Everyone in Ravenglass invested in the scheme, and pretty soon after the mining operation got going, the town was big enough to establish itself. New businesses opened up, schools, all that. Dad says the records get a little fuzzy after that—but at some point after the gold frenzy, things sort of just dried up. Maybe the gold ran out, maybe Mr. Brand got tired of the place and moved on. There isn't much mention of the town hero after 1857, so he must've. Anyway, the miners set down their pickaxes at some point after that, moved on to jobs at the sawmill. And after that shut down during the Depression, my great-great-grandfather came back from the war and found granite deposits in the mountain. He started the quarry and brought Ravenglass back from the brink of extinction. Been that way ever since."

"Huh," Evie said. "They really held on to all that gold stuff, didn't they?"

"Yup," Desmond agreed. "Put up a statue and a plaque for good old Wallace Brand and imported a truckload of little gold nuggets for the gift shop. It's good for business, I guess. Lots of people from New York and New Jersey come through here in the summertime for the Gold Festival to buy jewelry and all those little gold nuggets. They don't care if they're just rocks painted gold. They come here to see a place stuck in time, and that's what Ravenglass delivers."

"It sounds like you feel stuck, too," Evie said quietly.

Desmond looked at her, surprised.

"I'm sorry," she said abruptly, her cheeks burning. "That was rude. I don't know why I said that."

Desmond looked ahead, his profile outlined in afternoon light. Evie thought again of ancient statues carved from stone, noble and unmarked, and was seized by a desperate desire to run her fingers down his jaw, to cup his face in her hands.

"No, you're right," he said. "I do feel stuck here. Being who I am, I have a certain duty to stay. Sometimes I just want to be a regular guy and melt into the crowd, but I can't. I always have to be Desmond King. A lot of times people just try to say what they think will impress me, or get them in good with me and mine." He paused, licking his lips. "It just feels like I don't really know anyone at all."

He looked at her, and she felt ashamed. He didn't really know her, either, not really.

"That's why I like hanging out with you, Evie," he went on.

Please, she thought miserably. *Please stop talking.*

"Because you're real."

Evie said nothing, and hated herself for it.

Desmond smiled and looked down, wiping a hand across his mouth. "Listen to me, complaining. Poor little rich boy, right?"

"Not at all," Evie replied. "Sometimes I want to disappear, too."

"Well, here we are," Desmond said as they crested the last hill. "King Quarry. Home sweet home." He led her to the edge of the tree line, where the land dropped off so cleanly that it looked like it had been sliced by a knife. The quarry spread out below them, a wide gray canyon with a pool of dark green water on one side. The stone was cut into giant steps, each one leading to another by a series of bright yellow ladders. Various trucks, loaders, and excavators sat at the bottom, dusty and still, along with a few regular cars parked next to an office trailer. "What do you think?" he asked as they continued down along the road, which wound down to where the cars were parked.

"It's incredible," she said. "I've never seen anything like it before."

A moment later, a man emerged from the trailer. He was dressed in jeans and a brick-red flannel shirt, and shielded his eyes from the sun as he walked toward them, his boots crunching on the gravel. "Des?" he called out. "That you?" He was tall and broad, with deep brown skin and a short beard peppered with gray. Evie saw his expression change when his gaze moved to her, from curiosity to something like horror. His jaw went slack; he gibbered, not words but noises.

"Dad?" Desmond called. "What's wrong?"

Mr. King took a step back and slipped on a muddy patch. With a little cry, he fell. His head hit the ground with a crack.

10

"**D**ad!"

Desmond dropped his bag to the ground and ran toward his father. Evie did the same. By the time they reached him, Evie was relieved to see him moving, groaning with pain and irritation.

"Damn clumsy of me," Mr. King muttered, and he gingerly touched the back of his head. When he pulled his fingers away, there was blood on them.

"Let me see," Desmond said, getting down on one knee.

Mr. King waved him off. Evie could see that the fall had wounded his pride. "Stop your fussing, son—I'm *fine*."

"You could have a concussion, you shouldn't—"

"Didn't I just say I'm fine? Just—"

It was at that moment that he noticed Evie again, standing close now, looking down at him with worried eyes. Confusion stole across his face before he could stop it. "Who are you?" he asked, his voice soft and strange.

Evie felt like an insect pinned to the spot. "Evelyn Archer, sir," she said haltingly. "My family just moved here a couple of weeks ago."

Desmond was looking back and forth between them, unsure of what exactly was happening. "She's in one of my classes, Dad," he said. "She's living in the old Hobbie place, and I've been meaning to show her around—"

At this, Mr. King's lip began to tremble ever so slightly. "Hobbie House?" he mumbled. He struggled to get to his feet. Desmond tried to help him, but Mr. King shouldered him off. He stood up, swaying, his eyes never leaving Evie's face. "You . . . you—" he stammered, and swooned.

Desmond shot forward to catch him. This time, Mr. King didn't fight when Desmond pulled him over to a large boulder and leaned his back against it. "I'm going to get Mom," he said, panting. "You need a doctor, I don't care what you say." He turned to Evie. "Stay with him, okay? I'll be right back."

Evie nodded, bewildered by how quickly things had spiraled out of control. Desmond ran for the trailer, his long legs pumping like pistons. She kneeled next to Mr. King on the dusty gravel. His eyes were closed, his breathing labored. A thin sheen of sweat covered his face and neck. She was relieved to see that he wasn't bleeding—the wound was superficial, not deep. But if it was a concussion, that could be serious. *I should keep him awake*, she thought, and placed a hand gently on his knee. "I'm here, Mr. King," she said softly.

After a moment his eyes fluttered open, focusing once more on her face. He licked his lips. "You look," he said in a rasp, "just like her."

Evie felt her stomach give an uncomfortable twist. "Like who?" she asked. But she already knew the answer.

"Like Holly."

Evie had to say something, had to break the terrible silence. "She was my mother's cousin," she finally managed.

He pointed, and she saw that he was looking at the golden locket, which had slipped out from under her shirt and lay against her chest. *Strange*, she thought. *I don't even remember putting it on.*

"That was her locket," he said. "She wore it every day, near the end." He swallowed and looked back at her face. "Up close, I can see the differences," he said. "Your hair is darker, your eyes are brown, hers were . . ." He broke off. "But when I first saw you, I thought . . . I thought—"

At that moment, the door to the trailer slammed open and a woman came tearing out, followed closely by Desmond. Like her husband, Mrs. King wore jeans and boots, but her blouse was a loud magenta, a color she also wore on her lips. She came toward them, not running but walking quickly, as if to run would be un-dignified. Everything about her—her hands, her expression, her black curls pinned to the side—seemed tightly coiled. "I've called Dr. Rockwell. He's expecting us," she said to Mr. King as she approached. "C'mon, let's get you in the truck." She took one look at his wound and sucked her teeth. "C'mon," she said again.

It was only then that she noticed Evie.

Mrs. King looked at her with undisguised suspicion. "Who is this?" she asked Desmond, keeping her eyes on Evie's face.

Desmond chuckled lightly, as if to ease the tension. "She's just a friend from school, Mom. Evie's new in town, so I brought her up to see the quarry."

Mrs. King's nostrils flared. "This isn't a playground, Desmond," she said, flicking a look at her son. "Walk your friend back to town and hurry to the office right away. I'll need you to watch the phones while we're gone." She motioned for Mr. King to rise, and he did so wordlessly. Mrs. King put an arm around his waist and led him toward a blue pickup truck parked next to the trailer.

She never said a word to me, Evie thought, feeling chilled. She and Desmond watched them drive up the road and away.

Desmond rubbed the back of his head, clearly embarrassed by everything that had just happened. "I'm sorry," he said. "That was weird. My parents aren't normally like that. I don't know what—"

"It's okay," she said, cutting him off. She couldn't help but feel like it was all her fault. The romance of their walk had given way to something sinister and ominous. She wanted to go home. "I should head back," she said, picking up her bookbag.

Desmond's shoulders fell, almost imperceptibly. "Yeah," he said. "Yeah." He retrieved his own bag from where he had dropped it and led her back down the mountain road to town. The walk seemed much shorter and darker in the silence between them.

"Your dad," she asked after a while. "He knew Holly? All those years ago?"

Desmond shrugged. "I guess so. I think they were at RHS around the same time—most everyone probably knew her. Small town, you know? Never mentioned her before, though. Most folks don't like to talk about what happened. Why?"

Evie shook her head. "No reason."

By the time they reached Main Street, the sun was sitting in a pool of red light, just above the horizon. It colored the world a deep shade of pink, making the town and everything in it look strange and otherworldly. "My house is down that way, on Blue Stone Court," Desmond said, pointing down a manicured road toward a stately gray colonial. "Granddad wanted to be close to the quarry but still close to Main, so it's the same house where my dad grew up. My great-granddad used to live in the old place up on the mountain, but that's empty now." He kicked at a rock with his sneaker. "You'll be okay getting home?"

Evie nodded. She felt desperate to salvage the moment, to somehow recapture the earlier bliss she'd felt walking next to him.

He stood, looking at her, the pink light outlining him in stark relief against the dark mountain. She wondered if she should kiss him. But then, it didn't seem like the right time for that. If there was such a thing. Instead, she said, "I really liked walking with you."

Desmond smiled, and she knew she'd done the right thing. "I liked it, too," he said.

"See you soon?" she asked.

"I hope so."

She turned, and felt his eyes following her as she walked away. It wasn't a kiss, but it was enough.

Evie heard footsteps behind her on the narrow lane. It was getting dark, and whatever sunlight was left was obscured by the trees that stood on either side of the road. She stopped, both to see who it was and to rest for a moment—her feet ached from all that walking.

At first it looked like a shadow was stalking her, but she quickly realized it was only Stan.

He peered up at her as he approached, his face a pale moon inside his black hoodie. "Hey," he said.

"Hey." Together, they walked toward the house. She wrinkled her nose as an acrid smell filled the air. "Ugh," she said. "Why do you smell like smoke?"

"I don't," he said.

She sniffed him. It wasn't cigarette smoke—more like a campfire. "Yes, you do. What have you been doing?"

"None of your business." He started walking faster and reached the door first.

She followed him inside. "Who are these boys from the Glade you've been hanging out with, anyway?"

But he didn't stop, didn't turn as he made his way upstairs. A moment later she heard a door slam. She sighed. Mom was at work, and probably would be all night. And Evie had better things to do than worry about her brother.

She had too many questions, too many bits of information, and no idea how they all fit together. If she could only sit down and sort them out, like pieces of a jigsaw puzzle, she thought that maybe she'd be able to see the bigger picture. She took a can of Coke from the fridge and sat down at the kitchen table. She sipped at it, listening to the house grumble and creak around her.

It seemed clear that whatever was happening to her had everything to do with Holly Hobbie and her disappearance from the house. *She's still here*, Evie thought. *Maybe she never really left.* Was Holly a ghost? If so, what did she want? Somehow, that seemed too simple. Too easy. There was more to it than that, Evie was certain.

She spun the can around and around on the table, leaving a ring of condensation behind. It was too hard to try to figure all this out alone, but she didn't want to tell anyone about it. Not all of it, at least. *They'll think I'm crazy.*

There was one person she could talk to about Hobbie House, though. Someone who would be more than happy to tell Evie everything she knew.

Evie pulled her cell phone from her bookbag and started a new text conversation.

> Hey Tina, I know I said I didn't really want to know anything about Holly and the house, but I've changed my mind. Will you help me?

Evie waited, but after three minutes and no response, she was about to give up when the three little bouncing dots appeared on her phone. A moment later:

> Aww yiss. 🔥 🔥 🔥

> What do you want to know?

Evie thought about it for a moment, and then wrote

> Everything.

I'll put together some stuff and bring it to birdie's tomorrow.

But you realize that it's not just holly and the house you need to know about. if you want the whole story, you have to know about the patchwork girl.

Evie looked up from the phone, racking her brain to remember what in the world the Patchwork Girl was. And then it came to her—it had been in that article Tina had shown her, that first night in Ravenglass. What had it said? She quickly opened an internet browser and found that same article from the *Boston Globe*.

"The original occupant of the home in the 1850s," she read, "was discovered inside the home, dead from a shotgun wound. The mystery surrounding his death was never solved, and his only child—a young girl colloquially called the Patchwork Girl for the dress she had always worn—disappeared the same day, never to be found."

With trembling hands, Evie opened the locket around her neck and looked once more at the picture within. The girl without a face, the girl in the bonnet. Could this *SF* be the Patchwork Girl? But what did she have to do with Holly? How were the two girls connected? She replied to Tina.

Like I said, tell me everything.

Evie took a drink of her soda, feeling satisfied. She'd tell Tina she was interested out of pure curiosity—that she'd found Holly's things in the attic. Her dolls, her diary. That was the truth, after all. Part of it, anyway. She would have to be careful not to lie; Tina was too smart not to see it. Evie would merely tell her enough of the truth to keep her from asking too many questions.

Feeling too tired to make more than a turkey sandwich for her dinner, Evie took her Coke and plate and sat down on the old couch to eat and watch TV. There were only reruns playing on the local channels—Mom hadn't had time to set up Netflix or anything else yet. Evie pulled a blanket over herself and watched, letting her mind drift. Eventually she must have dozed off, because the next thing she remembered, she—

was standing outside in the front yard again, coming up the narrow lane. Hadn't she already come home? She couldn't remember. The light wasn't pink anymore, but the color of an old penny that deepened the shadows that lay long across the grass.

There was something on the porch. Something big, and very still. She walked closer, her footfalls as silent as a cat's.

It was Desmond. He was lying on his side, one arm under his head and the other across his hip. She would have thought he was sleeping if his throat hadn't been torn out. His white T-shirt had absorbed most of the blood; it looked like a gruesome Rorschach test as the stain spread in ever-changing shapes.

She fell to her knees beside him. "I can fix it," she found herself saying. "I can fix it." There was a sewing needle in her hand, threaded with black. She imagined she could sew him back up, like a little doll, and he would be good as new.

She realized that someone else was standing on the porch, leaning against the railing. It was the tall girl in her dress and bonnet, her face turned away, staring into the woods. "It's too late for that," she said. "Don't blame yourself, though. You couldn't help it. It's your nature."

"I didn't do this," Evie said.

"Didn't you?" the girl replied.

There was a metallic taste in Evie's mouth, like old pennies. She raised her fingers to her lips and touched them, and they came away red with blood. The needle fell from her fingers onto the ground.

Desmond opened his eyes and looked at her. Milky, sightless eyes. "Evie," he said, his voice a gurgling moan. "What's wrong with you?"

11

"**O**f course I can work Saturday night," Mom was saying. She had her cell phone pinched between her ear and shoulder as she poured coffee into a Blue River Inn travel mug. "Absolutely, Fiona. We can talk about the brochure redesign and the revamped menu—I'm so glad you liked my proposal!"

It was Tuesday morning, and Evie sat at the kitchen table staring into a bowl of quickly softening Cheerios. She'd spent half the night on the couch and the other half tossing and turning in her bed after Mom had gotten home from work and sent her upstairs. She'd probably slept for ten hours or more, but it felt like she hadn't slept at all. The nightmares were more frequent now. Almost every night, it seemed like. She lifted a spoonful of cereal into her mouth and ate it without pleasure. It tasted like wet sand.

Stan sat next to her, eating his cereal quickly, mechanically. He was wearing his army-green hoodie and jeans—probably because his smelly black one was in the wash. Once he was done eating, he put his dishes away and slung his backpack over his shoulders. "I'm leaving," he mouthed to Mom as he made for the door. She waved him off with a smile. "Uh-huh," she said into the phone. "Oh, I agree. It isn't fall without a butternut squash bisque . . ."

Where is he going this early, anyway? Evie thought. *Middle school doesn't start for, like, two hours.* She felt, faintly, that she should pay more attention to her little brother—clearly her mother was too busy with this new job to do it herself. But at the same time, Evie was overwhelmed by her own troubles. *Stan's all right,* she told herself. *He probably just wants to hang out with these new friends of his, whoever they are.*

She took her half-eaten breakfast to the sink, rinsed the bowl and spoon, and set them in the dish rack. The smoky perfume of her mother's coffee intoxicated her. Pulling a ceramic mug from the cabinet, she poured what was left in the pot into it and added four spoonfuls of sugar.

Mom was watching her. "Hey, I'm just getting out of the house now," she said into the phone. "I'll see you soon, okay?" She set the cell phone on the counter and turned her attention to Evie. "Since when do you drink coffee?" she asked.

Evie shrugged, and took a long drink from the mug. The piles of sugar covered up the bitterness of it—she almost liked it. And it was already making her feel more awake. Falling asleep at school wasn't an option.

"You look tired," Mom went on, scrutinizing. "And pale. You know, I'm trusting you to take care of yourself while I'm at work, honey. If you can't—"

"I'm fine," Evie said, cupping the warm mug in her hands.

"Okay," her mother said lightly. She pulled a lipstick and compact out of her purse and began applying a deep pink shade to her lips. "Do you want to use some of my foundation and rouge? I know you're not into makeup, but a little color might—"

"I don't need makeup, Mom," Evie said. She could feel heat rising at the back of her neck.

"All right, all right," Mom said, raising her hands in surrender. "Excuse me for trying to help." She put the makeup back in her purse and zipped it closed with finality. "Why don't we go dress shopping after school today? I'll be home early. I told Fiona I can work over the weekend, so I have some extra time. We can drive to the next town over and check out the boutiques. I've heard they have some really nice homecoming gowns you can choose from. Wouldn't that be fun?"

Evie sipped some more coffee. "I don't need a dress. I'm making one at school."

"Oh!" Mom said it in the exact same tone as someone who'd just been shown an ugly baby and was trying to be polite. Evie waited for the other shoe to drop. "Well, that's very ambitious of you, honey. But don't you want a nice dress like the other girls? Something with chiffon—or sequins, maybe? It's going to be such a special night for you!"

Mom could disguise her disapproval under as much sweetness as she liked; Evie could still taste it. "It *will* be a nice dress, Mom," she said.

Mom nodded, unwilling to push the subject further but clearly unhappy about it. "Of course it will."

Other than saying a quick hello to Desmond, Evie barely noticed anyone else in the room that morning in FCS. She went straight to her table, sat down, and got to work. The coffee had done its job, and she felt possessed by an intense need to create.

She had already cut most of the large pieces of the dress, including the bodice and the underskirt, and was working on the ruffles for the voluminous sleeves. As she worked, her mind kept drifting back to her mother's words. *Don't you want a nice dress like the other girls?* Even now, it set Evie's teeth on edge.

Mom had always supported Evie's sewing hobby until Evie had made it clear that she considered it much more than that. Her mother had never said it directly, but Evie knew that she thought a career as a seamstress or dressmaker was something stale, obsolete. She couldn't fathom why her daughter would want to spend her days toiling in front of a sewing machine when she had the world at her fingertips. But Evie loved the *realness* of it. The feel of the pedal under her foot and the rhythmic thrum of the machine through her body. The satisfaction of fixing rips and tears and making things new again. The thrill of taking bits of fabric and thread and making something beautiful. She had no interest in coding, finance, or any of those supposedly "good" careers that her mother put up on a pedestal. What did you actually make in those jobs?

Nothing you could touch, that's for sure. Nothing *real.*

Evie needed the thrumming, solidity of sewing. She held it like a life preserver, whether her mother understood that or not.

Ms. Jackson wandered over halfway through the period and studied Evie's progress. She'd managed to finish pinning the ruffles and was measuring how much more she would need to cover the area. "It's very unique," the teacher commented. "Like something from the nineteenth century—especially with that beautiful old fabric you've brought in. Where did you get the pattern for it?"

"It's my own design," Evie said. "It's like a prairie dress, but with a modern twist."

Ms. Jackson raised her eyebrows in surprise. "Impressive," she said. "I assume you've made one like it before? You're not just doing this from scratch, are you?"

"I've made one like it before," Evie said, although she couldn't explain why. She'd never made another dress like this. So why did it still feel like the truth?

For the rest of the period, her hands seemed to move of their own volition, working toward completing the vision that was so clear in her mind. It might have been the coffee, but it felt like more than that. Her foot on the pedal, she pushed the bodice slowly under the flashing needle, which hummed in its tireless, brutal work.

Birdie's was pretty quiet when Evie and Tina arrived that afternoon—the lunch crowd had been gone for a couple of hours, and the early-bird dinner folks hadn't yet arrived. Birdie and her mother weren't even there, either. Without them, the place seemed even more empty. A couple of elderly men sat at the counter eating sweet potato pie and drinking coffee. Evie stood nearby, waiting for one of the servers to point them to a booth.

"Got pulled outta the shop to put out that fire yesterday," one of the men was saying. He had a leathery, pinched look to him like someone who'd spent too many years staring into the sun. "'Member the old Dutton place, down at the end of Knickerbocker Road? Well, it's not there no more, I'll tell ya that."

The other man took a gulp of coffee and smacked his lips. With his shiny, pink face and round body, he reminded Evie of a teapot. "Oh yeah?" he said. "How'd that happen? Brush fire or somethin'?"

"Somethin'," the first man said meaningfully. "The other guys in the RFD think it was prob'ly some kids."

"Hmm," the teapot man grumbled, lifting his mug for more. "Can't blame kids for bein' kids."

"Sure can. Ruined my afternoon, little brats. Now I gotta work late to finish rotating the tires on that Buick."

Evie listened with interest, and suddenly had a theory of why Stan might have come home yesterday smelling like smoke.

"You girls can take the far booth," said the waitress, gesturing with a sloshing coffeepot after refilling the man's mug.

Evie and Tina settled themselves in a booth by a window overlooking the mountains. Low clouds clung to the tops of trees there, threatening a murky night. Tina ordered a strawberry milk and kimchi fries, and Evie got the same. As they waited, Tina folded her fingers on the yellow Formica table and regarded Evie with eager eyes. "So," she said. "Is it haunted?"

Evie blinked. She still hadn't gotten used to just how direct Tina really was. "The house?" she said lamely.

Tina rolled her eyes. "Yes, the house. I just assumed that you wanted to talk about all this stuff because you've been hearing things go bump in the night. Have you . . . seen things?"

Images flashed through Evie's mind. The reflection in the mirror that was hers and wasn't hers at the same time. The thing in the bathwater. The nightmares. She worried that those stories would make Tina less interested in ghosts and more interested in Evie's sanity. She worried even more that Tina might somehow find out about Evie's past. But she still needed Tina to help her, so she'd have to give her *something*.

"Holly's diary," she said. "One day, I found it on my bed, but no one had put it there. And I do sometimes feel like I'm being watched. I just . . ." She faltered. "I just have this feeling that I'm supposed to figure out what really happened to her." It was easy to say, because it was the truth.

Tina's eyes widened. "Holly had a *diary*?" she said. "And *you* have it? Evie, this is huge. I don't know how it's possible, but the police must never have found it—or else it would be in a box in the station along with all the other evidence from the case. And you're saying it just appeared on your bed one day?"

"Seems like it."

"Did you read it?"

At that moment, their food arrived, and Evie gave Tina a rundown of the contents of the diary while they ate. Holly's relationship with her parents, her involvement with someone named J, and the arrival of a mysterious "secret friend" shortly before Holly's disappearance. Tina was so captivated that she burned her tongue on the hot fries.

"Well, a creepy 'secret friend' who encourages you to defy your parents certainly seems to support an abduction or runaway scenario," Tina said after cooling her mouth with some strawberry milk. "The problem with that theory was always that neither her parents nor anyone else saw her leave the house—no less the town. Not too easy to just walk out of Ravenglass." She gestured toward the mountains outside the window.

"She could have snuck out of the house and died somewhere outdoors," Evie argued.

"True." Tina gestured with a fry. "But at the time, the police chief had his officers and an entire search party out combing the woods for days. Not only did they not find her, but they didn't even find a single piece of evidence. No tracks leaving the house, no nothing. And it had been raining that week, so the ground was muddy. If she'd left on foot, there would have been something."

"But she had to have left the house . . ."

"Right, well, that's the whole problem. It's like one of those locked-room mysteries. Which is probably why this story got so much attention back when it happened. That, and the connection to the Patchwork Girl."

"Tell me more about her. The Patchwork Girl."

The bell tinkled as the two older men headed out the door to their cars. Tina licked the spicy red salt off her fingers and leaned in close. "It's a local legend, but it does have some basis in reality—although you'd have to go through some historical papers in Town Hall to find out just how much. I think the story stuck around for the same reason Holly's disappearance did. First you have the grisly, unsolved murder of the father, then you have the little girl who disappears without a trace. Did he commit suicide, only to have his daughter find him and run away in anguish? Or did the little girl kill her father herself—either on purpose or by accident—and then run away to avoid being caught? They mystery alone is captivating. But the idea that the specter of this little girl was still haunting the house? That's a whole other thing. It became this bogeyman story that kids would talk about around a campfire or at sleepovers to scare each other."

"Is it really so scary?" Evie asked, more to herself than to Tina. "The ghost of a sad little girl?"

Tina glanced at her darkly. "It is if that little girl was a murderder who doesn't want to be alone anymore." She swallowed. "The Hobbies had to deal with it, too, when they moved in. The stories and the superstition. There was even a song—kids would say that the Patchwork Girl would sing it as she wandered the woods."

A frisson rippled up Evie's spine. "A song?" she asked.

"Yeah. I think it was something like, '*Playmate, come out and play with me, and bring your dollies three*'— Evie, what's wrong?"

Evie's world had tilted sickeningly, like a ship nearly overturned by a sudden wave. She felt her stomach clench, and almost knocked over her glass of strawberry milk as she reached out to steady herself. Tina was staring at her, horrified. "Evie!" she said again. "Are you all right?"

With great effort, Evie got ahold of herself and nodded. "Sorry," she murmured. "I . . . just had a dizzy spell. That's all. I haven't been sleeping very well."

"I can imagine," Tina said, leaning back into the booth. She didn't look entirely convinced by Evie's story, but at least she wasn't going to call an ambulance.

That song, Evie thought. The mere idea of it made her feel hysterical. *It's that same song.* But there were eyes on her now. Even the waitress had looked over to see what the fuss was about. She had to stay calm. There was more to be learned here. She drank the strawberry milk down to the dregs—the cold sweetness helped her focus. "Both Holly and this girl disappeared from the same house. Is there something special about it? Something that could explain that connection?"

Tina considered the question, swirling her drink with a straw. "It's the oldest building in town, so there's that. Not the whole house—a lot of that was rebuilt or renovated several times over. But most of the first floor and the root cellar is still the original. Built about a hundred and seventy years ago—around the time all that mining started up. Only a few families lived there over the years, and never for very long. The Hobbies stayed the longest. Holly pretty much grew up there."

In all the excitement, Evie had neglected her fries, and they were getting cold. She dug in. They were crispy, and the seasoning had a tangy, spicy flavor. She ate them thoughtfully, trying not to let her frustration show. All of this was interesting—and terrifying—but it didn't seem to help her get any closer to understanding what had happened to Holly. Clearly, there was some connection between her and this other missing girl. But that only presented another mystery, and did nothing to solve either of them. Where else could she find information?

An idea came to her—a crazy idea. But desperation made her bold.

"Tina," she said after a moment. "Do you ever hang out at the police station?"

The girl looked back at Evie with curiosity. "Sometimes. Dad's usually out in the field, though, so I only drop by when he's around. Why do you ask?"

"Just wondering if you know where they keep old case files."

Tina scoffed. "You can't possibly think that we could—" She stopped talking, her gaze flicking to something right over Evie's shoulder.

"Well, hello, ladies." The voice was so close to Evie's ear that she could feel the person's hot breath on the side of her face. Startled, she turned to see Kimber Sullivan leaning over the low, frosted glass divider between booths. Her hair was pulled up into a bun, and she wore a periwinkle blouse with a big pussycat bow at the neck. "Fancy meeting you here."

"Hey, Kimber," Tina said. Her voice was light, placating. Evie said nothing.

"So, Evie," Kimber said, not acknowledging Tina at all. "You know, I could have *sworn* we had an understanding. About Desmond. You agreed to stay away from him, and in exchange, I agreed not to ruin your life." The heavy mascara she wore made her eyelashes grotesquely long. Up close, they looked like spiders. "But it's the strangest thing—I keep hearing that you're hanging around him in class, and after school, too. Well!" She laughed, venomous. "It's almost as if you *want* me to ruin your life. Is that it? Did you come to Ravenglass with a death wish?"

Evie imagined herself grabbing a fistful of that stupid pussycat bow and yanking it hard, trapping Kimber's scrawny neck across the divider and holding her there like a chicken on the chopping block. She imagined the choking sounds Kimber would make, and the way her manicured hands would scrabble at the vinyl of the booth as she struggled to break free. She imagined leaning so close to Kimber's ear that she could smell the coconut-scented hairspray, and whispering, "It's not me who has the death wish."

"Evie!" Tina exclaimed.

The alarm in Tina's voice broke Evie out of her reverie. Soft periwinkle fabric was clutched in her fist, and Kimber was clawing at it now, her eyes rolling with panic. In that instant, Evie realized that she hadn't *imagined* doing those things. She had done them. All of them.

In shock, she let go of the pussycat bow. Kimber tore away from her, coughing, purple with rage.

Evie watched her, mystified. "I . . . I didn't mean—" she stammered.

Kimber composed herself quickly, got up, and walked around to stand at the head of Evie and Tina's booth. Her artificial sweetness was gone, and she glared at Evie. But before she could say anything, the bell jingled again, heralding the arrival of Birdie and her mother. The waitress came out of the kitchen and waved. Kimber sent an irritated glance their way before placing both of her palms on the table, leaning forward until her face was only inches from Evie's.

"You're dead," she said simply. Then she adjusted her pussycat bow and left.

Moments passed in silence. Evie's pulse was racing. What had come over her? How had this happened? She was losing control . . . Tina was looking at her, her mouth open, eyes wide. *It's over*, Evie thought. *She's going to get up and leave.*

"I can't believe it," Tina finally said.

She thinks I'm crazy.

"No one has ever stood up to Kimber like that before," Tina went on. She looked at Evie with something that resembled admiration. "I didn't think you had it in you."

Now it was Evie's turn to be confused. "What?"

"First you propose we break into the police headquarters and steal case files, and then you give the mayor's daughter a taste of her own medicine. I seriously underestimated you." Tina shook her head in amazement, a curious glint in her eye. "Evie Archer, who are you?"

Evie chuckled nervously. She expected to feel mortified or full of regret for what she'd done. But instead, she felt good. *Very* good.

Who am I? she thought. *I'm not so sure anymore.*

12

When had she let it in?

Evie asked herself that question with every passing day. Was it when she opened the diary? Or was it when she first went into the attic and looked into that mirror? Was it then? Or had she let it in the moment she first walked through the door of that house?

She didn't know. Perhaps it didn't matter. After all, she couldn't go back. Something had gotten into her, planted itself deep inside her mind. And it was growing.

Sometimes she felt it lurking in the shadows, just out of view. Sometimes it whispered from the corners of her thoughts. She lost time, too. Hours spent working on the dress went by like minutes, so many of them that even at home in her bed she could still feel the machine humming under her fingertips.

What was it, this thing? She couldn't pinpoint it exactly—to try to describe it felt like trying to hold on to smoke. She often thought, however, of the word *haunted*. A house could be haunted, and certainly the thing seemed to strengthen whenever she was home, but it didn't end when she walked out the door. It followed her. It haunted her, not only like a ghost but like a memory. It was frightening but also somehow familiar. Like an old friend. Or a new one.

Tina texted her all the time after that day at Birdie's. They talked about Holly and the house—Tina wanted to know if Evie was actually serious about getting those case files, because if so, they needed a plan. They talked about school, too. Apparently, Kimber had been busy spreading nasty rumors about Evie after their confrontation, but according to Tina, all it had accomplished was to make her go from being virtually invisible to the most interesting girl at Ravenglass High. The mysterious girl from the Big City, who moved to the Horror House and managed to attract the eye of Desmond King and the ire of Kimber Sullivan, all in a matter of a couple of weeks. Evie felt their eyes on her as she walked down the hall between classes, but it all felt like background noise. Static. Other than finishing the dress and finding out more about Holly, there was only one thing that pulled her out of the fog.

Evie never would have labeled herself "boy crazy." That wasn't her at all. In fact, she'd always chafed at the idea of needing a man for anything. Growing up in New York, she was an independent young woman with skills and ambitions, and no one else factored into that.

But with Desmond, it was different. She didn't need him. She *wanted* him. Even just looking at him made her feel calmer, happier. His energy warmed everything around it like sunlight, and she wanted that light shining on her always. She looked forward to seeing him smile at her every morning when she walked into class, and to the afternoons when he would walk with her all the way to the bottom of the narrow lane, watching her until she was up the hill and out of sight. Like the nameless thing that haunted her, she could not explain what it was about Desmond that kept her captivated. He was handsome, funny, kind—but more than any of those things, he was a magnet that drew her to him. She often wondered if he felt the same way, but she was always too afraid to ask. Too worried that putting the feeling into words would shatter it like glass. So it remained unspoken between them, except in quiet glances that nevertheless spoke volumes.

On Saturday Evie woke up to bright morning light streaming into her bedroom. She'd managed to doze off around 4:00 a.m., and her bedside clock showed a few minutes after nine. She rubbed her eyes. Five hours was probably the most sleep she'd gotten all week, but it still wasn't nearly enough. Sitting up in bed, she reached for her phone and saw several text messages from Mom.

> Could really use your help with something at the inn.

> Come by around 10. Won't take long.

Being around a bunch of people was the last thing Evie felt like doing—she'd planned to scour the house for more artifacts left behind by the Hobbies while her mother was at work. Stan would probably be out with his friends all day, so he wouldn't be around, either. For the past few weeks since they'd moved in, the three of them had been ships passing in the night. Evie figured it was better that way. Her mother wasn't there to hover over her and ask questions, and Stan didn't get in her hair. Whatever was happening, it was easier to deal with when no one was there to watch. Because she was terrified that if anyone looked too closely, they would see it and give it a name of their choosing.

Evie shook the thought away, fingering the locket at her throat. She was getting closer to the truth. She could feel it. But it would probably be easier to just go to the inn than to argue with her mother over text. That would only make Mom wonder what she was doing all day, alone in the house. She texted her mom back.

> Fine. I'll be there.

A huge vase bursting with wine-colored dahlias and tiger lilies on a little wooden table greeted Evie when she walked into the lobby of the Blue River Inn. The place was wood-paneled and fashionably cluttered, and had a warm, cinnamon-scented homeyness. Mom stood behind a large wooden desk at the back of the room, and looked up from her computer when Evie walked in.

"Oh good, you're here," Mom said. There was a small gold name badge pinned to the lapel of her tan blazer, and the silk camisole she wore underneath was so close in color to the dahlias that Evie almost believed she'd planned it that way. Stepping out from behind the desk, she took Evie by the arm and led her down the hall. They passed a door to the greenhouse out back, where Evie caught a glimpse of two girls in jeans and gloves potting dozens of seedlings. One of them was Kimber.

"What is she doing here?" Evie asked, relieved that Kimber hadn't seen her.

Mom squinted at the girls. "Kimber and Anne? They help out on weekends in the greenhouse—it's too much work for the staff to keep up with, so some of the high-school kids volunteer for extra credit. Now, come on." She led her to the end of the hall, which opened up into a large dining area. It was a bright room alive with the chatter of guests seated at half a dozen tables, eating plates of eggs and salad and potatoes. Each table had a small vase of the same dahlias and lilies that had been in the lobby.

"So, what do you need my help with?" Evie asked.

But Mom merely gestured toward the center of the room, where Aunt Martha was seated alone at a two-person table. "Sit," her mother said. She gave a quick, uncomfortable smile. "You two have a nice breakfast." Then she turned crisply and walked back to the lobby.

Confused, Evie turned to call after her, but Aunt Martha had caught her eye before she could. She waved, and Evie had no choice but to make her way to the table and sit down. "What is going on?" Evie said, irritation clear in her voice.

"Good morning to you, too," Aunt Martha replied evenly. She took a sip of her tea.

"Mom told me to come here to help with something, she didn't say anything about—"

"Your mother thought that if she told you we were going to talk, you would make an excuse not to come. She's worried about you, Evie. She says you . . . haven't been yourself lately."

Evie snorted. "How would she know? She's never home. And anyway, why isn't *she* talking to me, if she's so worried?"

Aunt Martha sighed and leaned back in her chair. "You know how your mother is. She has trouble with, ah . . . difficult conversations. Anyway, she's under the impression that I'd have better luck getting through to you than she would."

A waiter came around with menus. Evie ordered coffee, and Aunt Martha asked for fruit and pastry. When he went away, Evie stared at the menu, stalling for time. If she left now, it would only confirm her mother's suspicions that something was wrong. But what could she say? Aunt Martha would see straight through her lies—Mom would have known as much.

There was a long silence. Finally, Aunt Martha cleared her throat and said, "Evie—"

"Why won't you go in the house?" Evie interrupted.

The question was so direct that it caught her aunt off guard. Her mouth opened and closed like a fish out of water. "What? I . . . Evie, this isn't about *me*, this is—"

Evie felt the power shift in her favor. It felt good, just like it had when she'd confronted Kimber. She charged on. "If you really cared about me," she said, "you'd tell me the truth."

Aunt Martha sighed and pulled her violet shawl tighter around her shoulders. "I suppose you're right." She drained her cup and wiped her lips with the linen napkin. "Do you know why I became a professional psychic?"

Evie shrugged. "I guess I figured you had a knack for it. A gift."

"Some might call it a curse, but yes. I've had it all my life, since I was younger than you are now. I'd walk into doctor's offices as a child and know who was about to have a heart attack. When someone in my class would lose their favorite eraser on the playground, I'd always be able to find it. It wasn't something I learned, it was just *there*. As easy as touching an ice cube and knowing it was cold. It was wonderful sometimes, but most of the time it was isolating. Your mother was normal—smart, charming—nothing odd about her. She was the lucky one, if you ask me. They say that this sort of thing—this gift, as you call it—runs in families. But as far as I ever knew, as far as anyone ever told me, I was the only one." She looked down at her hands, looking lost. "We'd come to visit the Hobbies, back when we were kids. I never said anything at the time, but I *hated* those visits."

Evie sat up straighter in her chair. She'd never heard her aunt talk like this before.

"Every time I set foot in that house," Aunt Martha went on, grimacing, "it felt like spiders were crawling down my back. It was this overpowering sense of . . . need. Like the house wanted something. And it was just biding its time until it could take it. Once I was old enough and had moved out of your grandparents' place, I'd always find an excuse not to go. Your mom was still living at home back then, so she'd go and hang out with Holly. But she never noticed anything about the house. She liked it, in fact. That's probably why she was so happy to come back here after the . . ." The word *divorce* hung unspoken in the air between them, like a balloon. She cleared her throat and went on. "When Holly disappeared, it was a shock to everyone. Obviously. But the thing that hurt the most, the thing that I'll never forgive myself for—is that I wasn't shocked at all."

She sniffed. "I knew," she said bitterly. "I knew about that house, but I never told anyone. I kept it to myself and stayed as far away as I could."

"That's why you moved back here, isn't it?" Evie said after a moment. "Because . . . because you—"

"Because I felt guilty, yes. Because if I had done something all those years before, Holly would still be here. And so, I came to pay my penance. To watch over the house, and to try to help other people in the only way I know."

"Even if you had said something," Evie argued, "no one would have believed you. It wouldn't have mattered."

"Maybe not," Aunt Martha admitted. "But I would have known that I *tried*." She reached out and put her hand over Evie's. "I'm trying now, Evie. You can tell me everything is fine, but I can feel it on you. I felt it when you came to my apartment, and I feel it now. Stronger than before. You're carrying something, I can sense that. But you don't need to carry it alone. Let me help you. Please."

Evie felt her resolve waver. *If anyone would believe me, it would be Aunt Martha*, she thought. *She knows something is wrong with the house.* But then again, everything she told Aunt Martha would probably get back to Mom. And if her mother found out about the things Evie had seen, she might call Dr. Mears. The waiter arrived with food and drinks, and refilled Aunt Martha's teacup to the brim. After he left, Evie stirred four sugars into her coffee and plenty of milk before taking an experimental sip. She held the cup in both hands, letting it warm her.

Aunt Martha seemed to sense Evie's indecision and grabbed her knit handbag from the back of the chair. "Let me at least finish your reading," she said, pulling the familiar box of cards from the bag. "You took off before I could tell you the most important part. Even if you won't tell me what's going on, the cards already know. Okay?"

After a moment of hesitation, Evie nodded.

"Good," Aunt Martha said. She moved the plates of food to the side and took four cards out of the box, laying them in a vertical line in front of Evie. Evie leaned forward to study them, curiosity eclipsing fear. As before, the tarot cards—with their bold, cryptic designs—seemed as close as she'd ever been to real magic. "Why are these cards more important than the others?" she asked.

"The first six cards in a Celtic Cross represent the questioner's current situation—that's the cross. These four cards are the tower. They represent the message the cards want to send you about that situation. Think of it as advice from the universe."

Evie pointed to the card closest to her, which showed a man in red walking away from eight golden cups arranged in an uneven stack—with five on the bottom and three on top. In the background, a full moon looked down on him and a group of dark, craggy rocks in the water. "Another moon," Evie noticed.

Aunt Martha nodded. "Yes, there's an aspect of illusion to this card, just like the Moon card. But the Eight of Cups is more about delusion than illusion. It's about turning away from difficult or painful things that you don't want to deal with. But as you can see, the cups are set up in such a way that it looks like one is missing. This card is telling you that you must face the pain you've been avoiding or remain incomplete forever."

Evie squirmed in her seat with how accurate the reading was. It was almost as if Aunt Martha were peering into her thoughts and simply listing what she found there. Then she looked at the next card and blushed. It showed a naked man and woman standing beneath a celestial angel emerging from the clouds above them, like Adam and Eve. Behind the man was a tree all aflame, and behind the woman stood an apple tree, a large snake curled around its trunk.

Aunt Martha saw the color rise in Evie's face and gave a small smile. "The Lovers. This card largely explains itself—you have found new love in your life. Someone who fills you with excitement, and with whom you already feel a close bond."

The image of Desmond looking out over the town, fading sunlight on his face, came powerfully to Evie's mind.

"The Lovers card calls on you to be open and honest with this new person in your life, who may turn out to be vitally important to your future. Even the strongest bond cannot withstand deception. And it urges you, in your darkest hour, to remember that you are not alone. Choose the best version of yourself to face others and the world."

A trickle of sweat dripped down Evie's spine. The room began to feel uncomfortably warm. *How could she know?*

Aunt Martha moved to the third card, which showed a blindfolded woman tied with rope, walking on uneven ground among eight swords. She glanced up at Evie, and her eyes were serious. "This card is a warning. There may come a time when you feel trapped by your circumstances, when you believe there's no way out of whatever you're facing. You're in a prison of your own making. Your heart can see what your eyes cannot." She glanced at Evie. "Are you all right? You look—"

Evie shook her head. "I'm fine. The last card . . ."

"Yes," Aunt Martha said carefully. "This card represents what the tarot believes is the likely outcome of the matter at hand."

The card showed a skull-faced rider on a white steed, a black flag gripped in one hand. Women and children fell on their knees before him, and a man lay on his back under the hooves of his horse. "Death," Evie whispered. "Well, that seems pretty clear to me."

"But it isn't, Evie. Tarot can sometimes be straightforward, but more often than not, it compels us to look beyond the surface for meaning." She became animated, her dark eyes sparkling. "This card is one of the most powerful in the entire deck—and one of the most misunderstood. Instead of signaling the ending of life itself, it often suggests the ending of some part of your life that isn't serving you anymore. Transformation." She pushed the card across the table and pointed to it. "Do you see? Death rides a white horse and all fall before him. Not only because he is invincible but because he is pure. He carries the flag of a white, five-petaled rose because change is natural. The rose blooms, the rose dies. And because it dies, we appreciate the blooming all the more. Change is coming, that much is certain. And I know that's hard to hear, especially after all the change you've already been through these last couple of years. But whether this new change is for good or ill—that's up to you. You've got to let go of the past. The past is gone. Find a way forward."

She paused, her eyes searching. "Am I getting through to you, Evie? I know this is a lot, but I want to help. Whatever this is, whatever you're not telling me—you can't get through it alone."

"I—I . . . ," Evie stammered. She wanted to tell Aunt Martha everything. To start from the beginning and go through every terrifying detail until it was all out in the open. Exposed to the air instead of sitting inside her head, slowly putrefying and poisoning her mind. No matter how insane it might sound or what consequences might befall her, it would still be such a relief to let go of it all.

Yes. She was going to tell her. She had to. "Okay," she said, and Aunt Martha leaned back in her chair, a look of relief on her face. Evie gathered her thoughts and began to speak. "Ever since we first moved to the house, ever since that first day—"

Evie stopped. Her throat was parched, and she was sweating more profusely now. The room felt like an oven, and the sunlight that had seemed so pleasant when she'd arrived felt harsh and glaring. The spicy-sweet scent of flowers and cinnamon had turned rancid, and was so pungent, she could hardly breathe.

"Hey," Aunt Martha said, relief turning to concern. "What's wrong? You're pale as a ghost."

Evie took a sip of her coffee, and it was bitter despite the spoonfuls of sugar she'd dumped into it. The cup rattled in the saucer as she set it back down with trembling hands. "I don't know," she said. "I don't feel right."

"You probably need to eat," Aunt Martha said, but her voice had become strange, distorted. Evie watched as she picked up a danish and pushed it toward Evie on a small plate. The cherry filling looked dark and horrid, like congealed blood. It made Evie's stomach turn.

"I can't," Evie said, pushing the plate away. She became aware of other people in the room looking at her, whispering. Their faces seemed grotesque, but Evie couldn't put her finger on why. Everything about them was just too big, too much. The noise of their whispers was deafening.

Right outside the window, a shadow stood, impossible in the morning brightness. A small, lithe shadow. A girl with a bonnet. And although Evie could not see her face, she could see the shadow raise one dark finger to her lips.

Shh.

Paralyzed with terror, Evie's throat seemed to close up, and it was only after she thought to herself that she would not speak, that she would keep this terrible secret, let the thing that haunted her remain at home inside her mind for just a little longer, that she was able to breathe again.

"You are scaring me," Aunt Martha muttered, flicking a reassuring smile at the waiter as he passed by, delivering glasses of ice water. "Tell me what's going on right now, or I'm going to get your mother."

Evie grasped the glass of water and drank until she felt better. The dining room had regained its normal cool, pleasant quality. The guests chatted among themselves, paying her no mind at all. The shadow in the window had gone. Aunt Martha was watching her, expectant. She racked her mind for an answer. "I want to tell you," she said, "but I can't. Not now."

"That's not good enough, Evie—"

"I know. I'm sorry. But I need you to trust me. And I need Mom off my back so I can figure this out. Tell her I'm fine. Tell her I'm just stressed about the move and being at a new school."

"But that can't be what all this is about. Don't ask me to do this—"

"She'll buy it. Believe me. Mom loves a simple answer. Look, I have to go. I have to get back to the house. Thanks for breakfast." And before Aunt Martha could say anything more, Evie had walked out of the dining room, leaving her food on the table, untouched.

13

As she walked down the windy street toward Hobbie House, she pulled out her phone to text Tina.

> Hey, you still want to come see the house?

Tina's response was almost immediate.

> I absolutely do. Name the time and i'll be there.

> How about tonight? You can sleep over.
> We'll watch a movie or something.

> Haunted sleepover FTW! can't wait!

Evie slipped the phone back into her bag and stuffed her hands into the pockets of her shearling duffle coat. The crisp air felt good after the stifling heat of the inn and helped clear the remnants of fear and confusion from her mind. She would go home, pour herself a bowl of cereal, and spend the rest of the afternoon combing the house for clues. During the daytime it wasn't as frightening, so she'd do it for as long as the light lasted. By the time night fell, Tina would be there. Tina still thought all of this was a fun game, like they were playing Nancy Drew and solving a mystery together— and that was fine. Good, actually. It kept Tina from asking too many questions that Evie couldn't answer. And she knew that having Tina there with her would be reassuring. She might even get some sleep, with her friend nearby. She didn't know how many more sleepless nights she could take, how many more nightmares she could stand before she—

Stop it, she thought angrily. *Keep it together. If Mom noticed, then who else might have? Keep it together, and maybe you can figure this out. Maybe you can get out of this.*

"It's fine, you're fine," she muttered to herself as she reached the narrow lane. Above, on the hill, the house watched her approach with both faces. She went in through the kitchen and closed the door behind her. Stan still wasn't home, so the only sounds were the creaks and sighs of the house shifting and moving with the wind. And despite her dread of that place, Evie felt her body relax. Why? she wondered. When the house was the source of all her terror, how could she possibly feel relief in being there?

Because it welcomes you, something inside her said. *Because it knows what you keep hidden in the dark, and still it wants you. Because here, you don't have to hide.*

"Wow," Tina said. "Just . . . wow. This is exactly how I imagined it." She had arrived through the living room door, with the bloody sunset streaming in behind her. Evie watched as Tina moved through the rooms on the first floor, stopping to look at everything. The butter churn, the plastic phone, the wooden sign that Mom had picked up at some little shop that read, annoyingly, TOGETHER IS OUR FAVORITE PLACE TO BE.

"You imagined *that*?" Evie said, pointing at the sign.

Tina snorted. "Your mom drinks pumpkin spice lattes, doesn't she, Evie? Admit it."

"Like her life depends on it," Evie said.

Tina chuckled and continued her tour back into the living room, examining everything like a police detective at a crime scene. Her green curls were windblown and wild, and fell in front of her eyes as she leaned down to look at a glass bluebird on the kitchen shelf. She tucked the stray locks behind her ears, revealing a row of silver stud earrings. "I didn't imagine cobwebs and ghouls in closets, if that's what you're asking. I figured that you guys had fixed the place up but retained some of the house's original"—she stopped short of saying "charm" and instead went with—"spirit. And that's exactly what you've done. It's cool! Very atmospheric. Very cottagecore. The perfect setting for a lovelorn milkmaid like yourself."

Evie rolled her eyes.

"What's down there?" Tina asked, pointing to a door right outside the kitchen. An old fabric draft blocker sat on the floor in front of it. It was designed in the shape of eight different-colored cats sitting in a line—orange, yellow, white, four shades of gray, and blue, all featureless except for black dots for their eyes and nose.

"The cellar," Evie said. "I actually haven't gone down there yet. I kept forgetting about it, I guess."

Tina's eyes widened. "The root cellar? That's the oldest part of the house, remember? We should go down there and check it out!" Before Evie could stop her, Tina grasped the doorknob and threw the cellar door wide, pushing the eight cats along with it. Evie winced, anticipating—well, she wasn't sure what—but *something* happening. Something getting out.

But nothing happened.

The two girls peered down into the murk, and Tina reached out to flick a metal push-button light switch on the wall. Two bare bulbs strung across the stairwell sputtered to life, casting weak yellow light down the dusty wooden stairs.

"C'mon!" Tina said, her eyes alight with excitement. She started down, placing one careful foot on each stair, checking whether it would carry her weight. The old wood whined, but seemed to be solid. Tina crept down into the shadows, and Evie followed close behind, fighting the urge to reach out for Tina's hand like a frightened child.

"I'm surprised you haven't been down here yet," Tina said, her voice sounding small inside the darkness. "After all the exploring you've done."

There was no railing, so Evie pressed her hands against the walls for balance as she descended. The walls were stone, rough and cold to the touch. *Why didn't I come down here?* she wondered. She had spent the afternoon searching the house but had never thought to come down to the cellar. Perhaps it was some kind of subconscious fear that kept her away, like it was with the attic. She wondered, in that moment, why people always seemed to be afraid of attics and cellars. Maybe when things lie dormant for too long, either above our heads or below our feet, people worry about what might come skittering through the cracks, or grow, or wake.

Tina didn't seem afraid. Either her ignorance gave her courage or she was putting on a great show of being unfazed for Evie's sake. They made it to the bottom of the stairs, stepping into a dank, cavernlike room with a low ceiling and dirt floors. A single light bulb hung in the center, buzzing like a dying bumblebee. Its feeble light managed to dispel only the deepest shadows, leaving many still lurking in corners. One wall was dominated by heavy wooden shelving, mostly empty aside from several wine bottles and half a dozen large Mason jars filled with cloudy gray liquid and vague, fuzzy shapes. Some rusty tools—a shovel, a sledgehammer, a rake with bristling tines like a cockscomb—leaned against the shelf as well. The hulking HVAC unit sat in one corner next to the stairs, grumbling like a cranky old beast. Several tarnished and cracked air ducts stretched out of the thing and up into the house through vents in the ceiling. A few wooden crates lay stacked about, too, but other than that, there wasn't much to look at. It had a musty, vegetable smell, like old cabbages, which was probably what led Great-Aunt Liz to think it was plagued with "bad air."

Evie pulled her phone out of her pocket and walked the perimeter of the cellar, swinging the beam of the phone's flashlight into the corners where the light didn't reach. Something on the floor sparkled as her light passed over it, so she went over to the far wall to investigate. But it was just some bits of gold tinsel—likely remnants of a birthday party or Christmas decorations from decades before.

"Well, that's disappointing," Tina said. "Just some dusty old junk, mouse poop, and what appears to be some jars of eyeballs. Let's go back upstairs. It's freezing down here."

Her casual attitude banished Evie's anxiety like a spell. "Yeah, okay," Evie said, relieved. "Why don't we make some hot chocolate? Then I can show you the rest of the house."

They thumped back up the stairs, switching the lights off as they went. But Evie didn't feel truly comfortable until the door was shut tight behind them and the eight cats were pushed back up against the bottom, preventing anything—even air—from creeping up out of the cellar. In the kitchen, she pulled two earthenware mugs from the shelf, and they caught up about school while a saucepan of milk warmed on the old-fashioned stove. After a few minutes, Evie heard the sound of voices approaching.

"Who's that?" Tina asked.

"Stan, probably. My little brother. But it doesn't sound like he's alone."

A moment later, the kitchen door burst open and four boys piled into the kitchen, all of them talking at once. One of the boys, a tall kid with blond hair, was carrying an orange DEAD END traffic sign under one arm. Evie thought he looked kind of familiar, but she couldn't place where she'd seen him. "It's gonna look awesome in my room," he was saying, and the other boys laughed. Stan was the first to notice Evie and Tina standing there, staring at them.

He was carrying a sign under his arm, too. A green street sign that read CONWAY ST.

"Oh," Stan said, and then the other boys noticed them, too. "You're home."

"Sorry to disappoint you," Evie said. "What is this, anyway? Did you steal those signs?"

Stan hesitated, and in that moment the tall blond boy stepped up to throw an arm around Stan's shoulders. "Let me handle this one," he said to Stan.

"But, Dylan—" Stan started to say.

"It's cool," Dylan broke in. He turned his attention to Evie. "Whether or not we *appropriated* these signs is none of your business, okay? So you can just back right off."

"It's a criminal offense, you know," Tina said, stirring the milk. "Stealing road signs. You could be arrested." The blond boy started to scoff, but Tina went on. "You do remember who my dad is, don't you?"

Dylan's smirk curled into a sneer, and he gripped the sign a little tighter. "I do. And I'm sure you remember who mine is, too."

It was at that moment that Evie realized why Dylan looked so familiar. He looked like Kimber. All this time, Stan had been hanging out with Dylan Sullivan, the mayor's son.

Mom would be thrilled, she thought darkly.

No one said anything for a minute, and the tension in the kitchen was palpable. Finally, Dylan sucked his teeth and said, "Man, let's get out of here and go to my house. This place is lame, anyway. Creepy old dump . . ." The other two boys nodded and made their way back toward the door, following Dylan like a couple of ducklings.

Stan glared at Evie, a mixture of embarrassment and anger on his face. "Thanks for nothing," he said coldly, and started to follow his friends out.

"Stan, it's late," she called after him. "You can't walk home in the dark."

"Whatever. I'll ask Mom to pick me up from the Glade after work," he said. He went to pull the door closed behind him and gave Evie one last scathing glance. "What do you care, anyway?"

After he'd gone, Evie set about aggressively spooning cocoa powder into the mugs.

"Well," Tina said. "That was . . . something."

Evie threw the spoon into the sink with a clatter. "Of all the people in this town, Stan picks the brother of that—that—"

"Shrew? She-devil? Miscreant?"

"Yes, all those things—he picks *her* brother to be his best friend? And now he hates me, too. God, at this rate, I'm going to be run out of town with a scarlet letter pinned to my back."

"What, M for *Milkmaid*?"

Evie smirked. "No."

"*F* for *Farmgirl*?"

"Tina!" Evie laughed, which felt nice after all that unpleasantness. She poured the steaming milk into each mug, retrieved the spoon, and stirred. Tina's good humor had restored the mood, and Evie was hopeful for a fun night. Something that felt in the realm of normal.

But Stan's accusation needled at her. *Does he really think I don't care about him?* True, they hadn't really talked much since the move, but that was just as much Stan's fault as hers. She was a little worried about him, though, especially now that she knew exactly the kind of company he was keeping. "You know that shack that burned down last week? The Dutton place, I think it was called?" she said.

"What about it?" Tina asked.

"I think . . . ," she said slowly. "I think Stan and those other boys were the ones who set it on fire. I don't know for certain, but I'm pretty sure."

Tina took a sip of her hot chocolate and nodded. "Really. Well, I can't say I'm surprised. Do you want me to tell my dad about it?"

"No—I mean, I don't know. What good would it do, if the Sullivans get away with everything? I don't want Stan taking the fall for something that probably wasn't his idea." She shook her head. "Why are those rich kids hanging around with Stan, anyway? They've all got to be at least two years older than him."

Tina shrugged. "Who knows? Younger kids make good scapegoats. And Stan would probably do quite a lot to impress those guys. Probably just some extra entertainment for them."

"Hmm," Evie mumbled into her mug. She didn't like the idea of Stan going along with whatever stupid schemes those boys came up with. Stealing signs was illegal, for one thing, and if they really did burn down that shack, Stan could have been hurt. *I should tell Mom*, she thought grimly. If she didn't and something were to happen—the responsibility would fall on her.

"Oh! Who's this now?" Tina was smiling at the tabby cat, who had appeared in the doorway to the hall, watching them with its inscrutable green eyes.

"Oh yeah, he was here when we moved in," Evie said. "He seems to come and go as he pleases—I honestly have no idea how he gets in or out of the house. I give him some food sometimes, but

I think he likes to hunt for his meals. Keeps showing up with these little moles."

"Moles, huh?" Tina said, kneeling down to stroke the cat. He allowed it, but then made his way over to Evie and wound about her ankles. "He must be a pretty good hunter—most of the cats I've had over the years have stuck to killing mice and baby rabbits. Moles take some work to get out of the ground."

"I guess Schrödinger knows where to find them."

Tina cocked her head. "Schrödinger? What kind of name is that?"

Evie bent down and gave the tabby a scratch behind his notched ear. He purred like a motorboat. "I guess it was what I was thinking about when I first met him. And I think it fits—he lives here, but he also doesn't live here. He's a mystery."

"Huh. Just like everything else in this place." Finished with his greetings, Schrödinger turned around to head back out of the kitchen, his fluffy orange tail waving like a flag. Halfway down the hall he stopped and turned back to stare at them, offering one plaintive meow. "I think he wants to give me a tour," Tina said.

They quickly drained their mugs and followed the cat around the rest of the house. Tina asked a lot of questions, and Evie tried as best she could to answer them. They even went up to the attic, where Evie showed her Holly's trunk and the strange dolls. The doll remained mute, despite how many times Evie pulled her string. They ended in Evie's bedroom—Holly's room—which captivated Tina most of all.

Tina sat in the fanback wicker chair in the corner and looked around like a girl in a museum. Schrödinger made himself comfortable on the bed, watching. "Wow," Tina breathed. "This is crazy.

I grew up on stories about Holly, and now here I am, in the room where she grew up. Where it all happened."

Evie turned to look at the room, too, trying to see it through Tina's eyes. The soft pink walls with the sun-blasted ghosts of posters left behind; the rose, moldering and black, still lying on the dresser atop the old photograph. To her, Holly's disappearance was a tragic family story, not some tabloid scandal. Then again, Tina's family were longtime residents of Ravenglass, so in some ways, they were closer to Holly than Evie's family was. And yet, neither of them seemed any closer to understanding what had happened to her.

"So, I spent all day looking around the house," Evie began. "And other than uncovering some more of Holly's old stuff, I couldn't find anything. I mean, it makes sense. It's been forty years. Plus, whatever actual evidence there might have been was almost certainly taken away by the police." She said the last word with particular emphasis.

Tina's wandering eyes flicked to Evie's. "You're still thinking about getting your hands on those case files, aren't you?"

Evie's gaze was steady. "I never stopped thinking about it. But only you can tell me if it's possible."

The wicker chair creaked as Tina leaned back, the fingers of both hands pressed against her mouth in contemplation. "I'll admit, I've been thinking about it, too," she finally said. "I mean, no one has looked at those files in decades—who knows what the police back then might have missed? And honestly, it wouldn't hurt anyone, so . . ."

"So you'll do it?"

"Here's the thing," Tina replied, leaning in. "I think we've only got one chance with this thing. If we're going to get those files, it will need to be on a day when the station is empty—or at least nearly empty. Which hardly ever happens—there's always a couple of officers either at the desk or coming in and out from their beat. *Except*—the day of the homecoming parade."

Evie's mind raced. "That's . . . that's this Friday!"

Tina nodded. "Right, so we only have a week to plan. The parade is such a big deal, with the road closures and the crowd control and all that—basically the entire police department has to be out on the streets to work the event. They only leave the clerk behind to man the phones. A clerk who I happen to know quite well. He was my math tutor back in middle school. And he loves to talk."

Evie was starting to understand. "I take it this is a two-person job?" she asked.

Tina grinned. "Definitely."

"All right then," Evie said. "Let's get to planning."

They never got to watch a movie or eat popcorn, because they stayed up all night just talking. Evie learned about Tina's mom, who was a flight attendant and wasn't home very often, and about her older sister who was in her third year of college in California. Tina talked about her internal struggle between wanting to travel like her mom and her commitment to Ravenglass, like her dad.

Evie was happy to keep the focus on Tina—she wasn't really up for sharing details about the divorce.

Mom peeked in to say hello around eleven when she got home from work, but only for a moment. Evie considered going to tell her mother about what had happened with Stan, but Mom looked tired, so she figured it could wait until the morning.

By the time Evie got into bed, it was close to 2:00 a.m. Tina was curled up under a pile of blankets on a cot mattress Evie had brought from the spare room, and was already asleep by the time Evie turned out the light. In the quiet darkness, Evie snuggled under her quilt and listened to Tina's rhythmic breathing. She was calm, warm, and safe. Sleep came on soft paws and carried her away.

Evie wasn't sure what it was that woke her up. The cat, perhaps? Schrödinger had gone out before they went to bed—maybe he'd been scratching at the door. But when she listened for a sound, there was nothing at all.

She squinted at the clock—3:09 again. *Strange.*

And then, a whisper. "Are you awake?"

Evie turned toward the pile of blankets where Tina was lying. "Yeah, something got me up," she whispered back. "You too?"

"Yes." And then, "Are you lonely?"

It was a strange question, but they'd been talking about all sorts of things that night. "Sometimes. I miss my friends back home—though I'm happy I got to meet you. Sometimes it just feels like no one really understands me, you know? Like I don't know who to trust."

"You can trust me."

Moonlight cast skeleton shadows of trees on the ceiling, and Evie watched them tremble in the wind. The dusty, floral smell of the dried rose filled the room. Had it smelled so strongly before, and she just hadn't noticed? "I appreciate that," she whispered.

"I understand you. You're just like me."

"Oh, I don't know about that. You're so—"

"Yes. Just like me."

Evie frowned. "Are you okay, Tina? You sound like you might be coming down with something."

"If you come with me, you'll never be lonely again."

Evie sat up and was about to ask what she was talking about when the bedroom door creaked open. A figure stood silhouetted against the dim light from the hallway.

"Sorry, did I wake you?" Tina said, walking in. "I had to go to the bathroom, so— Evie, are you okay?"

Evie said nothing, her body shaking with sudden, paralyzing terror. She glanced back down at the cot mattress, visible now in the dim light. Blankets there, nothing more. A tiny, strangled moan escaped her lips as Tina ran over, asking questions that Evie could not hear through the roar of panic in her ears. Only one unavoidable, horrible, impossible question made it through the storm inside her mind to what was left of her rational thought.

If Tina wasn't in the room, who was I talking to?

14

Evie was already awake when the sun rose. Dully, she watched the light grow and lengthen as the minutes passed. The glass of water that Tina had brought in the night stood half empty on her nightstand. There was a chip in the rim, and the sun caught there and refracted into a thousand motes across the white nightstand and onto the floor. She had heard the glass clatter in the bathroom sink as Tina had filled it. Tina had been shocked to find Evie in such a state. Her shock had eventually penetrated Evie's haze of terror, and at that moment, Evie had realized that if she did not calm down, Tina would run to get her mother, and then— And so she had gotten ahold of herself and asked for water.

A nightmare, Evie had told her. She had woken from a nightmare and thought the horrors of it were still happening. But she was all right now. She just needed some water.

Tina's hands had probably been trembling as she stood at the sink. And the glass was slippery in her clammy hands. She likely didn't even notice the glass breaking, didn't see the fresh, sharp edge as she handed the water to Evie, who drank half of it in one go. The chip was so small, even if it had cut Evie's lips as she drank from the cup, she might not have even noticed until she tasted the blood.

But the crack was already growing. Tiny fissures had opened and were trailing down from the chip, spreading, turning something whole unstable, a little at a time.

Is that how it's going to be with me? she wondered. *How long do I have before it's too late? How long before I fall apart?*

Tina got up a little while later. Evie closed her eyes and pretended to be asleep so she wouldn't have to talk. She listened as Tina moved about the room quietly, folding blankets and getting dressed, and then washing up in the bathroom down the hall. When Tina returned, she came to the bed and shook Evie gently by the shoulder. When Evie opened her eyes, Tina's expression was apologetic.

"Hey, Evie," she said. "Look, I hate to do this, but I gotta go. Dad wants me home to help with yard work, and we've got to get it done early before he goes in for his morning shift. He's working double duty this week to get ready for all the homecoming events." She paused, looking cautious, hesitant. Evie could plainly see that her sense of fun and adventure had been replaced by worry. It was the same way her mother looked at her. "Evie, um—are you sure you're okay? You kind of, well . . . you scared the hell out of me last night."

Evie sat up against the pillows and made herself offer a comforting smile. "I know," she said, her voice carefully controlled. "I'm sorry. Like I said, it was a nightmare. I have them sometimes.

Especially in this place." She gestured vaguely at the house, as if it were a scary video game that she really should stop playing before bedtime.

Tina's shoulders relaxed a little. She returned the smile. "Oh, it's okay. You don't need to apologize. I was just, like, worried about you. Doing all this Holly Hobbie stuff is cool and exciting, but there's got to be an explanation for all of it. I mean, it might be really sad or gruesome or whatever, but . . . you don't really think this place is haunted, do you?"

"Of course not," Evie said without hesitation. "It's just easy to get caught up in all the stories and everything, you know? Easy to get spooked in a place like this."

"Yeah, absolutely," Tina agreed, her posture relaxing further. "Text me later, okay?" she said, collecting her bags.

"Will do," Evie said. "The plan is still on, right? For Friday?"

Tina nodded, but there was a sliver of uncertainty there now, a tiny crack in her resolve. "Still on," she said, and waved goodbye.

After she'd gone, Evie picked up the glass and drank the rest of the water, not caring if the sharp edge cut her or not. She'd have to be even more careful from here on out. Vigilant. If she let the fear take over, even once, she knew she was lost.

She had been truthful to Tina about one thing. The nightmares hadn't stopped when she woke up. In fact, they never stopped at all.

The kitchen door was open when Evie finally came downstairs later that morning, allowing a crisp autumn breeze to blow through the house carrying the smell of fallen leaves. She could see her mother outside on the porch, sitting in one of the new rocking chairs she'd bought in town. Before Evie could pour herself a cup of coffee, Mom called out to her. "Come here for a minute," she said.

Sensing trouble, Evie went outside. Mom was wrapped in her forest-green dressing gown, her iPad in one hand and a steaming mug of coffee in the other. Without her makeup on and her hair styled, she looked softer, less intimidating—but Evie knew better than to let her guard down. "Yeah?" she said, wary.

Mom took a sip of her coffee, the steam cloaking her face in clouds of vapor. "Stan spoke to me this morning. He's . . . well, he's concerned about you, Evie."

Alarm bells immediately started ringing in Evie's head. Stan could be a brat, but he wasn't stupid. What had he done?

"He said you've been staying up every night until past midnight, wandering the house, crying out in your sleep—whenever you *do* sleep. He said that he overheard you and that friend of yours talking last night. All this stuff about Holly. Now, I know when we moved into this house, we accepted that we would be surrounded by its . . ." She hesitated. "Its history. But, Evie, getting obsessed with what happened to my cousin—" Mom stopped, considering her next words carefully. "It's not *healthy*, honey. Not for anyone, but especially not for you."

"Mom, I'm not—" Evie started to say.

"Don't try to deny it," Mom broke in. "That episode in the bathtub happened right after you were reading Holly's old diary, so it isn't the first time this Holly business has been a problem." She shook her head. "And clearly this friend of yours isn't helping if she's encouraging this kind of behavior."

"That 'friend of mine' is Tina Sànchez, the police chief's daughter," Evie retorted.

Her mother seemed surprised by that, which gave Evie a moment of satisfaction. Mom had obviously taken in Tina's green hair and grunge clothing and made assumptions. But her mother, never one to stay down, recovered quickly. "Be that as it may, she isn't doing you any favors right now, Evie. You become who you're with, so you'd be wise to spend your time with people who make you better, not worse."

Evie gripped her hands into fists, but tried not to let the anger show on her face. The irony was staggering. Stan was out there literally committing petty crimes with his gang of well-dressed delinquents, but Evie was the one getting the third degree from her mother about her choice of friends. Stan must have realized that Evie would tell Mom about stealing the traffic signs, so he'd decided to head her off at the pass. If Evie tried to tell Mom about it now, it would look like she was making something up to try to turn the attention to her brother. Stan knew that, too. *That weaselly, sneaky, horrible, little—*

"Promise me that you're going to drop this," Mom said. "I have enough to deal with at the inn and here at the house—I don't need to be worrying about you, too. Okay?"

"Okay, Mom." The lies came so easily now. Evie barely had to think before they just flowed out like water. The truth was impossible. Lies made everyone happy.

"Good girl," Mom said with a satisfied smile. "Here's something to think about: homecoming weekend! I'll be working the parade with Fiona for the inn. You really should come—it's supposed to be a wonderful event. Then the home game that night, and the dance the following evening. If you haven't gotten your tickets yet, you can grab some cash from my purse and buy them tomorrow." She patted Evie's hand. "Better days ahead, yes?"

Evie nodded. "Better days ahead," she echoed, and went back inside.

She grabbed some coffee and a bagel and took them upstairs to her room, passing Stan in the hall on the way there. He smirked when he saw her, but before he could open his mouth, she said, "Don't talk to me," and slammed her bedroom door in his face.

She ate her breakfast in bed, scrolling mindlessly on her phone. It had been days since she'd received a message from one of her friends back home. They were all busy, she supposed. Too busy for a friend who they'll never see again. When you leave, people say, "Oh, we'll keep in touch! We'll visit!" But they don't really mean it. It's just something polite people say. When you're gone, you're gone.

Are you lonely?

On a whim, Evie opened her nightstand drawer see if Holly's diary was still there. She wouldn't put it past her mother to come in and take it while Evie was asleep. But the little white book was just as she had left it. She brought it out and flipped through it, feeling particularly sympathetic to the parts where Holly complained about her controlling mother.

I understand you.

Evie began to wonder if Holly had experienced something similar to what she was going through. Maybe Holly couldn't talk about it, either, which is why she had chosen to write it all down in a secret diary. Maybe her "secret friend" wasn't a person after all, but something else?

You're just like me.

Evie set her half-eaten bagel down on the nightstand. She wasn't hungry anymore. She stared across the room to where her mother had hung one of the framed pictures they'd brought with them from the apartment in New York. It had been a gift from Miss Olive when both Evie and Stan were old enough to go to school and didn't need a nanny anymore. It was a print of the illustration of Alice staring up at the Cheshire Cat sitting high up in a tree. Below, the words from the book were printed:

"In *that* direction," the Cat said, waving its right paw round, "lives a Hatter: and in *that* direction," waving the other paw, "lives a March Hare. Visit either you like: they're both mad."

"But I don't want to go among mad people," Alice remarked.

"Oh, you can't help that," said the Cat: "we're all mad here. I'm mad. You're mad."

"How do you know I'm mad?" said Alice.

"You must be," said the Cat, "or you wouldn't have come here."

"Good morning, RHS!" a voice boomed over the PA system. "And welcome to the beginning of this year's annual Spirit Week! Well, homeboys and homegirls, I hope you've brought your freshest, funkiest threads today because as you know, it's Mall Rat

Monday! The day we go back to the future and party like it's 1989! And don't forget: Today is the last day to buy your tickets for Friday's home game and for Saturday's homecoming dance. Get 'em before they're gone! Have a great day, Miners!" A moment later, the sound of Culture Club's "Karma Chameleon" blasted through the speakers.

The day outside Ravenglass High School was as dark as the students' outfits were bright. Girls in neon pink, green, and orange sweatshirts paraded the halls, their hair sprayed into feathery, chemical-scented manes and their faces shining with glitter eyeshadow and bubblegum-pink lip gloss. There were T-shirts sporting MTV, *Ghostbusters*, and *Teenage Mutant Ninja Turtles* logos, MC Hammer pants, and denim jackets. The hallways were loud and raucous, and in the classrooms the teachers mostly gave up and handed out busywork or showed a movie, because everyone knew very little got done during Spirit Week. It was all noise and spectacle, like ancient soldiers preparing for the coming battle and the victory celebration that was sure to follow.

Evie floated through the day like a specter, running on coffee and little else. She was afraid to sleep, afraid to let her guard down, but sometime in the night sleep took her, anyway. It was only for an hour or two—sleep that wasn't really rest. She woke up confused, fuzzy-eyed, and unprepared for the important week ahead. As she poured four spoonfuls of sugar into the black coffee that morning, she wondered if perhaps she was becoming addicted to it. She'd never really liked coffee before, but now it seemed to be the only thing keeping her going.

Never mind that, she told herself. *You have to be ready for Friday.* She realized that she'd put too many eggs in that particular basket—for all she knew, there would be no new information at all in the police files. But it was the only thing she had, and she desperately needed something to hold on to. In the meantime, there was the dress.

At the end of the day, after all the loud, bright things had gone, Evie sat at her humming machine in the FCS classroom, her foot on the pedal and her mouth bristling with pins. The voluminous skirt and bodice were finished, although she still needed to add the cornflower-blue ruffles to the hem and the ribbons around the waist, which would take time. She'd never made anything like it before, but the movements still seemed so familiar that she barely had to think about them at all. She'd been acquainted with the muse before—there had been times in New York when she'd seen a bolt of fabric on a shelf and designed the piece in her mind in an instant—but this muse was different. It was direct, insistent. It demanded her attention like an impatient customer. And so she worked, happy at least to have her mind taken off of everything else.

"Hey."

The word was like a penny dropped into a deep well. She heard it distantly, and it sent ripples of pleasure through her as she realized who the voice belonged to. She looked up from her machine, blinking in the dimness at the figure in the doorway. "Hey, Desmond," she said.

"Watch those fingers, Sleeping Beauty," he said, raising his eyebrows.

"Oh!" she said, realizing she still had her foot on the pedal. She quickly raised it, and the machine stopped humming. "Sorry, I was, you know—in the zone." She took a closer look at him.

"Wow, you really take Spirit Week seriously, don't you?" He wore a black-and-red-striped windbreaker, acid-washed jeans, and white high-tops.

"Got to," he replied. "With me on the starting team and all. Even got my pop's Air Jordans from 1985. Still look pretty good, considering." He stuck his foot out so she could get a better look.

"You probably look just like him," she said, remembering how similar Mr. King's and Desmond's features were.

"Yeah, probably. You like the cut?" He gestured to his hair, which had been styled in a flat-top fade.

"I like the whole ensemble," she said with a grin.

"Why didn't you dress up?" he asked. "I thought you'd jump at the opportunity."

She put her hands on her hips in mock offense. "Excuse me, I *did* dress up." She did a slow turn for his benefit, showing off her soft pink top, long brown skirt, leather belt, and white silk neckerchief. "I'm obviously Molly Ringwald from *The Breakfast Club.*"

He held his chin between thumb and forefinger and studied her up and down. "If you say so," he said. "To be honest, it doesn't look any different from what you usually wear." She threw him a dirty look, and he laughed. "Don't be mad. All I'm saying is that your style is classic, Evie. You'll never go out of style."

She chuckled and looked back down at the dress, still under the foot of the machine.

"You've been working on that dress nonstop," he said, watching her gaze. "It's not due for another couple of weeks, you know."

"I really wanted to get it done this week," she said. "Before homecoming."

"Oh yeah?" he said. "You got plans, then?"

Evie shrugged. "Not really. I honestly don't even know if I'm going to go. I just . . ." She hardly knew how to finish the sentence. "I just feel like it has to be done by Saturday. I don't really know why."

Desmond pressed his lips together and nodded. "No, I get it. You like to stay on top of things. So do I. In fact, I already finished my project."

"Really?" Evie said, surprised. "Last time I checked, you were still trying to figure out how to do a blind stitch."

Now it was Desmond's turn to throw a dirty look her way. "Listen, you're not the only one who can sew, okay, princess? I got it."

"All right then," Evie replied. "Let's see it."

Desmond smiled. "I thought you'd never ask." Stepping farther into the room, he unzipped his windbreaker and opened it to reveal the handmade black jersey underneath. It wasn't perfectly made, but it was certainly good enough in length and cut. But it was what was on the shirt, not the shirt itself, that caught Evie's attention. A message, sewed on with evenly spaced, yellow felt cut-out letters.

EVIE ARCHER

WILL YOU GO

TO HOCO WITH ME?

Evie stood frozen, one hand covering her mouth in amazement, the other pressed against her chest, where her heart was beating wildly.

"Well?" Desmond said, watching her carefully. "What do you think?"

"I think," she began.

Desmond leaned forward, expectant.

"I think your stitching has really improved," she said, her voice breaking.

Desmond slumped, and he gave her a wry smile. "Cute," he said, and walked closer to her, putting his hands on her shoulders. "Now seriously, what do you think?"

Evie sniffed, and rubbed at her nose, trying to retain her composure. "But, what about Kimber?" she asked. Sure, she'd given the girl something to think about at Birdie's, but Evie wasn't so naive as to think that was the end of it. Knowing the type of person Kimber was, she was already planning some diabolical scheme to get back at Evie. Showing up for the dance on Desmond's arm would only add fuel to the fire.

But Desmond only shrugged. "Kimber? What about her? We're not dating anymore—despite what she's telling everyone. She seems to think she's entitled to have whatever she wants in this town, including me. She may be the mayor's daughter, but whose family do you think pays her daddy's salary? Hmm?"

"But . . . your mom didn't like me, either," Evie stammered. "She looked at me like I was something she'd found on the bottom of her shoe. What if she gets upset when she finds out I'm your date?"

Desmond sucked his teeth. "My mom doesn't think there's a girl in the world good enough for me. That's just how she is. Now," he said, his voice softening, "I want you to listen and listen good. I don't care if they don't like you. I like you. I like your smart mouth. I like the way your hair looks when the wind blows through it. I like how you see beautiful things in your mind and then make them real. I like your soft grace and the way you look at me when I walk into a room. I like the way you seem like a girl who belongs in another time but ended up with me, right here, right now. I like all of that."

Evie swallowed and worked hard to meet the intensity of his gaze. "I like you, too," she said.

"Then say yes."

There was danger in this. She could feel it in her bones the way some people feel the coming of rain. There was weight in that moment, in her answer, that would carry into all the moments that followed. But her mind had been made up long ago. The moment he'd opened his jacket. The moment he'd held her injured hand like a dancer in a ballroom. The moment he'd sat next to her on her first day.

"Yes," she said.

He grinned, laughed. "Yes, she says!"

She laughed, too. A moment later, lightning flashed, illuminating all the classroom windows with sudden brightness. And then, a crash of thunder.

"Man, it got dark fast, didn't it?" Desmond said. It was true, the room was almost completely in shadow now, aside from the pool of light radiating from Evie's sewing machine. "We'd better get out of here before it gets worse. C'mon, I'll walk you home."

"Are you sure?" she asked.

"Of course," he replied. "What kind of homecoming date would I be if I just left you to face the storm alone?"

She quickly turned off her machine and packed up her dress and materials in their cubby for the next day. After she'd grabbed her coat and bookbag, they made their way outside. Mountains of dark clouds were gathering above the town as they walked quickly down Main Street toward Hobbie House, and every thirty seconds or so, another flash lit up the sky. "It's getting closer," Evie said as a crack of thunder followed close on the lightning's heels.

And then, the rain came.

At first it was only a few fat drops, but it quickly turned into a downpour. They started to run. Their feet splashed through the puddles that had almost instantly appeared in the streets, and Evie began to laugh again, unguarded, like a child. It came down in sheets and sounded like applause, like the sound of her happiness come alive. Desmond grabbed her hand and pulled her along with him, splashing through the very deepest puddles on purpose. She shrieked and pushed against him, breathless and playful.

By the time they reached the bottom of the narrow lane, they were completely soaked through, their hair and clothes plastered to their bodies, their faces dripping. She stopped and turned to him. "Bet you're regretting walking me home, huh?" she said.

"No regrets," he said, "except maybe one."

"What's that?" she asked.

"I regret not doing this sooner," he said, and cupped her face in his hands, pulled her close, and kissed her.

And as the rain streamed off them in rivulets, she reached for him, raising herself on tiptoes just to be that much closer to him. She kissed him back as the world tilted and shifted around her, and she felt as if this not only had always been meant to happen but that it had happened before. She wished she could capture the moment in glass and look at it whenever she wanted, feel again the way she felt as the storm raged around them.

Something pricked at her senses, and she opened her eyes, just a little. Over his shoulder, thirty feet away in the forest, the dark figure stood, her face shadowed by her bonnet. She seemed unaffected by the rain, which fell around her but not on her, and she did not move, but simply watched. A sense of hunger and longing radiated off her like heat.

Evie closed her eyes, melting back into Desmond's arms. *Not now*, she thought. *Not now.*

When she opened her eyes again, the figure had gone.

15

Monday's rainstorm blew itself out by Tuesday morning, taking the clouds along with it. The rest of the week was clear, bright, and unusually warm, one last wave of summer heat before the cold set in for good. Evie made sure to finish all her work in class, so she could spend the rest of the time on the dress. Now that she had a ticket and a date to the dance, her self-imposed deadline to finish it had become very real. Other than that, she spent most of her time with Tina, who was obviously relieved to see Evie behaving more like herself again. She wasn't the only one. Ever since Desmond's proposal, Evie had felt a weight lifted from her shoulders. Nothing strange had happened—no visions of shadowy figures or nightmares keeping her awake. For the first time since arriving in Ravenglass—actually, for the first time in a very long time indeed—Evie felt free.

She didn't see much of Desmond—he spent every minute he wasn't in class at football practice, gearing up for the big game. He texted her every day, though, sending sweet messages and links to romantic songs on YouTube that he said "reminded me of you." Songs by Billie Eilish and Khalid, Frank Ocean, and even Lionel Richie—songs that made her smile and blush when she listened to them on her earbuds while walking to school. She passed Kimber in the hall on Wake-Up Wednesday, standing with her cronies in pink flannel pajamas, whispering as she walked by. In fact, a lot of the students had begun taking notice of her, their curious eyes watching her in the cafeteria and the classrooms and hallways. Tina attributed it to Evie's newfound status as Desmond King's date to homecoming. It had only happened on Monday afternoon, but by Tuesday morning it was a rumor, and by Wednesday it was a well-known fact. "Even Kitty wants to get to know you better," Tina told her at lunch. "And Kitty hates everyone."

Evie's past and current addresses were of much interest to the RHS student body, and mutterings about them both seemed to echo through the hallways of the school.

"She moved from some chic neighborhood in Manhattan to the Horror House, of all places . . ."

". . . I heard her mom's working at the inn on Main, but her dad's not around as far as I can tell . . ."

". . . wonder what it's like to live in that weird old house— although she *is* a little weird herself, always puttering around on that sewing machine . . ."

". . . what does Desmond see in her, anyway?"

Depending on the hour, Evie vacillated between being secretly thrilled with her newfound popularity and being completely mortified by it. She had intended to move like a shadow through this town, to avoid as much attention as possible. It was better that way—safer that way. But all of that became impossible the moment Desmond asked her to the dance and she said yes.

She tried not to let it bother her, though—focusing instead on her excitement about homecoming and about her plans for Friday. Tina had overheard her dad talking on the phone to an officer on Thursday evening, confirming that he and most of the police department would indeed be manning the streets, managing traffic and crowd control during the parade. The schools were all dismissing classes at lunchtime, so that everyone could participate in the big event in the afternoon and be ready to attend the football game that evening. Tina sent a text to Evie.

> I think we're good to go. You sure about this? There's still time to back out if you want to.

Evie stared at the screen for a moment, and her fingers instinctually found the locket that still hung around her neck. The thing, whatever it was, was leaving her alone for now. But she knew that it could—would—come back. It wanted something from her, just like it had wanted something from Holly forty years ago. And she knew it wouldn't rest until she understood. Understood what happened to Holly, what happened to the Patchwork Girl, what happened in this house to make its heart so black. She couldn't stop now. She wrote back to Tina.

> I'm sure.

There were already hundreds of onlookers lined up on Main Street by the time Evie arrived after school on Friday afternoon. Mothers stood on the sidewalk with babies in sunshaded strollers, while white-haired men sat in plastic folding chairs, sweaty cans of root beer gripped in their hands. The two men she'd seen at Birdie's were among them, drinking and talking. Birdie herself was there, too, making a killing selling fresh doughnuts. Evie stopped at her yellow-painted booth to buy one. Mama Bird was snoozing in a folding chair behind the booth, a Ravenglass Miners baseball cap shielding her face from the sun. After taking Evie's money, Birdie came back with a steaming, cinnamon-scented twist of dough wrapped in wax paper. She handed it to Evie and said, "Eat it while it's hot, okay? No good cold."

Evie nodded, thinking that with a smell like that, it would be impossible not to eat it immediately.

"You look funny," Birdie said, squinting at her. "What's going on with you? You sick or something?"

Birdie's bluntness took Evie by surprise. "No," she said. "I'm fine."

The woman wiped her hands on her apron and scoffed. "Don't be stupid. Your mouth says fine, but your face says different." She leaned over the booth counter. "Take a bite of that kkwabaegi," she demanded.

Evie did as she was told. It was unspeakably delicious.

"Now, you still want to lie to me?"

Evie shook her head vigorously.

"Then tell me: Why do you look so funny?"

Evie swallowed the sweet dough and said, "I can't go into the details, but—since I moved to Ravenglass, there's been this . . . thing that I can't figure out. It's keeping me up at night, and it seems to follow me wherever I go. I can't seem to make sense of it. I'm hoping that I'll get some more answers today, but I guess that's probably why I look . . . funny."

Birdie narrowed her eyes and nodded slowly. "It's dark under the lamp," she said.

"What?" Evie asked.

"Sometimes when we're searching for something, we look everywhere but where we should. Sometimes the answers are right under our noses. Here—" She reached into a plastic bin near the oil fryer behind her and handed her a small, yellow plastic bird.

Evie studied it. "A toy canary?"

"Something for the kids," Birdie said, shrugging. "Good for business, you know. And a good guide for lost little girls." She winked and gestured for the next customer to step forward.

Evie spied Tina waiting on the corner in front of the All That Glitters restaurant, just as planned. The parade was about to start, and it felt like every citizen of Ravenglass had come out to watch. The sidewalks and side streets, which had been cordoned off from traffic, were clogged with men, women, and children jockeying to find a good spot. Evie had to squeeze between a pack of teenagers from RHS and two big families to reach Tina, who waved when she caught sight of Evie approaching.

"You made it!" Tina said. Her voice was cheerful, excited, but Evie could sense the tension below.

"Yeah," Evie replied, checking her watch. "Just in time. We'll wait until the parade is fully underway, and then go. Right?"

"Right."

Just then, a ripple of sound made its way down Main Street toward them. A steady beat, and the sound of horns. "Here they come!" someone shouted.

A red Cadillac Eldorado convertible drove into view, and the man riding in the back seat was standing up and waving to the crowd. "That's the mayor—Kimber's father," Tina said. The sandy-haired man was dressed in a crisp navy suit with no tie, the first button of his shirt left open—as if to indicate that he was both their leader and a "man of the people." He was handsome in a TV evangelist sort of way, and had a too-white, too-wide politician's smile that reminded her of the Cheshire Cat.

We're all mad here.

Walking beside the Cadillac was a broad-chested man in a navy-blue police uniform, his brimmed cap pulled low over a serious, handsome face. He had light brown skin and a thick mustache that made him look even more the quintessential small-town chief of police. When he took off his cap to wipe the sweat from his brow, Evie saw that his black hair was curly, just like Tina's. "Dad!" Tina called out and waved. Her father scanned the crowd, found them, and waved back with a smile and a stiff nod. Evie imagined what his face would look like if he found out what they were planning to do, and quickly stopped those thoughts in their tracks.

Behind the Cadillac came the RHS pep band, marching in their black-and-gold uniforms, playing a thunderous rendition of "Ain't No Mountain High Enough." The drum major led the way, followed by the woodwinds and brass instruments flashing in the honey-colored light. The energetic drum line came next, and the color guard brought up the rear, their flags flying to the beat of the music.

The scene was so cheerful that the phantoms that lurked in Evie's memory seemed absurd and impossibly distant. Stricken with last-minute doubts, she wondered if the police department plan was worth the risk. *Homecoming is tomorrow,* she thought. *What if it all goes wrong? What if it ruins everything?* She had finished the dress just as the school day ended. It was in her bookbag right now, folded neatly and wrapped in wax paper and string. She'd never get the chance to wear it if they got caught.

"Here comes the homecoming court," Tina said, pointing.

Evie squinted to see the float coming up the road behind the pep band—a long trailer being towed by a black pickup truck. In the middle of the float, a six-foot-tall rocket ship with *RHS* painted on the side stood surrounded by piles of black and gold balloons, gathered around the rocket's base like clouds of smoke. Along the side of the trailer, a long banner read BLAST FROM THE PAST! Along the edges, four girls wearing gold dresses and four boys in black suits waved and tossed candy to the crowd. Evie saw Desmond—his white sash reading SOPHOMORE PRINCE—but he was facing the other side of the street. When he'd been voted onto the homecoming court that week—surprising no one—he'd texted Evie to tell her not to worry about it. He'd have to go up and stand with the others at some point during the dance, but the rest of the time, he'd be hers. Unfortunately, Kimber was on the court, too, and she was facing their direction. Despite the size of the crowd, and despite Evie being nearly hidden by the family standing in front of her, Kimber seemed to zero in on her almost instantly. Their eyes met and locked, and Evie refused to be the first to look away.

Kimber, who must have been used to being in the limelight, didn't let her plastic smile drop even for a moment. She smiled and waved—but her eyes burned with hatred. After a moment, she turned away and walked to the other side of the float to stand with Desmond. Evie watched as she linked her arm into his. Desmond flinched a little in surprise, but didn't pull away.

It was Evie's turn to burn. Her anger upset her—she never wanted to be the kind of person to fight over a guy, to carry on some ridiculous, petty war with another girl like this. *But what else can I do?* she asked herself. *Just let her walk all over me?*

She felt a nudge. "Evie," Tina said, "if we're going to do this, we've got to go *now*."

Evie hesitated. Suddenly her supernatural problems seemed much murkier than the problems right in front of her. The last thing she wanted to do was get in trouble and give Kimber the opportunity to move in for the kill.

But this might be the only chance you'll get to look at those files.

She closed her eyes and turned away. It was so loud, so crowded with people pressed tightly against her on all sides. She just needed a second to think! But as soon as she moved, she bumped into a little girl walking with her father, knocking a toy out of her hand. "Oops!" she said. "I'm so sorry!" She bent to pick up the toy before it was trampled by jostling feet.

It was a doll. A very familiar doll, with auburn hair and a red, white, and blue sailor suit. When Evie saw it, she felt the blood freeze in her veins. *It can't be, not here* . . . But it was the same doll from the attic. It had the same bit of hair missing, the same grin, the same sidelong glance. And it was the same strange, distorted voice that she heard, impossibly clear even over the roar of the crowd.

"*Come out and play with me,*" it said, "*And bring your dollies three . . .*"

"That's mine!" said the little girl, and she grabbed the doll out of Evie's hands, grasping it in her arms possessively.

Evie blinked, the spell broken. She looked over at the girl, who looked nothing like the one from her dreams—this was a girl with copper skin and curly black hair tied into pigtails. "Don't mind her," the girl's father said, apologetic. "She's very attached to her little baby there." He gestured to the doll, which Evie now saw was a completely different doll altogether. A baby doll with blinking brown eyes and a round open mouth where a plastic thumb could go.

Evie nodded, and the father and child moved on, the little girl begging to be put up on his shoulders to better see the floats rolling steadily down the street.

If the doll had been a message, Evie had received it, loud and clear.

She turned to Tina and gestured to the alley that ran next to the restaurant and toward the center of town. "I'm ready, let's go," she said.

The Ravenglass Police Department sat just off Main Street on Bluebell Road—a squat, unattractive redbrick building that looked like it had been constructed in the 1970s and then promptly forgotten about. The flat green roof was rusty in spots, and the furniture Evie could see through the fly-speckled windows could have been called "vintage" if she was being generous. "Wow," Evie said, and was about to comment on how small and shabby the place was but then realized Tina might take that personally. "It's, um . . . really different from the buildings on Main Street."

"Yeah, it's a dump," Tina agreed.

There was only one car in the parking lot, which was just as they had planned. All the officers and squad cars were down at the parade, except for the desk clerk watching the phones. "The parade should go on for another ten minutes," Tina said to Evie. "And it'll take another ten for the first officers to start arriving back at the station to check in. But we don't want to cut it close, so we need to be in and out in no more than fifteen minutes. You know what to do?"

Evie looked at her watch and nodded. "Fifteen minutes, got it."

Tina looked at her for another beat, excitement and fear warring on her face. "Don't get caught," she said. And with that, she turned away and walked toward the glass doors.

As soon as Tina was inside, Evie searched the perimeter to make sure no one was watching, then slipped around the building to a side door. Four large garbage bins were lined up along the wall beside it, smelling ripe in the afternoon sun. Tina had planted the seed for this part of the plan the day before—visiting her dad after school and "accidentally" leaving her phone on his desk when she left. She would tell the desk clerk she'd realized it was missing and had come back to get it as soon as she was out of school. Being without her phone for almost twenty-four hours had been exceedingly painful—she had made that abundantly clear to Evie when she'd called her on the landline last night—but necessary. There just wasn't any other item she owned that would have made sense to go out of her way during the parade to retrieve.

Tina would ask the clerk to go into her dad's office to get the phone for her, and while he was looking, she would slip into the back and open the side door for Evie. To make sure she had enough time to open the door and get back to her original spot, Tina had hidden the phone under some papers on her father's messy desk, so that the clerk would have to spend a few minutes searching for it before he could return.

Evie stood at the side door, watching the seconds tick by. Two minutes, three minutes . . . She started to get nervous. What if the clerk asked Tina to come with him, and she didn't get the chance to open the door? What if her dad had already found the phone and had it waiting for her right at the front desk?

And then, Evie heard a click, and the side door inched open. Tina's face peeked through, and she waved her in. "Small talk!" she whispered, making her hand into a puppet mouth opening and closing. "At least I won't have trouble keeping him distracted while you look for the file. Now go—quickly!"

Evie nodded, and slipped through the door into a poorly lit hallway with white linoleum floors. Tina walked soundlessly ahead, turning right toward the front lobby. Evie swallowed and took a couple of deep breaths. Her heart was racing. *You get mad at Stan for stealing traffic signs and then break into the police department*, she thought. *Hypocrite.* It was so insane that she almost giggled. Instead, she made her way down the hallway and turned left to go deeper into the building, replaying Tina's instructions in her head as she went. "Go all the way to the back of the building and turn right," Tina had said. "The hallway before that will take you to processing and the holding cells, and you don't want to go there. It will be in that hallway. If you get to the IT room, you've gone too far." Evie walked briskly until the hallway ended at a large room with four desks in it. Turning right, she passed a mechanical room, evidence storage room, and finally a room labeled CID FILE ROOM.

As quietly as she could, she turned the knob, slipped inside, and closed the door behind her. She looked at her watch. Six minutes had passed. It would take her another three to get back down the hall and out of the building, which meant she had only six minutes to find Holly's file.

Other than a small, battered desk near the door, the room had nothing in it but rows upon rows of metal shelving, each one crammed from floor to ceiling with white cardboard boxes. They were labeled in black marker by year, so Evie quickly ran up and down the rows, scanning the labels until she found 1982. There were four boxes for that year, and luckily, she found the one labeled OCTOBER–DECEMBER on the lower shelf and easy to pull down. Throwing off the lid, she began flipping through the files.

She looked through all the files for October and didn't find it.

Her fingers began to tremble as she flipped through the files again. Nothing.

She wiped her face with the back of her hand, her forehead slick with perspiration. Three minutes left. *It has to be here, it just has to.* She decided to look through the entire box, just in case it had been misfiled somehow. The closer she got to the back of the box, still finding nothing, the more her hands shook. *No, no, no . . .*

And then, she flipped to the very last file. The label read HOB-BIE, HOLLY. OCT 30 1982.

Biting back a triumphant cry, she pulled out the file. It was surprisingly thin. With her phone in hand, she quickly flipped through the pages, snapping photos of all of them. When she was done, she checked her watch. Only thirty seconds before she needed to be out of this room and heading back. She shoved the file back into the box, and the box back onto the shelf. After checking that everything looked just as it had before, she opened the door and walked out. After only two steps, she heard the desk clerk's voice—so loud that it almost seemed to be on top of her.

"I can't believe your dad didn't show you the new computers when you were here yesterday," he was saying. "Got 'em through some grant from the state. Real cutting-edge stuff."

"Oh, I don't want to take up your time," Evie heard Tina say, her voice tense. "I really should be getting back to the parade, anyway—"

"It'll just be a second, they're back here in the IT room."

Evie gasped, and then covered her mouth with one hand. They were right around the corner, heading her way.

16

Evie knew she had only seconds to act before the clerk turned the corner and saw her. Her whole body had broken out in a cold sweat, and she stood rooted to the spot in panic. There wasn't enough time to hide; there was hardly enough time to breathe. She'd be discovered, and Tina would be caught up in the thing with her, and then, and then—

"Oh!" Tina's sudden exclamation broke Evie out of her spiral. There was a clatter as something hit the ground.

"Jeez— Tina, are you okay? What happened?"

Evie heard Tina suck her teeth. "I'm so clumsy. Must have tripped. Ugh, look at this mess!"

"Here, let me help you."

Finally able to move again, Evie took several steps back toward the file room and quickly slipped back inside. Tina must have faked a fall to give her time to get away. *Thank god*, she thought. *That was too close.* She leaned against the wall next to the door and waited for them to pass by. Once they had, she snuck back out into the hallway and padded softly to the side door. In another moment, she was outside in the sunshine. She walked past the garbage bins just in time to see a squad car turning in to the parking lot. Evie ducked into the trees beside the building and made her way down the street, putting as much distance between her and the police department as she could. By the time she made it back to Main Street, the parade was wrapping up, and the crowd had begun to disperse. Squirrels were moving in, inspecting the odd crumbs and bits of candy left behind, and all the vendors— including Birdie and her mother—were packing up for the day. Evie stood and watched, feeling her racing heart finally slow. Five minutes later, she felt a hand on her shoulder, and turned to see Tina standing behind her, cheeks flushed.

"Did you get it?" she asked, breathless.

Evie held up her phone and smiled. "I got it," she said. "You really saved the day when you hit the floor. Two more steps down that hallway and he would have seen me."

Tina's eyes widened. "No way. I just wanted to make a big noise just in case you were still around, to let you know we were coming." She shook her head. "He was so set on showing me those new computers . . ."

"Well, we did it. I have all the pictures. Why don't we go back to the house and look at them?"

Tina glanced up at her. Evie wondered if she noticed how Evie never called it "my house" or "home"—only "the house." If she did, she didn't say. "Sure," she said instead. "Let's go."

Twenty minutes later, they were sitting on the grass under the apple tree, the shadow of Hobbie House falling over them. The late afternoon sun was warm, almost baking, but it was cool in the shade. Evie pulled up the pictures on her phone and turned up the brightness full blast. "It's good that the file was as short as it was," Evie said as she scooted closer to Tina, "or else I wouldn't have had time to take pictures of all the pages. But still, it was surprising. For such a huge, national case, why wouldn't there have been more paperwork about it?"

"Maybe there was," Tina said in a low voice, "and someone made it disappear."

Their heads pressed together, they pored over each picture carefully. The initial reports were unremarkable, and recorded only basic facts, all of which they already knew. A description of Holly, her last known whereabouts, the statements given by her parents, teachers, friends. All of the statements were from people they expected—except one.

41 Y/O F, 9 WINDSONG WAY, RAVENGLASS MA, MRS. BONG KIM.

"Bong Kim?" Evie murmured. "Who's that?"

"That's . . . that's Mama Bird," Tina said. "Birdie's mother. But why would she have given a statement? I mean, she knew Holly, but if they'd interviewed every person in town who knew Holly, this file would be a lot thicker."

Evie swiped to the next picture, which included the text of Mama Bird's statement.

> *Mrs. Kim, who owns a dining establishment in Raven-*
> *glass, states that she was a personal friend of Miss*

Hobbie and had seen the girl only a day before her
disappearance. She notes that Miss Hobbie had seemed
unusually agitated during her visit to Mrs. Kim's estab-
lishment ["Birdie's Diner"], and spoke of trouble at
home with her mother and father, as well as an un-
named "secret friend" who was helping and advising
her. Mrs. Kim would not comment on whether she be-
lieved this "friend" could have been an adult preying
on Miss Hobbie, but instead offered vague theories
about something haunting and attaching itself to Miss
Hobbie before taking her away. When asked if she be-
lieved Miss Hobbie to be dead, Mrs. Kim replied, "No."
But when asked if she believed Miss Hobbie to be alive
and well, Mrs. Kim said again, "No." After extensive
questioning, it is the opinion of the RPD that Mrs. Kim
may not be a reliable source for this case.

"This is important," Evie said, excited. "I can feel it. Mama
Bird knows something about all this."

Tina sighed. "Well, you'll have a hard time getting through to
her now. The Alzheimer's has made it really difficult. Birdie says
the only ways she's found to bring her back are things from her
past—music, smells, things that she knew when she was younger.
But even then, it doesn't always help."

Evie read the statement again. "I wonder what Mama Bird
meant when she said that something was haunting Holly."

"It could be that she meant someone was stalking her?
Maybe she was trying to explain something in her own words but
couldn't," Tina said. "But we have something that he didn't have."

"What's that?"

"The internet."

Pulling out her phone, Tina started typing Mama Bird's words. The first result was a wiki article about something called Gwisin. Evie scooted closer to read over Tina's shoulder. "'Gwisin are a type of ghost in Korean folklore,'" she said aloud. "Yes . . . I think this is it!" She read on. "'A Cheonyeogwisin is the spirit of a young girl who becomes evil because she died before her life could be fulfilled. These spirits often attach themselves to other young girls, haunting and sometimes even harming them.'" She looked up from the screen and stared at Tina. "Mama Bird thought Holly was taken by one of these ghosts! Maybe the Patchwork Girl? And if she was, then maybe Holly then became one herself!"

And now she's coming for you.

The thought arrived unbidden in Evie's mind, and she quickly waved it away. She was close; she needed to follow this line of thinking as far as it could go.

Tina looked torn between excitement and discomfort. "Well, just because Mama Bird thought this doesn't mean it's true. And anyway, if she thought Holly was taken and had become a ghost, she'd be dead, right? But she said to the police that she thought Holly was neither alive nor dead."

"Maybe the folklore didn't quite fit," Evie argued, "but it was the closest thing to what Mama Bird knew—the only way she could explain her theory to the officers. Not that they listened to her. People like that never listen."

"Maybe," Tina said, but she sounded unconvinced. Evie wasn't surprised—Tina clearly loved the thrill of the supernatural, but didn't really believe it was possible. Like her father, she wanted proof. Only hard evidence would do. "Let's look at the rest of the stuff and come back to it."

"All right," Evie said. She was too excited to argue—if there was one tidbit of information in these files, there might be more.

After all the witness statements, there were photographs of the interior and exterior of the house—glossy prints in the oddly bright, hothouse colors of old 35 mm film. It was strange seeing the house look so different and yet so much the same—the outside of the house free of climbing vines and moldering wood, Holly's bedroom with all her posters in their place and the rose fresh and red on her dresser, the kitchen with the dirty dishes from their dinner still piled in the sink, the eight cats sitting at an angle by the cellar door. The last places Holly had been seen, the last things she'd touched. Evie stared at them, trying to see *something*, some detail that had been missed all those years ago . . . but there was nothing. Just empty places.

"Looks like that's it," she said after reaching the final image. She tried to focus on the lead with Mama Bird and not be discouraged. Of course, Tina was right. The chances of being able to have a lucid conversation with Mrs. Kim about something that had happened forty years ago were slim to none. But what else could she do?

She flipped back to the first few images and scanned through them a second time. Back and forth, back and forth. "Did you find something?" Tina asked.

"I don't know—it's weird. This page ends midsentence, and the next page doesn't finish it. We didn't notice the first time around because the writing is so small, and it was almost the end of the witness statement, anyway. But look." She used her thumb and forefinger to zoom in on the image, which clearly showed an incomplete thought at the bottom of the page. "That means the next page—or pages—are missing. I think you were right. I think someone did make part of this file disappear." She flipped to the next image and zoomed in again, squinting. "Wait a second," she said, her pulse beginning to race. "There's something here at the top. It looks like someone removed the page, but the very top inch or so was left behind when they ripped it out. There are a few words written there." She squinted and huffed in frustration. "It's too small to make out, and I can't zoom in any further."

"Send it to me, and I'll open it on my laptop," Tina said, excited. "I can isolate that part of the image and increase the contrast and definition."

Evie shared the file, and soon Tina had it up on her computer screen and was toggling with the controls. "I think I've got it," she said after a few minutes. "It looks like the top of another witness statement form. 'Eighteen-year-old male, Nine Blue Stone Court, Mr. James K.' The rest of the name is cut off." She looked up from her computer, an apologetic expression on her face. "Sorry, there isn't—" she started to say, but then she saw the look of shock on Evie's face. "What? What is it?"

Evie was electrified with wordless wonder as she felt the events of forty years before sliding into place, creating an impossible symmetry, like two mirrors facing each other and reflecting the same image over and over into infinity. "The boy in Holly's diary," she whispered. "J. The boy she loved in secret, the one she was supposed to go to homecoming with that night and never made it there. His name was James."

Realization dawned on Tina's face. "Oh my god," she breathed. "No way."

Evie remembered the look on the man's face when he saw her that day, standing at the quarry next to his son. His son, the boy who was a spitting image of his father in high school. The look of recognition—and horror, too.

"*You look . . . just like her.*"

"Yes," Evie said. "Holly was in love with James King, Desmond's father."

17

"**B**egin at the beginning, and go on till you come to the end."
She'd always thought the King of Hearts' words in
the Wonderland tale were silly when she'd read them as
a child, but now they echoed through Evie's head as she walked
through the darkening streets toward Ravenglass High. The
clear day had become clogged with mist that clung to her eyelashes and the furry edges of her coat in tiny crystalline droplets. Their last remaining leaves gone, the skeletal trees loomed
over the town, shiny with moisture and silhouetted before an
acid-yellow sky.

The hands of time were spinning backward with every step
she took, she could feel it. The synchronicity of that very moment
and another one forty years before. She was walking on a path
already laid out for her, she knew that now. She must go back to
the very beginning, and not stop until all was revealed.

It was almost 7:00 p.m. After Tina had left, Evie had gone to
her room and fallen asleep. She hadn't meant to, but she was so

exhausted by the events of the day and all the sleepless nights that her body hadn't given her a choice. By the time she woke up, she'd already missed the beginning of the game. Throwing on her coat, she ran out of her room and almost collided with Stan in the hallway. He had his hoodie up and his backpack slung over his shoulder. "Are you going to the game?" she asked.

"No," he scoffed.

"Where are you going, then?"

"None of your business."

"Stan, I need to know. Mom's always working, so—"

"So, what? So you get to be the one who pretends to be interested in my life?"

Evie rubbed her forehead with her fingers and looked at her watch. "I don't have time for this," she said.

"No, of course you don't," he said, and pushed past her down the stairs.

"Stan!" she said to his back.

He stopped, but didn't turn around. "What?"

She hesitated. There was so much to say, so much she hadn't told him. She'd told herself she was protecting him—he was only ten, after all. But she realized that by keeping him in the dark about Holly and the house, she'd kept him in the dark about everything. Mom was gone, and she was gone, too. A wave of guilt crashed over her. *You can fix it, but not now*, she thought. *Right now, you have to go.*

"I'm sorry," she finally said. "We'll talk later, okay? Wherever you're going, just be careful."

She watched his shoulders slump just a little. "Whatever," he said, clomping down the stairs and out the kitchen door.

Evie waited a couple of minutes, and then followed right behind him.

It was nearly dark by the time Evie reached the football field at RHS, but the enormous floodlights made it seem like the middle of the day. Like that afternoon at the parade, it seemed like everyone in Ravenglass was there. Evie pushed through clots of people gathered around the edge of the field or standing in line to buy ice cream and hot dogs from student vendors raising money for clubs. All around her, the stands were crowded with rowdy fans decked out in black and gold for the Miners, shouting at the field and waving pennants. Across the way, the pep band was blasting out "Are You Ready for This?" and moving to the beat. The team mascot, dressed in a black coverall and carrying a huge plastic pickax, cavorted about the field, riling up the crowd. His oversize costume head grinned wickedly, and the headlamp on his hard hat flashed with yellow light.

Evie squinted at the scoreboard and saw that it was already the beginning of the second quarter, and the opposing team—the Blue Devils—had scored a touchdown. The Devils had the ball and were about to start a play at the thirty-yard line. She scanned the field for Number 19 and saw Desmond crouched in the far corner of the defensive line. Her heart flickered at the sight of him, but he wasn't the man she had come to see.

She spotted James King sitting alone up at the top of the side stands, right at the fifty-yard line. Her eyes moved past the hundreds of faces to his, as if drawn there by some invisible thread.

As she walked toward him, she saw Mrs. King chatting to two other women down on the field, and was careful to avoid her. Desmond's father was so focused on the game that he didn't notice her until she sat down on the bleacher next to him. He was wearing jeans, a worn black-and-gold letterman jacket, and an RHS baseball cap.

"Hello, Mr. King," she said. It was quieter, high up in the stands, and her voice cut through the dull roar of the game below.

Mr. King dragged his gaze from the field to look at her. His eyes widened. Clearly he had been expecting someone—anyone—else. "Miss Archer," he said, recovering quickly. "How nice to see you again."

"How's your head?" she asked.

Mr. King touched the back of his head instinctively and shrugged. "Oh, it's fine. Just fine. What can I do for you?"

Evie pursed her lips. This man wasn't just Desmond's father. Aside from the mayor, he was the most powerful man in town. What if he got upset? One word, and her family could be disgraced. Her mother could even lose her job.

There's no turning back now.

She took a deep breath. "I know you were the last person to see Holly alive."

Mr. King recoiled. The file hadn't said as much, it had only had his name, but she knew it in her bones to be true. "What are you talking about?" he said carefully. His bottom lip was trembling.

"You were more than friends," she went on. "Or rather, you wanted to be. Holly's parents were too strict to let her date boys from school, and for a long time, she was too shy to admit how much she liked you. And then everything changed right before she disappeared. Isn't that right?"

Mr. King looked away, his lip curling like he'd tasted something bitter. "What does it matter now? That was a lifetime ago. It's over. Dead and gone."

"It matters," she replied. "It matters because it's the truth. And the truth is still buried somewhere, and I need to find it."

He looked back at her now. "Why?" he asked.

She swallowed. The world shifted a little, like it had tumbled off its axis and exposed something else underneath. Mr. King's face flickered to a younger, smoother version of itself, one that looked almost exactly like Desmond. Around her the sound of the crowd and the music slowed, distorted, and the light flickered from vivid to the muted sepia tones of her dreams.

It lasted only an instant before everything shuddered back to normal, like an old record player skipping across a scratch. Evie wavered in her seat, reeling. But she closed her eyes for only a moment, determined to give nothing away.

"Because it's not over," she said, her heart hammering. "It's still happening. It's happening right now."

An expression of confusion, with a touch of fear, passed over Mr. King's face, and Evie wondered if she'd gone too far. Did he sense a wildness behind her eyes? Could he see the edge of that haunted thing inside her? But instead of dismissing her, he wiped his lips with his hand, grimaced, and said, "If I tell you what you want to know, will you leave it alone? Just because you're living in her house doesn't give you the right to dig up her bones."

It does if those bones won't stay buried, she thought. "Yes," she said instead.

He nodded. "All right," he said.

Remembering the pages ripped from Holly's case file, Evie asked, "Tell me what happened. Homecoming night. I want to know everything."

He closed his eyes for a moment, thinking. "That week was a whirlwind," he began. "Like you said, Holly changed. Maybe it was gradual, but at the time, it seemed like a lightning bolt struck and she came alive. She'd always been so afraid of her folks, what they'd think—but all of a sudden, none of that mattered to her. It was like she was trying to cram in as much living as she could, like she was making up for lost time. This . . . *passion* . . . just flowed out of her. Passion for the things she loved. History. Old things. Books." He paused as a flash of pain passed over his face. "Me."

"I heard that she had a thing for history," Evie said.

Mr. King's face brightened. "Oh, yes. Holly was a bit of a nerd." He chuckled. "She hated when I called her that, but she was. She was obsessed with that house of hers. Scoured it like an archaeologist. Wanted to know everything there was to know about it. Pretty sure she spent days in the library and the museum archives, just poring over old papers and books and suchlike. Near the end she used to go on and on about this girl who used to live there a long time ago." He crinkled his brows. "What was it? Ah—Sarah Flower. That was her name. Holly was fascinated by that girl."

Evie's hand went to the locket around her neck. *SF. This locket must have belonged to Sarah Flower.* Could she be the Patchwork Girl that Tina had told her about? Could she be the girl from her dreams? "What did Holly say about her?" she asked.

Mr. King shook his head. "Not much, I'm afraid. She was thrilled when she found a record of her name—but it was near the end when all that happened. If she found out more about the girl, I never heard about it. And at the time, I didn't really care much about some girl from a hundred years ago." He sighed. "When Holly opened up and told me how she felt about me, the first thing I did was ask her to homecoming. I didn't know if her parents would let her go, but she said not to worry about it. Said she'd take care of it. But that day—something happened. I remember putting on my suit at home and then getting a call from Holly. She was . . . hysterical. Ranting about her parents and how they were punishing her. I said it was okay if she couldn't make it, but she told me she would still come. She said—" He paused, licked his lips, and swallowed. "She said that her secret friend would help her. Her secret friend had 'a beautiful dress for her, flowers for her hair, and a song for her heart.' I remember those words exactly, because I thought they were so strange. She said she just had to go down to see her friend, and then she and I could dance all night. She sounded like a stranger." He shook his head, his eyes dark. "It was the last time I ever heard her voice."

Evie looked down at her hands, solemn. But then, something occurred to her. "But you said you were the last person to see her. If you only talked to her on the phone, then . . . ?"

"I did see her that night," he said. "Or at least, I thought I did. I went to the dance and waited for her. I waited all night. My friends kept me company, of course. Tried to cheer me up. Gloria—my wife—was there, too. We were friends then, started dating a few months later, after everything with Holly had died down. She helped me recover." He smiled briefly. "But my friends never thought Holly and I were a good match, anyway, so they tried to get me to forget about her that night and enjoy the party. But I couldn't stop thinking—worrying—about her. At one point I went outside for some air, and I thought I saw her standing out in that field by the side of the school. She was wearing a long dress, and some kind of hood or something on her head. It was dark, but I could see the moonlight shining off her red hair. I went to her, but on the way I almost stepped on something in the long grass that howled like the dickens. A cat, probably. When I looked back up, she was gone."

Evie shivered.

"Maybe it was just a trick of the eye and she was never there at all. Sometimes, you see what you want to see. I didn't find out she was missing until the next morning, along with the rest of the town." He chewed his lip. "After everything that happened, those times with Holly feel like a dream I had. But just like a dream, I forgot about it all after a while. Gloria and I got married, and it just faded away." He looked up at her then. "But when I saw you, it all came back. And let me tell you something, young lady, it doesn't feel good. Let it go now. Please."

Just then, the crowd roared. Down on the field, the Miners had just intercepted the ball, and one of the players was making a mad dash toward the end zone. One of the Blue Devils' wide receivers went to chase him down, and it looked like the runner wasn't going to make it. Then Evie saw Desmond bolt across the field, dodging and weaving with the grace of a dancer, and tackle the opposing player. The Miners' runner kept running all the way over the goal line for a touchdown. The crowd roared even louder than before.

Mr. King rose to his feet, clapping. When he sat back down, he proudly said, "He's a cornerback, you know."

"I don't know much about football," Evie admitted. "But I can see he's very good at it."

"Everybody talks about the quarterback, but the cornerback is the toughest position on the field. You have to have strength, speed, brains, *and* guts. Gotta have it all. And my boy? He's got it all." His eyes glistened with pride.

After the kicker scored the extra point, they were tied 7-7. Evie watched Desmond pull off his helmet and celebrate with his teammates. His smile was dazzling under the floodlights. The sight of him squeezed her heart, whether with pain or joy, she couldn't tell. When she turned back to Mr. King, he was watching her. "What?" she asked.

"The way you look at him," he murmured. "That's just the way she used to look at me." He leaned in closer. "I don't know what you're up to, Miss Archer, but don't you bring Desmond into it. You will not hurt him, do you understand? He is everything to me. *Everything.*"

Just then, Mrs. King appeared at the end of the row and stared at Evie in surprise. Her eyes flicked back to her husband. "James?" she said, the rest of the question—"what is *she* doing here?"—implied.

"Miss Archer just came to say a friendly hello," Mr. King replied. "I'm sure she'd like to get back to her seat now."

"Yes," Evie said quickly, rising. "It was nice to see you again, Mr. King—Mrs. King. Enjoy the rest of the game."

"Thank you," Mrs. King said cordially, though her eyes were cold.

Evie found Tina sitting with Kitty Flores at the bottom of the bleachers, where the two were eating ice-cream cones. "Hey!" Tina said. "There you are. I thought maybe you weren't coming."

Kitty glanced up, her eyes behind the tortoiseshell glasses a mixture of curiosity and loathing. She licked a bit of vanilla from her lips, managing to make the gesture seem vaguely threatening. For the first time, Evie recognized that she must have been Tina's closest friend until Evie had come along, and that perhaps Kitty wasn't too pleased about it. Still, Tina had said that Kitty hated everyone, so at least Evie was in good company. "Evelyn," she said drily.

"Kitty," Evie replied with a nod. "I'm sorry to ask, but could I talk to Tina in private for a minute?"

Kitty glanced around them at the hundreds of people and then back at Evie. "Really? This is possibly the least private location I can imagine." Evie shrugged. Kitty rolled her eyes. "Fine. I will get up so Her Majesty can utter her secrets in confidence." With that, she devoured the remaining ice cream on her cone, swallowed it in one gulp like a snake, and handed the empty cone to Evie.

When she was gone, Evie stood holding the cone for a moment before sitting down. "She is terrifying."

"I know. I love Kitty, but she can be a bit much sometimes," Tina said. "So? What's this big secret you want to tell me?"

Evie leaned close so that none of her words would be stolen by the noise of the crowd, retelling everything Mr. King told her. "He was supposed to be her date for the dance, and then she called him right before to tell him about the fight with her parents. He says he thinks he saw her outside the school during the dance, too—but he can't be sure."

Tina nodded, but didn't look very impressed. "Okay, I mean, it's good to have confirmation about all that, but how does it help us? It doesn't really tell us anything we don't already know."

"There's more," Evie went on. "Mr. King says that before she disappeared, Holly was talking a lot about her research into a girl who lived in the house a long time ago. A girl named Sarah Flower." She pulled the locket out from under her jacket and showed it to Tina. "SF. I think she and your Patchwork Girl are one and the same. And now that we know her name, maybe we can figure out who she was, and what happened to her. If we knew that, it could help us understand what happened to Holly."

Tina nodded, but Evie could tell she was thinking very carefully about what to say next. "Evie," she began, "this is great stuff—I mean, no one has put a name to the Patchwork Girl in all this time, so Holly must have found something really special. In the house, maybe." She paused.

"But?" Evie said.

"But . . . I still don't understand how you think this would help us find out what happened to Holly. Sarah Flower lived and died more than a hundred years ago. Whoever was involved in her disappearance couldn't possibly have had anything to do with Holly vanishing from inside her house just forty years ago."

Evie scoffed. "What about Mama Bird's statement in the police report? The evil spirits. You can't just completely discount all the evidence—"

"I can when it's impossible!" Tina broke in. "Look, I love a good story—you know I do. But I'm starting to worry about you, Evie. The police department caper was really fun, but maybe we should take a step back for a bit—"

"Fun?" Evie blurted. "You think I wanted to break into the police department because it was fun? I thought you cared about solving this." She was starting to feel a little hysterical.

"I *do* care, Evie. Cool it, would you?" Tina said, glancing around to see if people sitting nearby were looking at them. "But the answer to Holly's disappearance lies in the real world, Evie. Not in some delusional fantasy of yours." She lowered her voice. "Do you want people to think you're crazy?"

Evie sat back abruptly, as if she'd been slapped.

What's wrong with you?

Tina must have noticed the expression on Evie's face, because she immediately softened. "I'm sorry. That was harsh." She sighed. "I want to help you figure this out. I really do. But I can't let it ruin your life. You see that, right?"

Evie shook her head. She felt dizzy with frustration. "You don't understand . . . ," she muttered, looking away at the field. She couldn't meet Tina's eyes. Didn't want to see the pity there—the same pity that had been in her mother's eyes in the bathroom as she sat wet and shivering on the cold tile floor. In Dr. Mears's eyes, too. She hated it, that superiority disguised as compassion. *I know what's good for you*, the look said. *I know better. What you feel, what you see—none of it is real . . .*

At that moment, the Miners' offensive line started a play. The ball was snapped to the quarterback, who hesitated for an instant before launching a pass. Evie was watching when a dark smudge in the stands near the forty-yard line caught her eye. A shadow among the bright yellow pennants and the glare of the floodlights. At first, she thought it was just someone watching the game, but when the wide receiver caught the pass and the crowd rose to their feet, the dark figure was motionless.

It was her.

But unlike every other time she'd seen the figure in the bonnet and the long, long dress, she wasn't facing away. This time she was facing forward, and looking straight at Evie.

18

Every fiber of Evie's being unspooled at the sight of the shadow. The wrongness of it . . . just looking at that dark, still thing standing amid such brightness and movement made her composure start to fray and come apart. She tried to make out details of the face, but it was far away and shrouded in darkness. It almost seemed to blur in front of her eyes, like the photograph of the little girl in Sarah Flower's locket. Although there were other people sitting in the row around the figure, no one seemed to notice it. Their eyes were all on the game.

When Evie blinked, the shadow was gone.

"No," Evie whispered. *Not again. Not this time.* She scanned the crowd, desperately trying to find it again. *There!* Somehow, in mere seconds, the figure had moved from the bleachers to the field and was moving away, slipping like water through the unseeing crowd.

Evie rose from her seat and made for the stairs, rushing to catch up with the figure before it disappeared again. "Where are you going?" Tina asked, looking concerned.

"I need to talk to someone," Evie said, and before Tina could ask any more questions, Evie hurried down to the field, trying not to lose sight of the shadow as she went. She pushed through clots of onlookers and cheerleaders, and the noise of the crowd and the band was nearly deafening. But the shadow was always too far ahead. By the time she reached the outer edge of the field, beyond the bleachers and the glare of the floodlights, she almost thought she'd lost it. It was quieter out there, darker, and Evie could finally hear her labored breath, her heart hammering in her ears. Looking out onto the solitary tree and tall grass, she realized that this was the same wild field that her FCS classroom windows looked out on. The same place she'd seen the figure that first day when she and Desmond met.

And there it was again. Out by the tree, still and waiting, facing away.

Evie had wanted so badly to catch up with the thing, but now that she had—she was filled with an unspeakable terror.

You can't run, she thought. *It will never stop this if you do.*

Her throat was dry. In a voice that sounded pitifully small in that wide open place, so quiet after the cacophony of the football game, she asked, "Are you . . . Holly Hobbie?"

The shadow said nothing.

Evie tried again. "What happened to you? I've been trying to understand . . ."

Again, nothing. But suddenly, the scent of flowers, sweet with decay, filled her nostrils.

"You were trying to find out about Sarah Flower," Evie went on. "Why? Who was she?" And then: "Was she your secret friend?"

At that, the figure began to hum. Evie recognized the song at once—it was the Patchwork Girl's song, the same one the doll sang to her in the attic.

"Why are you doing this to me?" Evie said, a dizzying feeling of madness rising in her.

"These spirits often attach themselves to other young girls, haunting and sometimes even harming them . . ."

Evie began to walk toward the thing. "Look at me!" she cried. "What are you?" As she got closer, the shadow began to sing in earnest. The voice was hollow, like the sound of a late autumn wind rushing through the trees. *"Slide down my cellar door,"* it sang, *"and we'll be jolly friends forevermore . . ."*

As she got closer, Evie could see more detail in the shadow's form—the ruffles at the bottom of its long dress, the patterns of it that seemed to blur and refocus with every step she took, like an old TV channel fractured by electromagnetic noise. Evie reached out for its shoulder to turn it around, and when her fingers touched the thing, it was like gossamer, like feathers or cobwebs except cold. Cold in a way that traveled down her arm and straight to her heart.

The shadow turned then, and moonlight lit the face of the thing that had haunted her since she had come to Hobbie House. It was the face of the girl in the newspaper, the face she'd seen in family albums and in her dreams. Holly's face, framed by the frills of a bonnet. A lovely, alabaster face with mournful eyes, full lips, and cheeks sprinkled with freckles almost identical to her own.

Or rather, half of it was.

The other half of her face had rotted away, leaving only a

gaping skull behind. Its exposed teeth grinned, made more grotesque by its nearness to such sweet loveliness.

Evie stumbled back, a scream caught in her throat. She tripped over the uneven ground and fell, pillowed by the tall grass.

Washed in moonlight, the white, ruined half of her face was terrifying. *"Playmate, come out and play with me,"* Holly sang. *"Sarah and Holly and Evie make three."*

"No." Evie wanted to scream, but the word came out as a whisper. Her breath wouldn't come. Nearby and yet impossibly far away, the crowd roared. "No . . . I won't . . ."

"Yes," the shadow said, and Evie stared into the darkness of its hollow eye. It seemed to grow larger with every second, until it was a black hole as big as the sky. She felt herself falling into it, head over heels. *"You will."*

"Miss?"

The voice was faint and distant. Evie was at the bottom of the ocean, or might as well have been.

"Miss, are you all right?"

She groped for the words, holding fast to them like a lifeline. Evie felt herself rising to the surface of consciousness, felt the grass underneath her body, insects crawling along her legs, the cool night air on her face. She opened her eyes.

A young man knelt beside her, tall and bent like a seedling that had grown too fast. He wore a matching blue cap and polo shirt and smelled like cigarettes. When he saw her looking at him, his shoulders slumped in relief. "Oh man, you're awake. You scared me. Thought I'd have to call nine-one-one. I thought you were dead, at first. You know, body in a field, like on TV. Almost tripped over you and fell on my face." He was talking very fast and was clearly shaken. Evie guessed that he was one of the food vendors working the stands and had come out into the field for a smoke break.

She sat up. Her head spun, but only for a moment. She glanced over at the football field and saw the cheerleaders performing the halftime show. That was a relief. It had been almost the end of the second quarter when she arrived, so she must have been unconscious for only a few minutes. "I'm fine, thanks," she said to the man, and allowed him to help her to her feet. "I came out here to get some air, and I must have fainted."

The man nodded. "Yeah, I get it." He paused, obviously unsure what he should say next. "You want a snow cone?"

Evie peered around him to the spot where she'd first seen Holly. The specter wasn't there, of course, but Evie still needed to make sure. She'd told the man that she was fine, like she wasn't a hairsbreadth away from a complete breakdown. She balled her hands into fists so that the man couldn't see them shaking. "Thanks," she said, "but I really think I should be heading home."

The man cocked his head and pointed his thumb back toward the game. "You don't want to see how it ends?" he asked.

No, Evie thought of saying, *I'm not sure I want to see how any of this ends*. But instead, she merely shrugged.

The man shrugged in return. "Okay then," he said. "Well, have a good night." Shoving his hands into his pockets, he walked away.

Evie brushed the dirt from her clothes and pulled her coat collar more tightly against her neck. It was fully dark now, and cold. She wanted to be back at the house, away from eyes that would see the disturbance in her own. But the house wasn't safe, she knew that. Holly had made that perfectly clear. But where else could she go?

She was walking down Main Street, just outside of town. She watched the sign above Birdie's blinking in the darkness, the yellow neon wings flapping rhythmically, flying but going nowhere. Just as she approached it, the sign blinked off. She was passing the diner itself when she saw Birdie in the window, counting money from the cash register. As if sensing her, the woman looked up and spied Evie outside. Within moments she was at the door. "You!" she shouted. "What did I tell you about walking in the night? Get in here, now!"

Evie had learned not to argue with Birdie, so she dutifully walked inside the dimly lit diner, wiped clean after the day. Birdie was grumbling. "Wait here while I finish up, then I'll drive you home. You keep Mama company."

"Okay," Evie said meekly, and walked over to where Mama Bird was sitting in her chair, staring out the window. The shadows that crept into the deep wrinkles of her skin made her look impossibly ancient. Evie approached her and sat in the booth opposite. "Hi there, Mrs. Kim," she said, using the name she'd learned from Holly's diary and the case file. "How are you?"

Mama Bird turned and regarded her. There was a cloudiness to her eyes that cleared after a moment, and she smiled. "Oh, it's you. Hello, Holly."

A chill ran down Evie's spine. She bit back the instinct to tell her *no, I'm not Holly*, and thought perhaps she could use this opportunity to ask a few questions. If Mama Bird wouldn't talk to Evie from the present, maybe she would talk to Holly from 1982 . . .

"Mrs. Kim," she began, "we're friends, right?"

Mama Bird nodded. "I've known you since you were just a little girl. I'm so glad you're all right, Holly. I was worried about you. I thought the spirit had taken you."

Evie's ears perked up. "The spirit?" she said.

"Oh, yes. You were so low that the spirit only needed to reach up just a little and pull you down with it. I told you not to talk to it. I told you it wasn't your friend. But you didn't listen, Holly. You didn't *listen*."

"I'm sorry," Evie said, and added, quite truthfully, "I didn't know what else to do."

"Those spirits, they aren't ghosts, you see—not like you'd think. They didn't die. Not in any natural way. They let the darkness take them and became part of it. They exist somewhere between life and death, between day and night." She blinked thoughtfully and stared back out the window. "Like a shadow," she added.

Yes, Evie thought, exhilarated. *That's it. That's exactly it.* "But why does it want to take me? What is it about Hobbie House?"

Mama Bird looked back at Evie, as if she had just remembered something. "Oh, yes! Do you want to know the secret?"

Evie swallowed. "Yes, I do," she said.

Mama Bird leaned in close, gripping Evie's arm with a strong, leathery hand. "There's a hole in your house, Holly," she whispered. "And it goes all the way down."

"A hole?" Evie said shakily. "What do you—?"

"All done," Birdie broke in, walking over to them with Mama Bird's soft blue coat and walking stick. "Time to go home."

"But—" Evie said, but the moment had passed. The clouds had gathered once again in Mama Bird's eyes, and she allowed herself to be helped to her feet and into the coat.

"Time to go home," she echoed her daughter, and shuffled with Birdie toward the door.

Evie rose and followed them, feeling numb. Was it possible that just that morning, she'd been at school finishing her homecoming dress? Before the parade and the police department and everything else? She wanted to think about everything that had happened, wanted to weave all the things she'd learned together in some kind of order, have them make some kind of sense. But she was exhausted. She knew she wouldn't be able to do anything at all until she got some sleep.

They piled into Birdie's old maroon Hyundai and made the short trip up the narrow lane to Hobbie House. The house was dark aside from a single kitchen light—Stan and Mom must not be home yet. Evie thanked Birdie for the ride and pushed through the kitchen door, walking straight up to her room. She hadn't eaten anything since that sweet she'd had at the parade, but somehow she wasn't hungry. She groped in the darkness of her bedroom until she found the lamp on her dresser and clicked it on. Schrödinger had been asleep at the foot of her bed, and squinted at her when light flooded the room. He yawned hugely, a gesture she felt deep in her soul.

"Hello there," she said, and set her bag down on the floor before slipping out of her coat and shoes.

After changing into her nightgown, she unzipped her bag and pulled out the finished dress. She found a hanger and hooked the dress onto the edge of the closet door, smoothing out the wrinkles. It was, by far, the most complex piece she'd ever made. The lines were even, the different fabric patterns meshing beautifully. She'd sewn three layers of tulle underneath the skirt to give it weight and shape, so that despite its folksy heart, the dress had the soul of a ball gown. She admired the wide, romantic neckline, the ruffles, the billowy sleeves made from the blousy, cornflower-blue fabric that was as delicate as silk. A thick sash belt in the same fabric was sewn around the waist, long enough to tie a bow around the back. The design was half bygone era and half contemporary, a fusion of old and new that was startling and beautiful.

She turned off the lamp and got into bed. In the moonlight, the dress was drained of its color, and she suddenly realized it reminded her a little of the one the specter wore. *All I need now is the bonnet*, she thought grimly, envisioning it lying in Holly's trunk above her head in the attic.

Her pride over the dress suddenly curdled like milk.

Evie felt as if she were riding her bike down an unfamiliar wooded trail, her wheels rolling in Holly's tracks. She could not stop or veer away now; she was plunging down this path too fast. She had to see what was at the end of it. She had to see it through.

19

It was Saturday.

Homecoming.

Evie woke from an oddly dreamless sleep with a sense of anticipation—though whether it was apprehension or excitement, she could not tell. Friday's second summer had given way to frost that crisped the grass outside her window and crept through the house's cracks in cold little drifts.

She picked up her phone and saw a text from Desmond waiting for her.

> Roses are red, violets are blue, we beat the devils,
> and i want to dance with you.

She replied with a laughing emoji, and then:

> Congratulations. On the game, not the poem.
> You're about as good with poetry as you are
> with a sewing machine. 🫠

> I have my strengths and you have yours. looking forward to tonight?

> > Very much. You?

> Even more.

> >

> I made a reservation at all that glitters for 6:00. pick you up at 5:45?

> > Perfect.

Evie set the phone down and sighed with pleasure. There, in the bright light of morning, the awful terror of the previous day and all that had come before it could almost be forgotten. Or at least, ignored for a little while. She was starving for good feelings and a sense of normalcy, and being with Desmond offered both.

I don't know about tomorrow, but tonight will be unforgettable. She wasn't sure of much at that moment, but she was sure of that.

Suddenly she realized she wasn't just starving for emotional well-being, she was regular old starving, too. She padded downstairs and found Mom at the kitchen table, reading the news with her coffee and a half-eaten bagel. "Morning, stranger," her mother said, her eyes bleary. "I feel like I haven't seen you in ages."

"That's because you haven't," Evie said, pulling down a plate from the shelf.

"I know. I'm sorry, honey, but Fiona needs me at the inn.

We're still at the tail end of the busy season. But now that the fall color is done, I'm sure we'll slow down again until Christmas . . ."

Her mother prattled on about work, and Evie stuck a bagel in the toaster, thinking, *Don't you think we need you here?* but choosing not to say it. It was nothing new. During the divorce, Evie couldn't count the late nights Mom put in at the hotel, just so she wouldn't have to face the wreckage at home.

"I hear you found a date for the dance tonight," Mom said coyly.

Evie stopped, a container of cream cheese in her hand. "Hear from who?" she asked.

Mom shrugged. "Oh, word gets around. People talk. Especially when it comes to members of the King family." She looked at Evie meaningfully. "Well done, honey."

Evie tossed the cream cheese onto the counter and grabbed a butter knife, clattering the silverware in the drawer. "It's not like that," she muttered. "I don't like him because he's popular or rich, I just . . . like him."

"Either way," Mom said, taking a sip of her coffee. "I'm sure you'll enjoy being treated to dinner at All That Glitters tonight. It got a Michelin star a few years ago, you know."

Her mother's intimate knowledge of their plans infuriated her. Mom somehow managed to be both absent and meddling at the same time. Evie spread cheese on her bagel with violence.

"And I'm sure he'll be a good influence on you," Mom said lightly.

"A good influence?" Evie retorted. *Like I'm some kind of wayward child that needs watching?*

"Yes," Mom said. "You need someone stable like that around—he'll keep your mind in the right place."

Evie took a big bite of bagel to keep herself from talking back. *Ignore her and think about tonight,* she told herself. *Ignore, ignore, ignore.*

Just then, there was a knock at the kitchen door.

"Who could that be?" Mom asked.

Evie set down her plate and walked to the door. But when she opened it, there was no one there. She scanned the frosted yard, the long driveway, the misty woods. Everything was still. She thought she heard some rustling sounds coming from the side of the house, so she stepped out onto the porch to look. As she did, her foot collided with something, a bundle tied with white string. She looked down. Someone had left a bouquet of fresh cut flowers on the doorstep. There were bright yellow chrysanthemums, orange lilies, and tiny five-petaled white flowers she couldn't identify. They looked almost wild, like something gathered from a field, still kissed with dew. She relaxed, her unease fading. With one more glance around, she picked up the bouquet and stepped back inside the house.

"Who was it?" Mom asked, looking up from her newspaper.

"I'm not sure," she said evasively. A little note tied to the bouquet with string read TO E, THE PRETTIEST FLOWER IN RAVENGLASS.

Evie smiled. It had to be Desmond. She pressed her face into the velvet-soft flowers and breathed them in. They smelled sweet and earthy, almost intoxicating. She sighed and imagined pinning some of the flowers to Desmond's lapel, touching his chest and looking up at him in the fading light of day. She imagined him wearing a light-colored suit and a thin silk tie, and shining like he was polished. She imagined how he would move like water on the dance floor, and she would flow along with him to the music, and—

Evie's face began to sting.

Just a mild prickling at first, but then the pain spread—hot and sharp—across her cheek, her nose, her eyes. Within ten seconds, it was excruciating, burning like one side of her face was aflame.

She gasped, and dropped the flowers to the floor.

Her right hand was burning, too. She looked at it and saw dozens of what looked like short, fine hairs sticking out of her palm and fingers. She stumbled back against the kitchen counter as a wave of dizziness crashed over her.

Alerted by the noise, Mom set down her coffee and turned around in her chair. "Evie, what is— Evie!" Her eyes widened as she saw her daughter's face. She shot to her feet, toppling the chair behind her. "What happened?"

"I—I don't know," Evie stammered, her voice tight with pain. "I just picked up the flowers and—"

Mom looked down at the scattered flowers and squinted at the tiny white blooms. "What are *those*?" she said. She kneeled and picked up one of the stems with a kitchen towel, examining it more closely. After a moment, she stood, grabbed her purse, and said, "Come on. We need to get you to the doctor."

"What?" Evie said. "Why? What is it?"

"Something that shouldn't be in a bouquet," Mom said cryptically. "Get in the car."

Twenty minutes later, Evie sat in the waiting room of the doctor's office on Main Street, trying without success to remain calm. The pain had not subsided in the least—if anything it had increased.

Her mother was stabbing impatiently at an office electronic tablet, completing paperwork. When she got to a certain screen, she placed it on Evie's lap. "You have to fill out this part—can you manage with your left hand?"

Evie nodded and looked down at it.

PATIENT HEALTH QUESTIONNAIRE—9

HOW OFTEN HAVE YOU BEEN BOTHERED BY THE FOLLOWING OVER THE PAST TWO WEEKS?

FEELING DOWN, DEPRESSED, OR HOPELESS?

TROUBLE FALLING OR STAYING ASLEEP, OR SLEEPING TOO MUCH?

FEELING BAD ABOUT YOURSELF—OR THAT YOU ARE A FAILURE OR HAVE LET YOURSELF OR YOUR FAMILY DOWN?

Two weeks? She'd moved to Ravenglass roughly a month ago, give or take. How many times had she felt hopeless, not knowing how to stop the horror from following her everywhere she went? *Nearly every day.* How many nights had she lain awake in bed, afraid to fall asleep because of what might find her in her dreams? *Nearly every night.* And how many times had she felt that somehow, like everything else, everything was her fault? *Nearly every day.*

But this questionnaire wasn't asking about shadows and nightmare creatures. It was asking about things that were happening only in the patient's mind. And Holly wasn't just in her mind.

Was she?

With a trembling finger, Evie went down the line of questions and tapped NOT AT ALL for each one, before giving the tablet back to her mother. Mom hurried to the receptionist's window and handed it back. "Will it be much longer?" she asked. "I would have taken her to the ER, but it's fifteen miles out of town and—"

"The doctor is still in with a patient, ma'am," the bespectacled receptionist said, not lifting her eyes from the computer screen in front of her. "If you'll just take a seat, we'll be with you as soon as we can." With no other avenue to vent her frustrations, Mom settled for sitting stiffly in one of the black plastic chairs and tapping her foot on the linoleum.

Her mother's behavior was doing nothing to lessen Evie's pain. Mom had refused to say anything more about what she knew about the flowers before she had confirmation from the doctor. "Dr. Rockwell will know what to do," she'd said in the car. "He's come to the inn for Sunday brunch several times—he's a very nice man."

Sitting there, waiting to be called, Evie wasn't comforted by her mother's words. Every doctor she'd ever seen back home had been a "very nice man," too, and yet none of them had done anything other than make her feel misunderstood and alone. Mom was too dazzled by their expensive wristwatches and degrees on the wall to see that they hadn't helped her. She'd hated doctors ever since, and done everything she could to avoid visiting them.

But now she didn't have a choice. The pain was too much.

She shifted in the hard plastic chair and cradled her injured hand in the palm of the other, trying not to let it touch anything. Brushing up against the stinging hairs stuck into her skin caused the pain to flare horribly, so she kept it very still. She gazed around the waiting room. Oddly, it looked more like an art gallery than a doctor's office—stark white walls, a low, modern black shelf with magazines and medical pamphlets, and a tall ficus tree in the corner by the window, potted in a simple black planter. The walls had over a dozen square watercolor paintings in black frames, hung at artful intervals around the room. At first, Evie thought the paintings were just abstracts, strange profusions of color and shape filling up the center of the canvas. But when she looked closer, she realized that they looked like those inkblot tests she'd seen in TV shows and movies. The ones that psychiatrists used to use to get a glimpse inside a patient's mind—Rorschach tests.

Upon realizing this, Evie's body became even more tense. *I thought this guy was just a regular family doctor. Why does he have these paintings on his wall?*

She had a desperate desire to get up and run. But before the idea could take hold, a nurse opened the interior door and said, "Dr. Rockwell will see you now, Miss Archer."

Evie and her mom followed the nurse down the short hallway to an exam room. Several more Rorschach paintings hung there next to a desk, examining table, and two hard plastic chairs. Dr. Rockwell knocked on the door only a moment after Evie had settled herself on the crackling paper that covered the examination table.

He rolled in on a stool with a laptop in one hand, which he was studying intently. "Miss Archer," he mused. "Age sixteen, possible severe contact dermatitis . . ." He looked up at her and winced. Evie did not think this was a good sign. "Well," he said, putting the laptop down on the desk. "I think we can safely change 'possible' to 'probable' right off the bat . . ." His voice had an odd quality, almost like an English accent that had faded into the background. He turned to wash his hands in the sink.

Dr. Rockwell was middle-aged, with pale skin, heavy-lidded blue eyes, and a mop of messy hair that was more silver that brown. A salt-and-pepper five o'clock shadow covered his face, which looked as if it had been carved with a dull chisel. If not for the white coat and stethoscope, Evie might have mistaken him for an old-timey prospector. He looked as if he were unfamiliar with the sun.

His brusque manner took both Mom and Evie by surprise, and for a moment, they said nothing. Then, Mom cleared her throat and said, "Um, hello, Dr. Rockwell. I'm Evie's mother. Thank you for seeing us on such short notice. I believe that Evie's reaction might have been to this—" She pulled the plastic bag out of her purse that contained the white flowers and handed it to him.

Dr. Rockwell pulled on a pair of latex gloves and opened the bag, quickly examining the contents. "Ah, yes. *Cnidoscolus stimulosus*, otherwise known as finger rot, bull nettle, or, my personal favorite: *tread softly*. Such a pretty little thing. But it can pack quite a punch." He came up to Evie and gently palpated her right cheek before gingerly examining her hand. "Grabbed it and took a sniff, did you? Looks like most of the stingers stuck into your hand, but there are a few in the face area as well. I'll need to remove them. The pain will subside within the hour, but the rash could last a week—and there might be blistering as well. I'll prescribe a steroid to deal with the inflammation, and you should pick up a tube of hydrocortisone, too."

Mom nodded and sighed. "Yes, that's what I thought."

Dr. Rockwell went back to his laptop and typed in some things. "I'm curious on how in the world did you come across *Cnidoscolus stimulosus*, anyway? They aren't native to this area."

"The inn imports flower seedlings from the south for our greenhouse," Mom muttered. "And sometimes they arrive with stowaways—weeds and things. I'm pretty sure I saw some mixed in with last week's shipment. The manager told me to make sure to warn the student volunteers not to put them in any of the rooms . . ."

The inn? Evie thought, confused. *But Desmond doesn't volunteer at the inn . . .*

Dr. Rockwell glanced over at Evie and tsked. "Didn't listen to your ma, did you, young lady?"

Evie shook her head. "No . . . someone put them in a bouquet and left it on my doorstep."

Dr. Rockwell blew out his cheeks. "Well," he said. "Either that person is not a botanist, or they are exacting some cruel revenge upon you."

"Doctor—!" Mom exclaimed, scandalized. "I'm sure whoever sent the bouquet didn't include those flowers on purpose. It had to have been an accident . . ."

Dr. Rockwell shrugged. "Perhaps," he said. And before Mom could say anything else, he said, "You may go back to the waiting room now, Ms. Archer. The nurse will prepare the prescription for you and handle payment. I'll take care of your daughter from here."

"Oh, but I usually—" Mom protested.

"It's okay, Mom," Evie said. She felt strangely comfortable with this shabby, rude doctor. "You can go. I'll be fine."

The nurse returned to escort Mom back to the waiting room, and after a moment's hesitation she followed, closing the door behind her.

"Now, I'm going to ask you to lie back a little, Miss Archer. Me and my tweezers will take a bit, so you just relax and be still." He pulled a bright light down from the ceiling and moved in close. Slowly, he began pulling the stingers out of her face, one by one. She gasped after the first one, but then realized that it wasn't so bad. Getting them out was a relief. "So, do you have any idea who left you this poisoned chalice?" he muttered as he worked.

"Yes," Evie said, trying not to move.

"A jealous ex-boyfriend, perhaps? Or a rival?"

Evie thought about seeing Kimber Sullivan working in the greenhouse, how she told Evie she was "dead" after the incident in the diner. "You could say that," she said.

Dr. Rockwell nodded. "A tale as old as time," he said. "Finished. Now your hand."

As he began plucking the stingers out of her palm, Evie said, "You're not . . . like other doctors I've met."

"I'll take that as a compliment," he replied.

"You're not from around here, are you?"

"Not originally, no. My son and I used to live in Oxford, England, while I practiced psychiatry."

"Your son?"

Dr. Rockwell nodded. "Yes. Nagasai. He's a senior at RHS."

"I haven't met him," Evie admitted.

"I'm not surprised," he said, but didn't elaborate further.

Evie remembered what he said earlier. "Is that why you have those paintings?" she asked, nodding at the yellow-and-black inkblot in front of her.

"Yes, it is," he said, plucking out a particularly stubborn stinger. "I painted them myself. Long time ago, when I was still 'tell-me-about-your-mother'-ing. Gave it all up for this bit. Liked the scribbles too much to get rid of them, though, so I hung them up. Old habits, I suppose."

"Why'd you give it up and move here?" Evie asked.

Dr. Rockwell glanced up at her with his limpid blue eyes. "Let's just say it was a controlled burn."

"Meaning what?"

"Meaning sometimes it's better to burn it all down and start over. Sometimes we need to go where our memories cannot follow. Although they do, anyway, don't they?" He turned to the painting she was looking at. "What do you see?" he asked.

The pain had begun to subside, and the doctor's open manner had put Evie at ease. She studied the painting for a moment, with its wide, arching angles in golden yellow above a flat black circle. "I see a bird," she said, "Flying out of a deep well." She looked back at Dr. Rockwell, expectant.

"What? Deep psychological analysis costs extra," he said with a wink.

"So that was just for you, I guess?" Evie retorted.

"Right into the lockbox," he said, tapping his temple. "Saved for later use. More helpful than that questionnaire you lied on, that's for certain."

Evie froze. "I didn't lie."

He gave her a sidelong glance. "Even the blissfully serene tend to have moments of fatigue and sadness 'several days' over the course of two weeks. A bad day at work, a fight with a loved one . . . they add up. Answering 'not at all' to every question breeds the suspicion that the patient doth protest too much." He paused. "I also have the benefit of your historical records at my fingertips, which I reviewed before entering this room."

Evie looked away. Dr. Rockwell's casual manner had left her open, vulnerable. She felt as if she'd been caught in a trap.

"No fear," the doctor said, plucking out another sting. "Your secret is safe with me. A little thing called the HIPAA."

"It's not a secret," she retorted.

"Isn't it?" he replied.

She licked her lips. "No. I just . . . I just want people to judge me based on what I am now, not what I was in the past."

"And what were you, then? Away with the fairies? A bad seed?" he suggested mildly.

She opened her mouth, but nothing came out.

"I don't think you were. Frankly, I think your Dr. Mears's certification isn't worth the paper it was printed on, and that's just after a cursory glance at his notes. But what's important is that *you think you were*. And that's all that really matters—what *you* think is real. So, let me guess, you took that girl, that bad seed, and you buried her deep, and tried to forget. Am I right?"

He seemed to take Evie's silence as affirmation.

"But you know what happens when you leave a seed too long in the dark, don't you?"

She looked up at him and swallowed. "It grows."

He nodded.

After a moment, he examined her hand, back to front, and said, "I pronounce you free of stinging hairs, young lady. You're under strict orders to go home and get some rest."

"Thank you," Evie said, relieved. It had become difficult to breathe in that room. She got up off the table and went to the door.

"Miss Archer," Dr. Rockwell said before she left.

"Yes?"

"I'm glad you came to see me today. Though I'm sorry about the flowers. If you ever need to talk—"

"Thanks," Evie said. She wasn't sure, but she thought she meant it.

"Oh, and the name of that flower," he said. "It's not just a name, is it? It's a warning. *Tread softly.*" He glanced at the paintings, saying, "When it wants to tell us something, the universe always finds a way."

Back home a little while later, Evie slowly climbed the stairs up to her bedroom. It wasn't even lunchtime yet, but she felt empty—sucked dry by the morning's events. She walked past the mirror over her dresser and stopped dead. One glance at her reflection in it and she nearly collapsed.

"Oh . . . ," she moaned, leaning close to the mirror. She touched the angry mottled rash that now covered the right half of her face, and winced. Her hand looked the same—red, raw—and in the places where the stingers had been, covered in pus-filled bubbles. The pain had dwindled to a constant low throb, but even brushing up against the rash caused it to flare once more with an agony that was nearly blinding.

The clock on her nightstand read 11:30 a.m. Homecoming would start in less than eight hours.

Evie placed her palms on the dresser and hung her head, stifling a sob. Kimber had done what she'd intended. Evie couldn't go to the dance like this. The night was ruined.

Grief came at her fast then, as painful and shocking as a knife in the back. She ground her fists into the hardwood dresser and sobbed. The tears burned her cheek and her hand throbbed, but she didn't stop. Now that the emotion had been let loose, it could not be put back in again.

Sadness and anger battled within her, until anger won and all she wanted to do was tear everything apart. In her anguish she went to the first thing she laid her eyes on: the dress.

It hung on a hanger from the closet door, clean and pressed and lovely. And suddenly she hated that dress. That dress was a dream that would never come true. A symbol of everything that she wanted but couldn't have. Its perfection taunted her. There was not a single thing wrong with that dress, but there were so many things wrong with her. It was cruel that she could make something so beautiful, when her life was so full of monsters.

She couldn't stand looking at it anymore.

Grabbing a pair of scissors, sobbing, shaking, she took the dress into her hands and ripped it apart.

20

A cold front was moving in.

As afternoon winds pummeled Hobbie House, and fast-moving clouds cast shadows across the walls, Evie lay in bed, staring at the dress. It was in a heap on the floor, curled up like some sorry creature, dead on the side of the road.

She held her phone limply in one hand before finally getting up the will to text Desmond.

> I'm sorry, but i can't come tonight.

He replied immediately.

> What?! Why?

> I'm not feeling well.

You're sick? but you didn't say anything about that this morning. What happened?

Evie considered telling him the truth—telling him that she believed Kimber had left the toxic flowers on her doorstep. But she had no proof, only guesswork. And if Desmond found out, he'd be angry. He might call Kimber and lash out, and knowing Kimber, that could only make things worse for Evie and her family. The mayor might get involved. Mr. and Mrs. King might get involved. And what would her mother say if Evie got her in trouble with the two most powerful families in town?

Evie had been foolish to think she could get away with it. With attacking Kimber in the diner, for defying her and pursuing Desmond. For trying to be happy.

Stupid, so stupid . . .

No, she couldn't tell him the truth. She'd already done enough damage.

I'm sorry. I just can't go.

Can't, or won't?

She could almost hear the hurt in his words.

She paused, unsure of what to say.

What aren't you telling me?

When she still didn't reply, he wrote again.

229

You think i can't tell that you're hiding something? you know so much about me, but i know hardly anything about you. every time i ask, you change the subject. i'm not stupid, evie. i thought i'd let you tell me in your own time, but i can't be with someone who won't be honest with me.

But all she wrote back was:

I'm sorry.

The three little dots had flashed on her screen for a full minute. Finally, he sent one final message.

I'm sorry too.

After that, she threw the phone on the bed and lay back on the pillows. She'd started feeling a little strange about an hour after taking the steroid pill her mother had picked up from the pharmacy. Her head felt fuzzy, like it was filled with cotton, and her thoughts drifted blindly through it as if she were walking through a cloud.

I've lost him, she thought dully. *Stan hates me, Tina thinks I'm crazy, I'm a disappointment to Mom, and Dad . . .*

With the anger and sadness gone, the only thing left in her was despair.

At some point after that she closed her eyes and fell asleep.

By the time she woke, the sun was low in the sky. The room was filled with a purple, crepuscular light—the color of a bruise.

Nothing looked right. The walls were crooked, none of the corners meeting at right angles. Evie felt even stranger than before, as if she were outside herself, looking in. She sat up slowly. The air felt as thick as water.

Schrödinger sat at the foot of the bed, watching her with golden eyes. So strong was the sense of unreality that Evie half expected him to disappear before her eyes, starting with the tip of his tail, until there was nothing left but a smile. Instead, he got up, stretched to what seemed like an impossible length, and hopped off the bed toward the closet where she'd first found him the day they moved in. The dress was no longer in a heap on the floor but back on its hanger in the closet, ragged and torn. How it had gotten there, Evie didn't know. The cat brushed his body against it, imbuing it with his scent.

The dress was captivating in the eerie light, and despite the windows being shut tight it seemed to move in the wind, the skirt fluttering sinuously, beckoning her. As she watched, intoxicated, a soft voice spoke to her in her mind.

"*Evie,*" it said. "*You're going to be late.*"

"Late for what?" Evie whispered dreamily.

"*The dance, of course. And look what you've done to your pretty dress! You'd better hurry and fix it now, before you run out of time.*" The voice seemed to be carried on the fragrant wind. It played at her shoulder and the ruined side of her face, cool and comforting, like a confidant whispering in her ear. It was Holly's voice. It always had been. Why had it taken her so long to accept that?

"But I can't," Evie said. "It's ruined."

"No, not ruined. All it needs is a little patching up. Go ahead. I know you can do it . . ."

Slowly, Evie rose from her bed and lifted the dress from its hanger. She took it over to her sewing table and laid the dress across it. Some of the bolts of fabric from the attic leaned against the wall nearby, and she thought dimly that she could use them to patch the tears and sew up the jagged lines she had made when she cut the dress apart. Yes, it could be done, of course it could.

She sat in front of her machine, with her fabric shears in hand, and got to work.

It was after 7:00 p.m. by the time she was finished. The dress lay before her, transformed. Where before it had been pure and perfect, now it was a wild thing—its skirt shot through with lines like scars and jagged shapes of alternating patterns of fabric. One sleeve was different from the other, and the bodice was a patchwork of uneven squares pieced together with black thread. It was not the dress it had been, but somehow, it felt more a part of her than before.

Stepping out of her clothes, Evie slipped the dress over her shoulders and let it settle against her skin. She tied the sash in a bow at her back and ran her fingers down the soft, scarred fabric.

It fit perfectly.

"Don't you want to see how it looks?" the voice asked.

She did want to see. There was a mirror in the bathroom, but it was small and too high. She wouldn't be able to get the full effect.

"There's one in the attic. Remember?"

Yes, Evie did remember. A full-length mirror, white like her bedroom furniture. Perhaps it had been Holly's mirror once.

Evie pulled down the attic ladder and climbed up into the gloom. Even with the single bulb lit, the attic was darker than the times that she'd been there during the day. Moving a few dusty boxes aside, she stood before the mirror and stared at her reflection.

She was luminous.

Now that she was wearing the dress, she could feel a wind blowing, furling and unfurling the skirt around her ankles and playing with strands of her auburn hair. It smelled sweet and intoxicating, like flowers in full bloom.

"Do you see now?" the voice said. *"Do you see how beautiful you are? I've only been trying to show you. But you didn't want to look. You were too afraid."*

"I'm not afraid anymore," Evie said.

"You understand now, don't you? I had to take everything away from you for you to see that I'm your friend. The only friend you'll ever need. The only one who understands you.

"You don't need to tell me your secrets because I already know them. They're my secrets, too. Because you're just like me."

"Yes," Evie said. "I'm just like you." Relief washed over her. She didn't have to fight it anymore. Confession lifted the burden from her shoulders.

"You have to go now, Evie. You're already late for the dance. He's waiting for you."

A pang of anxiety broke through the calm. "But my face," Evie protested, lifting a hand to her cheek.

Strange laughter, like the chiming of bells, echoed around her. *"You know what to do about that."*

Evie nodded. Yes, she did know. She kneeled on the floor of the dark attic and opened the trunk. The blue bonnet lay on top of the pile of Holly's forgotten relics, just where she'd left it. Pulling it over her hair, she fitted it on and regarded herself in the mirror. If she turned just right, it hid the horrible, angry rash completely.

"Now you're ready. Time to go. And when it's all over, we can finally be together."

Evie went downstairs, lifting her skirt so she wouldn't trip over the hem as she descended, feeling light and dreamy, like Cinderella going to the ball.

Her mother was in the kitchen, pacing. Her phone was at her ear, and after a moment she cursed and stabbed at the screen before putting it to her ear again. "I can't believe this," she was muttering. "Of all the days to—" She turned to see Evie standing in the doorway. "Evie, you're up." She lowered the phone from her ear, a wary expression spreading across her face. "What . . . what are you wearing?"

Evie cocked her head. "My homecoming dress, of course. I made it myself. Isn't it beautiful?" She made a slow turn.

Mom didn't react at first. Evie could see the gears turning in her mother's head, the mental calculations of how to *handle this situation*. Her face was a study in controlled emotion, carefully expressing nothing at all.

"You don't like it, do you?" Evie said, anger simmering just below the surface of her voice.

"It's not that," Mom said evenly. "I just . . . You're not actually thinking of going to the dance, are you? You're not well. You should go back to bed, and I'll—"

"I am going," Evie retorted. "It's a special night. You said so yourself."

"I did, but . . ." Mom sighed, rubbing her brow with her fingers. "Evie, I'm sorry, I can't do this right now. I can't seem to get ahold of your brother. He said he was going out with his friends, but that was hours ago and he's not answering his phone—"

"Can't do *what*?" Evie broke in. "I'm not asking you to do anything. I'm leaving."

"In that getup?" Mom said impatiently. "With your face looking like that? No, you're not. Can't you see I'm trying to help you? Or are you intent on embarrassing yourself?"

Evie inhaled sharply.

"She just wants to control you." The voice was in her ear again, whispering with honeysuckle-scented lips. *"She's unhappy and she wants you to be unhappy, too. You have to break free of her. Break free before it's too late . . ."*

"Embarrassing myself—or embarrassing you?" Evie said.

This took Mom by surprise. "What are you talking about?"

"You don't care about what happens to me," Evie went on. "You only care how this affects *you* and your precious *reputation*."

"Evie, stop it," Mom said. "You're not yourself. Just go up-stairs, and—"

"Oh, I am very much myself," Evie went on. "More than I've been in a long time. All the things I've wanted to say but was too much of a coward, you're going to listen."

Mom took a step back from her. Evie was amazed to see that she actually looked *afraid*.

"Tell her," the voice urged. *"Tell her how you feel so she can feel it, too."*

Evie looked at the shining kitchen—already transformed from the dusty, forgotten place it had been when they'd arrived about a month before. "I wondered why you wanted to come here, at first. You told us it was the only choice, the only place we could afford to live, but that wasn't true. You still had your job at the Hyatt. We could have downsized to a smaller place and stayed in the city. It would have been difficult, but we could have done it. But you didn't want that. Doing something like that might have been good for Stan and me, but to you, it would have *looked like failure*, wouldn't it? No, you needed a project. You needed something to fix. Because you couldn't fix your family."

Mom flinched, stung. "Evie—"

"But you could fix this house, couldn't you? And Hobbie House needed a *lot* of fixing. And whenever you weren't doing that, you could be out at the inn, fixing that, too. Making every-thing better. Right? Spending every bit of your time and energy working and mending this house, so you wouldn't have to spend any of it looking at the mess living inside it." Evie swallowed, her heart racing. "And when you couldn't help but notice something was wrong with me, you tried to shift that responsibility to Dr. Mears, or to Aunt Martha. Tried to get anyone to talk to me, fix me. Anyone but you."

Mom's upper lip was trembling. "That's not true!" she retorted. "I have tried so hard to help you! But you wouldn't *listen*!"

Evie laughed without humor. "You want to talk to me about listening? Two years ago, when it all started, I tried to tell you something was wrong. I tried to tell you what was happening to me, but instead of listening, you told me I was being childish. You said, 'Oh, Evie, stop trying to act out to get attention,' or that it was 'just a dream.' Do you remember that?"

"You were just a kid," Mom argued. "A kid with a wild imagination. You and your stories. . . . How was I supposed to know?"

"You were supposed to believe me!" Evie shouted.

"We called Dr. Mears," Mom said helplessly.

"Dr. Mears," Evie spat. "Useless, arrogant, stupid . . . You didn't believe me, and neither did he. You just wanted him to make it go away."

"Of course we wanted it to go away, Evie!" Mom shouted. "For God's sake, you were *seeing things! Things that weren't real!*"

"*Yes, they were!*" Evie shouted back, slamming her fist down on the table. At that moment the room shifted, as if it were a ship at sea. Evie swooned.

"Evie," Mom said, reaching out to her. "What's wrong?"

Steadying herself, Evie shook her head. "Nothing."

"You're lying."

"I've learned from the best."

Mom face turned stony. "That's enough. You're going to go upstairs, take off that costume, and get into bed. We can talk about this again when you've calmed down—"

"I'm going to the dance," Evie said with finality. "And if you cared about me at all, you wouldn't try to stop me." With that, she turned and threw open the kitchen door, and walked out into the night. Her mother called her name, once. But when Evie didn't stop, didn't turn, she didn't call out again.

A frigid wind blew through the dark trees, but Evie didn't feel it. All she could sense was the sweet-smelling breath in her ear, praising her and whispering:

"Time to dance."

21

Evie was still blocks away from Ravenglass High when the beat of the music reached her. It pulsed steadily, like the telltale heart of the town, drawing her in.

She produced a wrinkled ticket for the parent volunteer who sat outside the gymnasium, ignoring the woman's wide-eyed stare as she passed through the double doors and the hot-pink and electric-blue balloon arch.

Inside, the gymnasium had been transformed into a disorienting wonderland of color and light. The walls were lined in shiny pink, blue, and silver wallpaper, making the entire space feel like it was inside a mirror, reflecting the crowd of dancers in its surface. Above, a disco ball slowly turned, casting strange prismatic light down onto the people below. On the stage, a DJ riled up the crowd as he mixed Duran Duran and the Cure under a banner that read BLAST FROM THE PAST.

It was hot and loud and close, and Evie felt the room tilt under her feet as a powerful sense of familiarity washed over her, the sense that she had been there before.

Or maybe it's that I was always meant to come here, she wondered distantly.

Maybe both.

She walked slowly into the crowd, and it parted before her as if in a dream. She felt many eyes on her, like pinpricks, but she kept moving, searching for Desmond. The brim of the bonnet blocked almost everything from sight except what was directly in front of her. In the dimness of the gymnasium, her face lay in shadow. She looked for him. But the faces in the crowd blurred together, shifting and unfocused, blocks of moving color and not much more. She felt as if she were walking through water, the music becoming dissonant in her ears. Evie thought she caught sight of Tina and Kitty standing together nearby, Tina in a black polyester jumpsuit, her green hair dyed white at the tips like a cresting wave, and Kitty in a vintage forest-green A-line dress.

"He's right there, Evie," Holly whispered. *"You see? He's waiting for you."*

Evie's eyes fluttered and she looked up ahead. Sure enough, dancing in a pool of refracted light across the room, she saw Desmond.

He wore a champagne-colored three-piece suit, a single white lily pinned to his lapel. Evie felt a pang of guilt as she imagined Mrs. King affixing the flower to his jacket that evening, consoling him, whispering that it was *better this way.*

She started making her way quickly toward him, feeling suddenly that she'd already wasted too much time, and that perhaps at the stroke of midnight her gown would turn to rags and it would all be too late.

Suddenly, a girl in a white jewel-encrusted ball gown that looked like Cinderella's blocked her path. Her cheeks were pink with rage.

"What are you doing here?" Kimber sneered.

The sound of her voice cut through the blare of the music, and several dancers in the crowd turned around to look.

"Same as you," Evie answered. "I'm here to dance."

Kimber laughed. "You really can't take a hint, can you?" she said. She squinted at Evie's face beneath the bonnet and grimaced. "You really thought it would be a good idea to come to homecoming looking like that? You should really get that looked at." Behind her, her friends tittered. Kimber bent closer. "Hasn't anyone ever told you not to stick your face where it doesn't belong?"

"Oh, but I've been looking forward to this dance for a very long time." Evie said the words, but it was as if they were coming through her, not from her.

"Sure you have," Kimber said, shaking her head. "Where'd you get that dress from, anyway? Frankenstein's monster?" Another burst of giggles from the other girls. "Who do you think you are?"

Evie was feeling stranger and stranger, like she was a set of clothes being worn by someone else. "I hardly know," she said, thinking of Alice. "I know who I was when I got up this morning, but I think I must have changed several times since then."

Kimber snorted. "I knew you were crazy, Archer, but I never thought you were *this* crazy. Go home. Unless you want me to give you something more permanent than a rash." She started to turn away.

"I'm not going anywhere," Evie said.

Kimber stopped and then swooped in close to Evie. "Oh, really?" she growled. "Then why don't you take that stupid bonnet off and show everyone just how *pretty* you are?" With that, she grabbed the brim of the bonnet in her fist and ripped it away.

Evie pushed at her attacker, the hundred tiny crystals in Kimber's dress stabbing into her palms. But the bonnet was already in the girl's hand, and Evie felt the light shining on her swollen, reddened face. She raised a trembling hand to her cheek, waiting for Kimber to jeer and point, to make a mockery of her pain. But strangely, instead of a smile, Kimber's face wore a mask of horror.

Her pink, glossy lips parted. Her eyes, shadowed in blue, were wide with fear, staring at Evie's face. She took a halting step back, almost tripped, and dropped the crumpled bonnet to the floor.

"Kimber?" one of her friends said, confused. "What's wrong?"

Kimber said nothing. She could only stare, transfixed, at something it seemed like only she could see.

A ripple of confusion flowed through Evie, too. Surely her face was not so frightening to behold . . . But something brushed that thought away and replaced it with a feeling of deep satisfaction. *"Get out of my way."* The voice was hers, but not hers. She felt its words on her tongue, but the taste was unfamiliar. The words were cold. The words were dust.

A strangled sound escaped from Kimber's throat—something between a sob and a scream—and she pushed through the crowd and away, her friends following in her footsteps like abandoned puppies.

Her path clear, Evie picked the bonnet up from the floor and made her way toward Desmond, who still danced under the pool of light. The last song melted into a new one—a slow song. The chatter around her faded as couples began to sway. She wove through them, a patchwork anomaly in a tapestry of suit jackets, satin, and chiffon.

He had his back to her. She touched him on the shoulder and he turned, smiling broadly. But when he saw that it was her, the smile fell away. "Evie . . . ," he said. "I thought you weren't coming." He frowned and raised a hand to her face, but didn't touch it. "Your face . . . Is this what you meant when you said you were sick? God, what happened? And your dress . . ."

"It doesn't matter now," she said. "What matters is that I'm here."

"I-I'm glad that you're here," Desmond stammered. "But you have to tell me what's going on. I meant what I said—I don't like being left in the dark."

"I know," Evie said, a note of desperation in her voice. "But I've already wasted so much time, and we might never have this moment again. So will you just . . . dance with me?"

Desmond sighed, and he looked around the room as if searching for answers. Finally he looked at her again and said, "I want to, Evie. But you just don't seem like yourself right now."

Evie balled her fists in frustration. *He knows you're here, Holly*, she thought. *You have to go away. If you don't, you'll ruin everything!*

"No," Evie heard the voice reply. "*No, no, no! This is my moment, too. You can't take this from me. I won't miss this again!*"

This isn't about you, this is about me! Evie shot back. *This is my life!*

"Evie?" Desmond said, watching her face. "Talk to me, please."

"I won't go!" Holly's voice was distorted now and full of rage. *"I'm your friend, don't you remember? You would never have gotten here without me! You never would have stood up to that horrible girl! Without me, you're weak, useless—"*

Evie closed her eyes. *GET OUT!*

She waited. One moment. Two.

The voice did not speak again. All around her, the room seemed to settle again, like a carnival ride slowing to a stop. Sounds seemed sharper, colors clearer, as if she'd just broken the surface after being underwater. She looked at Desmond, who was watching her, wary. "I'm so sorry," she said. "I should have told you the truth from the start. I just . . . I didn't want to lose you."

Desmond shook his head. "Don't you remember what I said in class? Honesty, for both of us."

"It's not that easy," Evie said. "I was afraid that even if I'd been honest, you'd think I was making it up."

The last song came to an end, and a new song, something by Harry Styles, came on. Desmond gently took her injured hand in one of his and raised it high. He laid the other hand on her waist and pulled her close as they started to dance. "Let me be the judge of that," he said. "With the music playing, no one else will hear you but me."

Evie bit her lip. "Are you sure you want to know?"

"Very sure," Desmond replied. "Tell me everything."

She did.

She told him about the house. About Holly. About Kimber and the poison flowers. The shadows. The dreams. She told him about Dr. Mears and all that had come before.

It took four slow songs to do it, but she told him everything. Once she started, it was impossible to stop.

He only asked a few questions. Mostly he listened.

When she was done, she felt exhausted. But she also felt lighter. She watched his face, terrified of what she'd find there.

Desmond blew his cheeks out. "Wow," he said, clearing his throat. "I guess I don't blame you for keeping all this to yourself for so long."

"You don't believe me," she muttered, not meeting his eyes.

"No," he said, his face creased with concern. "The problem is that I *do* believe you."

Evie was astounded. "You do?"

"Don't get me wrong. If I hadn't spent my entire life in this town, I'd probably think you were crazy. But growing up here . . ." He licked his lips. "I always knew the Patchwork Girl was more than just a legend. More than just a story to scare little kids. I think everyone who's grown up here has seen her at least once. It's why you don't see a lot of folks walking around after dark. It's why the shops always close early in the winter when the days are short. It's why people steer clear of the Horror House. People were scared of it long before the Hobbies ever lived there. When Holly disappeared, it only deepened that fear. Made it more real."

"But why didn't anyone say that?" Evie asked. "Why didn't anyone tell us?"

Desmond shrugged. "Because if they told you, they'd have to admit it to themselves. It's easier to pretend it isn't there. Easier to just put it out of their minds, change it into a good story." He looked at his feet. "I know because I did the same thing. Until now." He paused. "I should have known something was going on just from the way you've been acting. But I told myself it was just a coincidence. If you had told me earlier about what was really going on, I would have—"

"I know," Evie said. "I'm sorry. I just didn't know who I could trust."

"No, I get it. But now that you've told me, what are you going to do?"

"I don't know," Evie said miserably. "Mom would never believe me, so it's not like we can move out of the house. If I told her what I just told you, she'd, she'd . . ."

Desmond nodded. "Well, you don't have to deal with this alone anymore. Okay? We'll figure it out. You and me."

"Okay," Evie said. She felt faint with relief. She had no idea what Desmond could do about any of it, but just knowing that someone in the world believed her was enough to give her hope. She reached out and touched his face wonderingly.

He turned his brown eyes to her and smiled, self-conscious. "What?" he asked.

"Nothing," she said, tamping down the swell of emotion rising within her. "You're just—I just—"

"Last dance of the night, RHS!" the DJ announced. The crowd whooped and cheered. "Better make it a good one!"

"I'm just what?" Desmond asked.

"You're just wonderful," she finished.

Desmond chuckled and looked at the floor. "You're just wonderful, too, E," he said.

As the music swelled and the lights dimmed, Evie laid her head on Desmond's shoulder and closed her eyes, wishing she could hold on to that moment forever.

And then, under her feet, the world moved off-balance.

She could feel the change, a sudden tingling at the back of her neck, like the inexplicable sensation of being watched.

No.

She knew it with a terrible certainty, knew that the immaculate moment was over.

Please no.

She didn't want to open her eyes. But eventually, she did.

The gymnasium was still in focus, but seemed soft at the edges. The faces of the other couples were lost in shadow as their heads bent together, swaying to the music. As they turned, Evie glanced at the mirrorlike, colorful walls. She saw her own and Desmond's reflection there, but no one else's.

She blinked and looked again.

It was the same. Despite there being dozens of couples pressing in around them, the walls reflected only one couple, dancing alone.

Evie heart began to race. Terror crept over her skin like spider's legs.

She looked closer at her own face in the reflection, and saw that it was not her face at all. Not the frightened, reddened face of Evie Archer. But instead, the half-rotted, grinning skull of the shadow.

Her breath caught in her throat, and she felt her blood turn to ice. *Is that what Kimber saw when she looked at me? Is that what I've become?*

In the reflection, her twisted mouth began to form words.

She and I and Evie make three.

Desmond noticed her distress and stopped dancing. "Evie," he said—his voice sounded like he was underwater—"what's wrong?"

She tore her eyes away from the monstrous vision of her own face and looked at him. His rich brown skin had turned to gray, and his eyes were milky white. Across his throat was a savage wound, encrusted with blood and roughly sewn up with black thread. He gazed at her curiously with dead eyes, cocking his head in grotesque confusion. *"Didn't she warn you this would happen?"* he said. It was his voice, but it was also hers. *"You shouldn't have pushed her away, Evie. That wasn't very nice. You don't want to hurt me, do you?"*

"Please," Evie begged, tears running down her face. "Go away . . . leave him alone."

"I told you to be quiet, but you had to tell him, didn't you?" Desmond's voice had gone now. It was only Holly's, honey-sweet and dripping with malice. *"Tsk, tsk, tsk. What an awful mess you've made. You don't want to make it worse, do you?"*

The room tilted sickeningly. The music blared. The press of bodies around Evie was suffocating.

Desmond's hand reached out to touch her face and she recoiled. The fingers were as cold as death. *"Better hurry now,"* Holly's voice said through his purpling lips. *"You'll be sorry if you don't. It's time to come and play."*

22

It was foolish to run. Where was there to go when the the rot was hidden deep inside? Like a worm in an apple, eating away at everything within?

But Evie had no choice. Fear overwhelmed her like a tidal wave, drowning her in breathless panic. Backing away from Desmond, she pushed through the crowd until she was free of it, and ran. She dimly heard someone calling her name. It sounded like Desmond, like the real Desmond, but she didn't stop. She burst through the double doors into the fluorescent light of a hallway. After the dimness of the gymnasium, the light was blinding. Stumbling forward, blinking, she nearly tripped over a trash can left outside a classroom for the janitor to empty.

It wasn't until she made it down two more hallways, until the sound of the dance had faded to a distant murmur of sound, that she stopped to catch her breath. She leaned against a bank of lockers, gripping the bonnet in her hands, with no idea of what to do next.

I'll run away, Evie thought. *She can't follow me out of Raven-glass. And if I'm not here, she won't hurt anyone . . .*

Somewhere nearby, a door slammed. Then, voices.

"Officer, we have a situation at the old mines. I'm going to need you to come with me."

"Chief? What's going on? I thought I was supposed to be on door duty here all night."

Curious, Evie crept down the hallway toward the sound of the two men. She peeked around the corner, which opened into the front entrance of the school. A young police officer and Chief of Police Sànchez stood near the door, both in uniform.

"It's a kid. Went into the mines a couple of hours ago—some kind of dare with his friends, apparently. Supposed to come back with a souvenir, but after an hour he was a no-show. The other boys were either too smart or too scared to go in after him, but they called down to him and didn't hear back. Took another hour for one of them to get up the guts to call for help."

"Who'd they call? Us?"

Sànchez cleared his throat. "Called the mayor, actually. Then the mayor called me."

The officer scoffed. "His boy again, huh?"

Dylan Sullivan. Evie remembered the smart-mouthed punk who'd stood in her kitchen, holding a stolen traffic sign. She wasn't surprised that he'd called his daddy to come help when one of his stupid pranks went horribly wrong.

"I'd appreciate you keeping that to yourself, officer. We don't need more trouble than we've already got. We need every officer right now. Our best map doesn't even cover half of the tunnels down there. I've got the fire department and the paramedics on their way to the site, and the guys back at the department are gathering all the equipment we've got. Depending on what happens down there, we might need to get County involved."

"Let's hope not," the officer said.

"C'mon, we've got to hurry. You can ride with me. I've already got Hassan in the car."

"All right, I just have to let the administrators know that I'm leaving," the officer said.

"Fine, but don't offer any details right now. I don't want a panic."

"Okay. Who's the boy that went missing, anyway?"

"New in town," the chief said. "About ten years old. Poor kid. As if living in the Horror House wasn't bad enough."

Evie froze. *No. No . . .*

"Stan, I think his name was. Stan Archer."

She put a hand over her mouth so that she wouldn't make a sound. Moments later, the two men had gone. Evie slid into a sitting position and put her face in her hands.

This is all my fault.

She'd known that Stan had fallen in with a bad crowd. She'd known about the fire, the traffic signs—the trail of destruction that he was leaving behind him, hoping someone would notice. Hoping someone would care enough to stop him.

It should have been me, Evie thought. *But I was too busy with my own problems to do anything. Sure, I could blame Mom for never being around, but she didn't know what was going on. I did. I knew, and I did nothing.*

Remorse cut through her, so sharp she gasped with the pain of it. What if they never found him? What if Stan vanished into the darkness, leaving them without even a body to bury? It almost reminded her of—

A tingling sensation climbed up her spine.

It almost reminded her of Holly.

But Stan going down into the mines . . . That had nothing to do with Holly. Nothing to do with everything that's been happening to me. Right?

Through the window above the banks of lockers, Evie could see the moon hanging low over the trees. The Moon . . . Wasn't that one of the cards in her tarot reading? *"It's a card of illusion,"* Aunt Martha had said. *"It warns us that things are not always what they seem. If we dig deeper, sometimes we discover that beneath the surface, everything is connected."*

At that moment, Holly's final words to her took on a different meaning.

"Better hurry now. You'll be sorry if you don't."

At first, she thought Holly was threatening more assaults on Evie's mind, more hauntings—but now Evie wasn't so sure. Maybe it wasn't just a coincidence that Stan had disappeared on homecoming night, right as Evie was meant to join Holly in the shadows. Maybe it wasn't a coincidence at all. Maybe she'd taken Stan just in case Evie tried to get away—which she almost had.

Evie stood up, suddenly resolute. If that was the case, Evie was the only one who could find Stan down in the mines, who could save him. If it meant she sacrificed herself for his safety, so be it. It was the least she could do, after everything that had happened. After she had failed him so completely.

Evie stepped outside into the dark, cold night, making her way beyond the reach of the school's streetlamps. But once she turned onto the road leading up the mountain to the mines, she faltered.

What am I thinking? The mine entrance is swarmed with police and fire trucks right now. They're not going to let me anywhere near it!

She balled her fists, feeling like she wanted to scream. How was she supposed to do what Holly wanted, when she couldn't possibly follow Stan down to the tunnels?

Stop. Breathe. She was never going to figure this out if she didn't calm down. Maybe Aunt Martha was right, maybe if she just dug a little deeper, she'd see that she already knew everything she needed to. She closed her eyes, relaxed her body, and tried to remember.

She breathed.

"*When they reached the bedroom, Holly was not there, nor was she anywhere in the house. Despite claims from Mr. and Mrs. Hobbie that Holly could not have left the house without their knowledge . . .*"

In.

"*But a lot of the first floor and the root cellar is still the original. Built about a hundred and seventy years ago—around the time all that mining started up.*"

And out.

"*Our best map doesn't even cover half of the tunnels down there.*"

In.

"*There's a hole in your house, Holly, and it goes all the way down.*"

And out.

"*Slide down my cellar door, and we'll be jolly friends forevermore.*"

She gasped and opened her eyes. Was that the answer all along? There was one more thing she needed to see. Pulling her phone from the dress pocket, she went into her photo stream and found the picture of the kitchen from Holly's case file. She zoomed in on the corner of the image, where you could just see the door to the cellar. It was closed, just as she remembered. But on the floor, she could see the old draft blocker with the multicolored cats. Instead of being pressed up against the door as it usually was, it was at an angle, as if someone had opened the door and pushed it aside.

As if they had closed the door behind them, but never came back up.

"Holly never left the house," Evie whispered to herself. "She went under it."

Evie turned around and started running in the opposite direction. As she passed the high school, she saw Tina standing outside the gymnasium with a couple of friends. "Hey!" Tina shouted when she saw Evie pass by. "Wait a minute!"

But Evie didn't slow. She kept running, stopping only when she'd reached the bottom of the narrow lane and her lungs felt like they were going to burst. Her phone was buzzing like crazy in her pocket.

There were texts from her mother.

Come home now.

The police called and stan is missing.
I'm going over there now.

Answer me! This is no time to play around!

There were about eight missed calls, too.

There were also messages from Desmond. Reading those nearly broke her heart.

She replied to her mother and to Desmond.

I'm sorry.

There were only two texts from Tina.

My dad told me about Stan. They're going to find him, Evie. I promise.

Where are you going?

To Tina, she answered with one word.

Home.

The woods around Hobbie House were eerily quiet. The crickets and owls had gone silent—even the whip-poor-wills had ceased their wailing call. The only sounds Evie heard as she walked up the narrow lane were her own footfalls and the susurrus of the wind blowing through the trees. The world was a held breath. It was waiting, she knew, for her arrival.

The pale moonlight shone down on the house, illuminating its western face and shrouding its northern face in shadow. As she walked toward it, fear thrumming in her heart, Evie wondered what might have happened if they'd chosen the other door when they'd first arrived here. *If we'd gone in through the light, would anything have been different?*

No, Evie decided after a moment. None of it had been her choice. Not the house, not the divorce, not the voices in her mind. She was hardly more than a figurehead on a ship at sea, choosing neither where to go nor the direction to get there, but prisoner to the crashing waves and storms along the way. No, she was always meant to be there, in that moment.

The porch steps sighed as Evie climbed them, her hand on the vine-covered railing. Her mother had cut back the vines with pruning shears when they'd first arrived, but already new ones were growing, not only around the railing, but along the pitted floorboards of the porch and up the burgundy siding. It seemed as if any attempts to free the house from its bonds were only temporary. Perhaps like her, the house was also a prisoner of its fate. *Mom couldn't fix this place any more than she could fix me.*

The kitchen door opened at her touch, as if it hadn't been closed all the way. The kitchen light was on, and it looked like someone had left in a hurry—there was a half-eaten bagel on the table, milk left out, and a mug on the floor, its handle broken off, lying in a pool of cold coffee. Some unopened mail lay scattered nearby, probably knocked off the counter when Mom grabbed her purse in a rush to get out the door.

Evie closed the door softly behind her. As soon as it clicked shut, the atmosphere in the house seemed to change, taking on that now-familiar sideways quality, like a ship in turbulent waters. She stumbled, catching herself on one of the high-back chairs. The blue-shaded light over the kitchen table flickered briefly, buzzing like an angry wasp, before going out.

Thrown into darkness, with only the thinnest rays of moonlight filtering in from the hallway, Evie struggled to breathe through the rising panic. She tried to use her phone, but the screen stayed stubbornly black, even though she knew she still had power left. She abandoned it on the counter—it couldn't help her now. Blinking quickly, she tried to get her eyes to adjust to the murk. She stood stock-still, listening, watching for any movement. A soft sound, barely noticeable, wound through the silence like smoke. A whispering. But where was it coming from?

She took a few tentative steps forward, feeling her way along the kitchen table. Yes, the sound was getting louder. She kept going, her own ragged breath threatening to drown out the whisper that was like eyelashes fluttering against her cheek. Leaving the table behind, she continued to lurch forward, her arms outstretched, moving more out of memory than sight. The sound grew louder as she went. It wasn't long before she realized what lay in front of her.

The cellar door.

She put her trembling hand on the doorknob. It was cold to the touch.

All she wanted to do was run away. Everything in her was screaming at her to stop, to call someone, to leave that place and never come back. But even as those thoughts were pouring through her, her hand was turning the knob, and then the door was open.

"Stan needs me," she said to no one at all.

The whispers flowed out from the dark portal, washing over her, loud and unmistakable as the voices of young girls.

"Slide down," they said. *"Slide down slide down slide down . . ."*

In a trance, Evie reached out to click on the light in the stairwell. The bare bulbs were as weak and flickering as candles, but it was enough. Evie had become accustomed to the darkness now, and she descended smoothly, her long skirt trailing behind her.

The cellar was just as she'd left it the day she and Tina had come down—the wooden shelves, the murky jars, the shovel, the rake. But where before she had seen nothing but junk, now all of it was infused with meaning.

She stared at the HVAC shafts rising up into the house and remembered the sounds she'd heard in her bedroom through the vents. The sound in Hobbie House, she realized, was deceptive. *Holly could have screamed down here in the cellar, and it could have sounded like she was in her bedroom, just like her parents said.* But even if she was here in the cellar before she disappeared, how did she get down into the old gold mines? There must be a secret entrance. But where?

She trailed her fingers along the stone walls, feeling for any loose stone, anything that might move, might trigger something. When she found nothing, she looked under the boxes, behind the shelf. But there was only more stone and more dirt.

Then her eye stopped on something twinkling on the ground. The pieces of gold tinsel she'd seen on her first visit. She bent to pick one up, meaning to inspect it, only to find it seemed to be stuck. She pulled harder. The tinsel stretched and snapped, leaving half of it in her hand and the other half still stuck to the floor.

Evie stared at it, her heart beginning to race.

No, not stuck *to* the floor. Stuck *in* the floor.

She knelt next to it and began brushing the dirt away around the tinsel, exposing the edge of . . . something. She followed it up and around, brushing dirt away as fast as she could, until she had exposed a square wood panel, about three feet across, flush with the cellar floor. With the dirt covering it and the dim light, it had been completely invisible.

"*Slide down,*" the whispers urged.

Evie couldn't find any kind of handle or latch on the panel, nothing that would allow her to open it. Standing, she grabbed the shovel from its resting place and wedged it under the corner of the panel. With the shovel in place, she was able to dig her fingers underneath it and get enough of a grip on it. Ignoring the pain as she scraped her swollen fingers against the wood, it squealed on unseen hinges and slammed back onto the floor, raising a cloud of dust as it did.

She fell back with the effort of it, and coughed as the dust flew into her face. Wiping her stinging eyes, she blinked and then stared at what the panel had been hiding.

Evie was reminded of when she had learned about black holes back in New York, during her first year of high school. Her physics teacher, Mr. Katz, had done an astronomy unit—it had been the only part of that class she really remembered at all. His words echoed in her mind, like a poem whose meaning she only came to understand at that moment:

A black hole happens
When a star dies.
It's a place where the gravity is so strong,
That no light can escape it.
It can be as small as an atom or as large as the sun,
And yet it is invisible.
But if you get too close to one,
It will pull you in,
And tear you apart.
Inside a black hole,

The rules of physics no longer apply.

There is only darkness,

Only mystery,

And there is no going back.

The hole in the cellar floor was the darkest thing she had ever seen. Staring into it made her head ache, and flooded her body with cold terror. She couldn't bear the thought of getting closer to it, and yet at the same time she felt it tugging at her with a kind of infernal gravity, pulling her in.

"*Slide down . . .*" The whispers were loud now, a chorus of them echoing in her ears.

"No, I can't," Evie moaned, sick with fear.

And then another voice joined in—a familiar voice, small and desperate.

"Evie!"

Stan's voice.

Evie gasped and scrambled closer to the hole, bringing her face near the edge and looking down. It was like looking into a solid mass, the darkness was so complete. "Stan!" she screamed. "I'm coming!"

"It'll be okay, it'll be okay," she chanted quietly, reaching her hand into the hole. It seemed to disappear at the wrist as it passed through the edge. She felt cool, damp air on her fingers below, and felt around—searching for a ladder, a foothold, anything that would allow her to climb safely down into the abyss.

Instead, she felt something else. Another hand, slender and smooth. Evie screamed and tried to pull her hand back, but it was too late. The hand grasped onto hers with inhuman strength and pulled.

Evie fell—down, down, down—into a darkness that was everywhere and everything and at the same time, nothing at all.

23

E vie could have been falling for a second or an hour. She could have fallen through the center of the earth and back out the other side, and it would not have surprised her. The darkness was so thick that she could not tell whether her eyes were open or closed.

When it was over, she didn't hit the ground, didn't smash her bones into a million pieces against the cold, hard earth, but simply stopped falling. Her feet felt something beneath them, and she was standing on it. The air was so odorless and still that she could barely feel it against her skin. It was a nothing-place. It was nowhere.

Just ahead she saw a door. A canary-yellow door, so bright in that nightmarish place that it seemed like a trick. Without any other choice, Evie walked up to it, her feet making no sound as she did. The door was a little crooked, a little small, a little not-quite-right, but when she turned the knob, it opened all the same.

When she stepped through the portal into darkness, the first sound that drifted out to her was the same as the last sound she'd heard before she fell down the hole. The sound of her own terrified scream.

A moment later, light blazed through the space, nearly blinding her. When the colors finally stopped dancing before her eyes, she was shocked to find herself back in her old bedroom in New York. She had apparently come through the closet door.

"Evie!" Mom cried out as she rushed into the room in her bathrobe, looking haggard and exhausted. She also looked about three years younger. "Stop screaming, honey, you'll wake the neighbors. What's wrong?" She went to the girl in the bed. It was Evie. By the state of her hair, and the purple-flowered pajamas she was wearing, she must have been thirteen.

Young Evie was sobbing. "H-he won't leave me alone," she said haltingly. "He says I'm not listening to him, but I *am*! I *am* listening! He scares me, I'm afraid he's going to hurt me . . ."

Mom, bewildered, sat on the bed and felt Young Evie's forehead, the same way she always did when things went wrong. "Who won't leave you alone?"

"The man in the red sweater," Young Evie said. "He says he's cold. Really cold. And the heat isn't working, but he can't leave the house."

Mom sighed in a way that Evie knew meant her patience was at an end. "Evie," she said in a strained voice, "we've talked about this. You're too old for these kinds of games, okay? This man, he's just a dream. No one is going to hurt you. You need to stop this and go back to sleep. You have school in the morning, and I have a twelve-hour shift at the hotel, so—"

"It's not a dream!" Evie cried. "I keep telling you, I can hear him talking to me. And not just while I'm sleeping." Evie leaned in close, and she could see the panic and desperation in her younger self's eyes. "Sometimes, I can *see him*. That's how I know he always wears a red sweater."

Mom rubbed her face with her hands. When she pulled them away again, her expression was passive, wiped clean of any emotion. She put on a small smile. "Okay, honey," she said. "Let's talk about it in the morning, all right?"

Young Evie was just sniffling now, tears drying on her cheeks. She rubbed the snot from her nose with the back of her trembling hand. "Okay," she said.

Evie stood watching this, remembering it like an old wound. She watched her mother stand up from the bed, pat Evie's feet under the quilt, and go to the door, turning out the light as she went. In the dark left behind, she heard Young Evie's ragged breaths, and knew there would be no sleep for her that night.

Outside the door, Evie heard her mother's and father's voices, quiet at first, and then rising in volume and intensity. *What are they saying?* Evie wondered, and went to the bedroom door, opened it, and stepped through.

But instead of the hallway of her old apartment, Evie found herself in another room—a plush office lined with bookcases, framed degrees on the walls, and a navy-blue armchair set next to a couch. Through a window she could see the busy streets of uptown Manhattan in winter, with passersby all bundled up in thick coats and scarves. Young Evie was sitting in the corner of the couch, looking uncomfortable. The armchair was occupied by a colorless, stoop-backed man who seemed more interested in cleaning his eyeglasses than in the girl sitting in front of him. Dr. Mears.

"Well, young lady," the doctor said, settling the glasses back onto the bridge of his nose, "you've made up quite the story for this Red Sweater Man of yours."

"I didn't make it up," Young Evie retorted. "It's what he told me."

"All right," Dr. Mears said patronizingly. "Can you tell me, then, when this man first started talking to you? Was it after something . . . strange happened, perhaps? Or something frightening?"

Young Evie answered immediately. "Yes," she said. "He started talking to me right after my friends and I went into that house, the abandoned brownstone a few blocks from school. We used the Ouija board in there and something talked back to us. I think it was him. I think he followed me home."

"Now, why would he do that?" Dr. Mears asked. "Why you? Why not one of your friends?"

"I don't know," Young Evie said miserably.

"Do you think it's because you're special? Do you think that's why he picked you?"

"No," Young Evie said, looking at the ground. "I'm not special."

"Maybe you thought that if something like this happened, your family might pay more attention to you? Are you lonely, Evie?"

"I mean, sometimes," Evie replied. "But that's not why I did this—I mean, I didn't *do this* at all. I'm not doing this. I'm not making this up, it's real."

Dr. Mears removed his glasses again, rubbing at an invisible smudge. "I know it might *feel* real, Evelyn. But people's minds, oh, they can do amazing things. If you want something strongly enough, you can make yourself believe it, make it as real as the chair I'm sitting on. But it isn't. And accepting that is the first step toward getting past this."

Young Evie's eyes became glassy. "I don't *want* this! How could I? Why would anyone want to feel this way? To be scared to go to sleep, or to be alone . . ."

"Young lady," Dr. Mears said, "I can't help you unless you want to help yourself. No one has the power to stop this but you. Your mother is very worried about you—you don't want that, do you?"

Young Evie shook her head.

"Well, then. Let's just see if we can't get rid of your imaginary friend, shall we?"

Watching this, Evie felt sick. After Dr. Mears had come into her life, everything had changed. Because she was a little old for "imaginary friends," Dr. Mears had filled her mother's mind with the potential for a series of psychological conditions down the line—*unless* she kept Evie under his expert care. Which of course, she did. Months and months of weekly appointments, persuading Evie to deny everything she saw and heard until they finally did stop speaking. But even after she stopped seeing the Red Sweater Man, Mom never treated her the same way. The way she looked at her, spoke to her, even touched her—like a bomb that could go off at any moment.

"Why are you doing this?" Evie cried out. She was dizzy, hysterical with grief and confusion. Neither Dr. Mears nor Young Evie seemed to hear her. "Why are you showing me this?" she screamed. Turning around, she pounded at the richly papered walls. But instead of being solid, they collapsed beneath her fists like tissue, and she stumbled through the rift with a terrified cry.

What was in front of her became the floor as the world turned sideways and Evie slammed into it. She gasped as the air was knocked out of her. Her cheek was pressed against something soft—a rug? She turned her face to look at it. It was soft blue, with whorls of violet running through it. She knew this rug. It was the same one that Mom had put under the coffee table in Hobbie House. They'd had it since Evie was a little girl. When she looked up, she saw that she was lying on the floor of her old apartment, right in the entranceway looking into the open living room and kitchen. Four people were sitting at their old glass-top table: Young Evie, who now looked about fourteen, Mom, Stan, and her father. No one was speaking. The only sound was the clinking of forks against plates.

Evie sat up and staggered to her feet. It was only when she saw what they were eating that the acid, horrible sensation of dread filled her. Italian takeout. Spaghetti and meatballs, garden salad, garlic bread. It wasn't just any dinner she was about to watch. It was *the* dinner. *The* night.

"Please," she said. "Please stop this."

But the scene went on.

"Gonna have go back to the studio tomorrow," her father said, his voice a deep baritone. Evie stared at him. She hadn't seen him in over a month, since they left New York and he flew off to Paris for work. She'd left half a dozen texts from him unopened, the missed calls unreturned. Hadn't even acknowledged to herself that they were there.

But there he was, in front of her, eating spaghetti with a fork and spoon. His hair, dark like Stan's, was a messy, curly nest, and his eyes dark and piercing like a hawk's. He still wore his work clothes—steel-gray utility pants and a black T-shirt with the word VITRUM printed across it in white gothic lettering. Below that was a line drawing of an elegant glass vase, its rim bursting up in a wild, jagged curve, like a wave cresting. An Ocean vase. It was the vase that had put her father's glass design studio on the map almost two decades before, the vase that was mass produced and shipped to offices and hotels across the nation—including the Hyatt in Manhattan. He'd hand-delivered that one himself. And while he was there, met a young, ambitious concierge named Lynne Hobbie.

Evie watched her mother glance up from her plate at him, but only for a moment. "Again?" she asked. "You worked last weekend."

Her father shrugged and rubbed his chin, which was dark with stubble. "Alexis and I have to finish up all the pieces for the new line before the end of the month. The vases and tables are done, but there was an electrical issue with the lamps, so we had to start over with—"

"Oh, Alexis . . . ," Mom murmured into her spaghetti.

"What about her?" her father said. There was an edge to his voice now. Evie watched her younger self stiffen at the sound of it.

"Nothing," Mom said.

Her father waited a beat before pressing her. "Spit it out, Lynne."

Her mother put her fork down and placed both palms flat against the glass table. It was one of her father's pieces, of course, from his original Ocean line. The base was a massive piece of driftwood, polished and positioned to perfectly hold the tabletop, which was made of a single piece of turquoise glass. She remembered being a little girl and staring down into that blue glass at the bubbles captured inside it and feeling like she was staring down into a frozen sea. "Kids, take your plates into your rooms, okay? Your dad and I need to talk."

Stan picked up his plate and glass of milk and scurried into the bedroom without a word. But Young Evie didn't move. "Go on, Evie," her mother urged.

But Young Evie sat back in her chair and crossed her arms. "Why should I?" she said. "We live *in an apartment.* You don't think we hear you guys fighting when we're ten feet away with the door closed? I'm still eating."

"Fine," Mom said through clenched teeth. She picked up her fork and poked at her food for a few seconds before setting it down again. "It just seems like you'd rather be at work than at home, Robby. That's all I'm saying."

A tight, ugly smirk stretched across her father's face. "Oh, really. Is that *all* you're saying?"

"Yes."

"You sure you're not saying something else? Because you better be real sure of what you're accusing me of before you—"

"Before I what? Ask you to be present in our lives? You *know* how hard these past few years have been, and I have been dealing with it all by myself, while you—"

"While I what? Support this family? You think we could afford all the extra expenses we've had on your salary?"

"Are you really trying to tell me you don't spend god knows how many extra hours in that studio every week?"

"I'm an artist, Lynne," Dad said harshly. "I'm committed to my work."

"Last time I checked, you're my husband, too!" Mom said. "How about being committed to me? To your kids?"

Her father's cheeks colored. "I have done *everything* for this family!" he shouted.

"Keep your voice down," Mom muttered angrily.

"Oh, are you worried about what the neighbors might think?" Dad said, even louder than before. "You accuse me of not being committed to this family, and all you care about is what the other ladies at the club say about you behind their cloth napkins—"

As the fight raged on, Evie's eyes were riveted on her younger self. Despite how hard she had tried to forget this night, every detail, every word her parents said, was seared into her brain. She remembered sitting there listening to them, and thinking

This is all your fault.

The past few years have been hard for Mom because of you.

All the extra expenses are because of you.

Dad doesn't want to come home because of you.

As Evie watched, she could see the cracks forming in Young Evie's control. Evie felt tears forming in her eyes. "Why are you making me watch this?" she asked softly.

No one answered.

"At least I actually care about someone other than myself!" Mom shouted.

"You think *I'm* selfish?" Dad yelled. "You're the most—"

"Stop it," Young Evie whispered.

But no one heard her. No one except Evie. The fighting continued.

"If you really feel that way, maybe you should go!"

"Maybe I should!"

Evie remembered the rising panic, her shaking hands, the sensation of the room spinning. She remembered the one thought that had drowned out every other in her mind.

Make it stop

Make it stop

Make it stop

Time seemed to slow as Young Evie stood up, her face a mask of anguish. She raised a clenched fist, and in a voice that cut through the noise like a knife, she screamed,

"Stop it!"

Her fist came slamming down on the glass table.

There was a moment of complete and total silence as her parents stared at Young Evie in shock, their mouths agape. And then, time resumed its normal pace, and the silence was broken by a deafening, thunderous crash as the kitchen table shattered into a thousand pieces.

Evie watched it happen with horror. The huge pane of glass was there one second, whole and blue, and the next second it had been transformed into crystal rain, a stilled wave finally crashing on the rocks below. The plates of food, the cups, the cutlery—everything on it came tumbling down, too, splattering all over the hardwood floor below in an unimaginable mess.

For a moment, the three of them just stood there, frozen in place. Stan's head came popping out of his bedroom door. He opened his mouth to speak but froze, too, when he saw the scene laid out before him. Mom was the first to speak.

"Oh god," she moaned, pushing her chair away from the mess. "Oh my god . . ."

Something like a strangled sob escaped Young Evie's throat, but she didn't move.

Her father's face had gone a terrible shade of gray as he stared at the wreckage of his beautiful handmade table. And then a spot of color appeared in both cheeks, and he stood, his chest heaving. He turned his eyes to Young Evie, and they were full of anger and confusion. When he spoke, the sound that came out was like nothing Young Evie had heard before, and the words cut her so deeply that they haunted her dreams.

"What is wrong with you?"

Young Evie shook her head. "I don't know, I don't know, I don't know," she babbled, tears streaming down her face. "I didn't mean to— I just couldn't— I'm sorry— I can fix it—"

"No," her father said, throwing his napkin on the floor with the broken glass and ruined food. He looked at Young Evie and her mother both. "You can't."

"I've seen enough," Evie said to the room, backing away. Her voice was shaking.

"Have you?" a familiar voice said in her mind.

"Evie, you're bleeding!" Mom rushed over to her daughter as tiny spots of blood appeared all over her hand and forearm. "Some of the shards must have cut you . . ." She began dabbing at the wounds with a clean napkin.

Evie looked down at her own hands and saw that they were bleeding, too. Tiny droplets of blood from a dozen invisible cuts, just enough to sting. *"Some wounds never heal, do they?"* the voice said.

"Enough!" Evie shouted.

The world shattered.

With the sound of a thunderclap, the apartment split apart in shards—the walls, the floor, the whole scene around her that had been so real a moment ago, fractured like a reflection in a broken mirror and collapsed. Evie screamed, fell to her knees, and covered her face—expecting the razor-sharp edges of the world to cut her to pieces as it fell upon her.

She waited, gasping, but the pain never came. When reverberation of the explosive sound finally faded, there was silence. And then, there was birdsong.

"Whip-poor-will?"

After a moment, Evie raised her head from her hands and looked around.

She was kneeling on the grass in front of Hobbie House. But something wasn't right. The world was stained the color of old things, and shadows gathered everywhere—in the woods, which looked different and strange; in the house, which seemed to be watching her from both its faces; and under the apple tree, which was smaller, as it was in her dreams. And there in the yard stood a figure she'd come to know very well. She wore a dress made of shadows, and under her dark bonnet, the face of a nightmare gazed out upon her.

"Whip-poor-will?" the bird cried.

"*Hello, Evie,*" Holly said. "*Welcome home.*"

24

Evie shivered, though there was no wind. The air was unnaturally still. When she was sure that the ground wasn't going to simply fall out from beneath her, she slowly rose to her feet.

Holly stood still as stone, watching her from the shadow of her bonnet. Evie could just make out the piercing green eye on one side and the black hole of bone on the other. *"Come along now,"* Holly said, and turned around to walk toward the apple tree, humming as she went.

Evie thought about running, about picking up a rock and hitting Holly with it, about screaming at the top of her lungs—but she knew none of that would matter. She was in Holly's world now, and she came willingly. She came for Stan.

Keeping a safe distance between her and the specter, Evie followed, looking around as she went. The wood was not as thick here, and so she had a decent view of Ravenglass—or what should have been Ravenglass—beyond a wooden fence that marked the border of their land. Instead of the patchwork of buildings and spiderweb of roads she was used to, below she saw only one road, and only a couple dozen cabins, barns, and other archaic buildings. There were fenced fields for horses, but no animals in them. In fact, there wasn't a single sign of life anywhere.

Evie got up the courage to speak. "What is this place?" she murmured.

"*A memory,*" Holly replied. "*Or a shadow of one. It was just like this when I arrived, and it hasn't changed at all. You're going to love it here . . .*"

"Where's Stan?" Evie demanded.

"*Frightened but safe,*" Holly said, picking up a daisy from the grass. She began plucking the petals from it and letting them drift to the ground. "*Wandering in the dark, like all children do.*"

"You said if I came to you, you'd let him go," Evie said. "Here I am, so—"

"*Oh, but I need to make sure you won't try to run away from me again,*" Holly said. "*Naughty Playmate. Spoiling all my games.*"

They were under the shadow of the apple tree now. A dark purple blanket was spread out on the lawn, and on it were set eight gold cups, each one small enough for a child. They were arranged in an odd configuration—with five on the bottom and three on top, with a space between the top cups as if one was missing. Evie stared at them. Why did they look so familiar? "What are those for?" Evie asked.

Holly turned her head to look at them and cocked it to the side, like a bird. "*They were not there before. Perhaps Sarah set* them out for a tea party. We'll have lots of time for games, now that you're here."

Evie shook her head. "Why?" she asked. "Why did you do all of this? What did I do to deserve—?"

At that, Holly spun to face her and closed the distance between them impossibly fast. Evie screamed and reared back from Holly's ruined face, now so close to her own, she could smell the flowery rot of her breath. "*I didn't do anything to you, Evie. You did that to yourself. If you had only welcomed me, understood what I was trying to offer you—*"

"Offer me?" Evie said, incredulous.

"Yes. A gift," Holly murmured. "*A great gift. The same gift Sarah offered me. Freedom from pain. From disappointment. From heartbreak. Once you're here with us, you'll forget all about those terrible memories you saw. You'll spend an eternity with friends who'll never betray you, never let you down, and never expect you to change.*" She searched Evie's face, and laid a cold, pale hand along her cheek.

Evie recoiled from her touch but stayed rooted to the spot.

"*You're thinking about those memories I showed you,*" Holly went on, caressing her hair now. "*I found them deep inside. Sarah and I played hide-and-seek and we found them where you thought no one would look. Aren't we clever? They hurt, didn't they? They cut you, right down to the bone, didn't they?*"

Evie's breath was coming in short, ragged gasps.

"*I know you didn't like to see them, but you needed to, so that you could remember the pain. So you could truly understand what we're offering you. We can take it all away, forever. You'll* never have to think about them again. Doesn't that sound wonderful?"

Behind her, a long green snake slipped through the grass and wound its body around the apple tree, climbing the gnarled trunk. Evie watched it go until it vanished into a hollow.

Holly didn't seem to take any notice of it. *"We'll have so much fun, we three,"* she was saying. *"And maybe one day, you can find us a new friend and bring her here, just like I did. But only special friends."*

"Special?" Evie asked, her curiosity overcoming her fear.

"Oh yes," she said. *"Only some girls will listen. I listened, that's why Sarah picked me. I tried to get Martha to listen, but she ran away and never came back."* Holly paused, her ruined face creasing in sorrow. For a moment, Evie could almost see Holly the way she used to look—vivid and beautiful—but after an instant, it was gone. *"But when you came, I knew you were special. My kitty told me. He said you would listen. And then you did. You saw me in the mirror, and I knew you were meant to be my new secret friend."*

"No!" Evie cried out. "I'm not like you . . ."

"But you are," Holly cooed. *"Your father was cold and heartless, just like mine. Your mother never let you do what you wanted, just like mine. You loved how I loved. You suffered how I suffered. Don't you see? You're my second chance, and I am yours. And now we can finally be together."*

Evie shook her head, tears in her eyes, and looked away. She could feel her strength failing; she could feel herself giving in.

She was just so, so tired.

In the distance, the wooden fenceposts looked like swords with their blades buried in the earth. She blinked at them—why did they seem so familiar?

Then the kitchen door opened, and a young girl in a patchwork dress and bonnet not unlike her own stepped out of the house. Her hair was dark brown, and hung in long plaits on each side of her head. When she turned to look at them, Evie saw with horror that unlike Holly, who still had half of her face, the little girl had nothing but a grinning skull. She looked at them for a moment, and then skipped toward the apple tree to kneel on the purple blanket. Out of her dress pocket she pulled a small brown satchel, which she opened and spilled out onto the ground.

Tiny white bones. Just like the ones from her dream.

"Sarah wants to play Knucklebones," Holly said. *"She loves games. Don't you?"*

The little girl began throwing the bones up into the air and trying to catch them again as they fell.

Evie stared at one of the pieces and bent to pick it up. Unlike all the other bones, this one seemed to be carved from a larger bone. It was shaped like a little white horse.

"Evie . . ."

The voice was distant, and so soft that she could easily have imagined it. But it, too, was familiar.

Holly took Evie by the shoulders and pushed her down onto the blanket next to the little girl with no face. The smell of rot was overpowering now, floral and so sweet that it made Evie want to gag. *"If you're going to stay,"* Holly said, *"you have to eat this. Then you'll be one of us."* She lifted a hand to one of the lower boughs of the tree and pulled a round, golden apple from it. She handed the fruit to Evie. It was cold and heavy.

"Eat," Holly said. "Eat and I'll let your brother go. I don't like him, anyway. He's too loud."

The little girl giggled and hummed as she played with her bones.

Evie held the apple in one hand and the little white horse in the other.

"Evie . . . ," the familiar voice called again.

It was too far away. No one could help her now. No one can fix this but me, she thought.

She raised the apple to her mouth and took a bite.

25

Juice flowed from the golden apple, filling Evie's mouth with sweetness. Holly and Sarah watched her in silence, their heads tilted like two carrion birds waiting for their prey to die. After a moment, the sweetness became cloying, and changed to the taste of rot. Evie gagged, but kept the fruit in her mouth.

Stan, she thought, *I won't let you down again.*

And then the rot turned bitter, the flavor of deep earth and things that grow in the dark. The taste of poison.

"Don't be afraid," Holly said. *"It will only hurt a little. And then you'll be free to play."*

A wave of dizziness sent Evie stumbling, falling to her knees on the purple blanket, nearly upsetting the neat arrangement of tiny golden cups. Staring at them, she suddenly remembered why they looked so familiar. They were just like the cups on one of Aunt Martha's tarot cards.

The Eight of Cups.

You must face the pain you've been avoiding or remain incomplete forever.

As the world lurched sickeningly around her, Evie put her hand on the trunk of the apple tree. The green snake emerged from the hollow and slid down toward her. It stopped at her hand, its forked tongue licking at her skin, before sliding over her arm on its way back down to the grass, its scales cool and smooth on her skin. Like the cups, this too reminded her of one of the cards, but which one?

A snake in the apple tree . . .

Of course—Adam and Eve, the Lovers.

Remember that you are not alone. Choose the best version of yourself to face others and the world.

Pain buried itself in her stomach like a knife, and Evie struggled to stay upright, leaning her body against the tree.

"*Stop fighting it!*" Holly scolded. "*You'll only make it worse for yourself.*"

But Evie knew now that this world was trying to tell her something, and she had to listen. She gazed up through watery eyes toward the distant fence at the tree line. It hadn't been a trick of the light; the fenceposts still looked like swords. Eight of them.

The Eight of Swords.

You're in a prison of your own making. Your heart can see what your eyes cannot.

It was getting hard to breathe. She could feel her throat closing, could feel the edges of her vision begin to cloud and darken. She didn't have much time.

With effort, Evie unclenched her fist and looked at the object nestled inside. The hooves and muzzle of the little white horse had left deep indentations in her skin, but it remained unbroken. The carving was quite miraculous, especially for being so small. It looked almost as if it would come alive at any moment and gallop away.

A white horse and rider. A black flag and a sun setting on the horizon.

Death.

Evie's eyes fluttered.

Let go of the past. The past is gone. Find a way forward.

Face the pain.

The voice calling her name was closer now. It sounded like her mother. Or was it Aunt Martha? They always did sound alike. She collapsed, her cheek against the soft purple fabric.

You are not alone.

She could have sworn it was Tina calling to her now. No, it wasn't her at all . . .

In a prison of your own making.

Out of the corner of her eye, Evie could see Holly standing over her, her half lips curled into a smile. The voice calling her name had changed again; it was clearer now. She knew who it was; of course she knew.

It was Desmond. He was calling to her.

Let go and find a way.

This was Holly's world, and Sarah's. A shadow land. So how was it that these pieces of Evie's own memories were seeping in? She felt the coolness of the locket against her chest. It had been Sarah's, then Holly's, and now hers. She gazed at the patchwork dress spread out around her like a faded blossom. She thought of all the things that had happened before, and were happening again.

"Just like me . . ." Her voice was featherlight now, her heart beating weakly. She could feel the flesh on her face beginning to shrivel and die, to pull away and reveal the curves of bone beneath. *Maybe Holly was right all along. Maybe the three of us are alike, just not in the way she thought.*

The idea gave her strength.

Just as the darkness was closing in, Evie raised herself onto her elbows and spit out the apple.

"*What are you doing?*" Holly screamed. A rush of cold air burst out from her, and her one good eye flashed with rage.

On the ground in front of her, Evie saw that the piece of apple that had been fresh and sweet was black and shiny with rot. The pain in her stomach ebbed but didn't stop—she was still dying. Holly and Sarah were descending upon her now, their white fingers tearing at her dress, pulling her toward them while they shrieked.

Evie scrabbled at the purple blanket beneath her, upsetting the little golden cups and spilling their contents on the ground. Only one remained standing, and she grabbed it before it could fall. Not caring what the cup contained, merely desperate to get rid of the taste of poison, she opened her mouth and drank.

Water. Cool and fresh and real.

She drained the cup to the bottom and then dropped it to the ground. Instantly, the pain vanished. She could breathe again. The muscles in her body, no longer rigid with panic, relaxed. With trembling fingers, she touched her cheek, afraid to feel bone instead of skin—but she was whole.

Sensing that something had changed, Holly and Sarah stopped shrieking and backed away from her, wary.

Evie slowly raised her head to look at them. For the first time, despite their grotesque faces, Evie saw them for what they really were—two lonely young girls. She struggled to her feet. "I'm tired of your games," Evie said. "So we're going to play my way instead."

The flesh side of Holly's face screwed up in confusion. *"You can't, only we can—"*

"Oh, but I thought I was just like you," Evie said. "If you can control what happens in this place, then so can I. She bent to pick up one of the fallen cups and held it out to Holly. "Now, drink."

"No. It's empty," Holly argued.

"Look again."

Holly took a few steps closer and gazed into the depths of the cup. It was filled to the brim. Her eyes flashed as she looked back at Evie with something like hatred. *"I don't like this game,"* she said. *"Maybe your little brother would be a better playmate after all. I could plant him in the ground and pluck his fingers from his hands like the petals of a daisy. 'He loves me, he loves me not, he loves me—'"*

Evie grabbed the two ribbons of Holly's bonnet and pulled her close. "You're not going to touch him," she growled. "You're going to drink." And with that, she lifted the cup to Holly's ruined mouth and poured the contents in.

Water spilled over Holly's face and when she opened her mouth to shriek, it only made it easier for Evie to force her to drink. Holly clawed at her face, tearing at her flesh, but Evie didn't stop until the cup was empty. When it was done, Evie threw the cup to the ground and stepped back, out of Holly's reach. Seeing this, Sarah turned her skull face away from them and ran, lifting her skirts as she made her way up the narrow lane and into the woods.

Holly's one eye was wild with panic. *"What have you done?"* she said, her voice strange and dissonant.

"You wanted to make me forget," Evie said. "So I'm going to make you remember."

Holly cried out, stumbled, and almost fell as suddenly the world around them changed again and again, like a television flipping rapidly between channels. Evie stood in the middle of it all with her, watching each scene switch from one to the next with dizzying speed and noise.

A young Holly making apple pie with her mother in the kitchen of Hobbie House.

Switch.

Holly stargazing with her father on the mountain.

Switch.

Camping in the front yard in a tent with her cousins Martha and Lynne during Thanksgiving break, telling scary stories with a flashlight.

Switch.

A hundred lonely nights alone in her bedroom.

Switch. Switch. Switch.

Meeting Sarah Flower after finding her locket in the attic.

Switch.

Kissing James King behind the high school after a football game.

Switch.

Holly's mother shouting at her in the same kitchen where they had made apple pies, and sending her to her room on the last night of her life.

Switch.

And then they were back in the shadow land with Hobbie House looming over them, and like before, everything was quiet and still except for the single bird hiding in the wood.

Evie's head was spinning like she had just gotten off a carnival ride. She turned to look at Holly, but she was facing away, her face shielded by the bonnet.

"I was never trying to hurt you," Holly said after a moment. *"I wanted to help you. Why would you do this to me? Why would you bring it all back? All those memories . . . the pain . . ."* Her narrow shoulders shook, and she put her face in her hands.

Evie shook her head. "I spent so much time trying to escape the pain. But . . . remembering nothing, feeling nothing . . . that's not life. That's death." She sighed. "I thought if I could make you remember, you'd see that it wasn't all bad. When you threw it all away, you threw away the good things, too."

Holly didn't reply.

"We're family, you know?" Evie went on, the words catching in her throat. "Me, Stan, my mom, Aunt Martha. She still thinks about you. She feels like she let you down. That's why she's never left Ravenglass. Because of you. You may have forgotten the pain, but you left a lot of it behind." She paused. "Don't make me do the same. Let Stan and me go."

Holly bent to pick up the golden cup from where it had fallen. She looked at it for a moment. "She made these, didn't she? Martha." Her voice was smaller, different somehow.

Evie thought about it for a moment. "I suppose she did. She's the one who put them in my head. Maybe she knew that when the time came, I'd need them."

"She always knew," Holly said, turning the cup in her hands. "Knew too much, I think."

"We're like her, in a way, you and I. Aren't we?" Evie asked.

Holly turned to look at her. Evie was shocked to see that the rotting flesh and exposed skull were gone. Her beautiful face was whole again, freckles and all. "Yes," she said, a sad smile touching her rosy lips. "We're girls who listen. Listen and get lost."

Evie felt an immense sense of relief seeing Holly brought back to herself. "What's lost can be found again," she told Holly. Then she added, "Please."

Holly looked across the yard to the old, empty version of Ravenglass below. "All right," she said, turning back to Evie. "But you have to go now, before he comes."

"Before who comes?"

"There's no time to explain. But you can find my notes, now that I remember where I left them. About Sarah. About . . . everything. Look in the mousehole in my bedroom. Maybe you can finish what I started." She reached out and grasped Evie's wrist. Evie was surprised to see fear in her eyes. "Sarah and I," Holly murmured, "we're not the only ones down here."

Suddenly the sky seemed to grow dark, as if a cloud had passed in front of the sun. The deep shadows grew deeper, and a cold wind began to blow. Evie shivered, wrapping her arms around herself as her dress billowed like a flag. Beyond the wood and the fence of swords, she could see the small silhouette of Sarah Flower cresting the hill. A moment later, another figure drew up behind her, a tall, dark shadow of a man. She could not see his face, but she knew he was looking right at her.

"Go," Holly urged. "Now. Into the house."

Evie dragged her eyes away from the shadow man. "What about you?" she asked Holly.

"It's too late for me," Holly replied. "I gave myself over to this place a long time ago."

Evie started to turn away, but before she could, Holly put a hand on her shoulder. "If you see James," Holly murmured, her eyes full of sorrow, "tell him . . . tell him I'm sorry."

Evie nodded and ran toward Hobbie House as thunder rumbled in the sky above them. She ran across the grass and up the porch steps. The kitchen door was bright and yellow. She opened it and ran through into—

Darkness.

Evie stopped short and looked behind her. The doorway she'd come through had vanished. The darkness surrounding her was complete, but it was different from the endless void she'd been in before. This darkness was close and moist, and in the distance she could hear the sound of water dripping. She reached out blindly with her hands and felt rough stone walls, and uneven ground underfoot.

I'm in the mines! she realized.

"Stan!" she shouted. "Stan, where are you? I'm here!" There was a horrible moment when she remembered that there were miles of tunnels running under Ravenglass, and the likelihood of her being able to find her brother was slim to none. But then, suddenly, a light came on ahead.

"Evie?" a small voice said.

"Stan?" Evie cried, and she ran in the direction of the sound and the light, her fingers running along the walls as she went.

As she got closer, she could see that the light was coming from Stan's cell phone. It illuminated his frightened, tearstained face, and Evie thought that he had never looked so young. "Oh my god, Stan!" she said, and fell to her knees, wrapping her arms around him.

"M-my phone is about to die," Stan mumbled into her shoulder. "And it was so dark. And I—I thought, I thought I was going to—"

"It's okay now," she said. "Everything's going to be okay."

"But how—? How did you find me?"

Evie closed her eyes and silently sent thanks to Holly Hobbie, the lost girl of Ravenglass. "I had a little help from a friend," she said.

26

Stan's cell phone battery was at 3 percent. Evie swung the thin beam of light left, then right. Both tunnels looked exactly the same.

"Listen, don't get me wrong," Stan said shakily. "I'm glad you're here, but—"

"But I don't know the way out of here any more than you do?" Evie finished.

Stan sniffed. "Yeah. I don't know which way to go. First I tried always going right, but that didn't work, and then I tripped over a rock and twisted my ankle, and it really hurts, and I can't walk, and—"

Stan's voice rose and rose until Evie interrupted him. "Shh," she said. "I know, I know. It's scary down here in the dark."

"We're going to die down here," Stan said thickly.

"No, we're not. We're going to get out."

"How?" The word came out like a sob.

Evie closed her eyes and took a deep breath, in and out. She thought of images she'd seen and conversations she'd had since she'd arrived in Ravenglass.

Dr. Rockwell's paintings.

What do you see?

I see a bird rising out of a deep well.

Birdie's toy canary.

A good guide for lost little girls.

And Holly. Her cousin Holly.

We're girls who listen. Listen and get lost.

What's lost can be found again.

Evie opened her eyes, and took Stan's hand in hers. "I'm going to listen," she said.

"Listen to what?" Stan asked.

"To whatever the world is trying to tell me." And with that, Evie did something she hadn't done since that day in the abandoned house with her friends, something that had terrified her ever since. She opened herself up to the unknown. To the strange, to the mysterious, to the impossible. She let go of her fear—and listened.

At first there was nothing but the sound of Stan's breathing next to her. But soon she became aware of the sounds of dripping water in the tunnels, and the skritch-scratchings of moles. And beyond those sounds, she could hear the rumble of cars far above her, the rush of river water, the distant passage of a train. But these general sounds weren't helpful. She needed more. She needed a beacon. Evie focused her mind on searching for something familiar, something that could lead her home.

And then, out of all the many sounds, one grew clear.

"Please," the voice said. "Please bring him home."

Evie's eyes widened. "Aunt Martha," she breathed. "I can hear her."

"What?" Stan said. "Where is she?"

"She's waiting for us, with Mom, probably. At the entrance to the mines. She's going to lead us out of here. Come on!" Evie pulled Stan with her down the left-hand tunnel, following the sound of Aunt Martha's prayer.

Evie followed her aunt's voice through the forks in the tunnels, Stan limping along behind her. She could swear that the voice was getting louder, but maybe that was just a trick of her mind. She had no idea whether she was going the right way or not.

"How much longer?" Stan asked, his voice tight with pain. "I can't . . . I can't walk much more."

"We're almost there," Evie lied. A moment later, the light from the cell phone went out and the screen went black. Evie and Stan were bathed in darkness.

Stan started to cry. Evie stuck the phone in her pocket and pulled his arm around her shoulders so she could help him walk. "We're almost there," she said again, half believing it herself.

"I'm so tired," Stan said. His voice was slurred, weak.

"I know," Evie said. "I'm tired, too." And she was. Her feet were throbbing, and her legs threatened to give out underneath her. She couldn't remember the last time she'd eaten or had any water. "But we can't stop, we have to keep going, okay?"

"Okay," Stan mumbled. He was leaning on her more and more, his body sagging against her shoulder.

The tunnel in front of them sloped down, which made Evie worry. They didn't want to go deeper down, they wanted to go up. What if she had been leading them the wrong way this whole time? The thought filled her with dread. She couldn't fail Stan now, not after everything they'd been through . . .

And then, up ahead, something flickered.

Evie squinted and blinked, uncertain if what she was seeing was real or a symptom of being in the dark too long. But then, she saw it again. A pinpoint of light, moving rhythmically in the gloom, getting closer.

"Hey!" Evie screamed, finding her voice. "Hey! We're here!"

Stan jolted to life beside her and began to shout, too. "Help! Help us!" he shouted.

The pinpoint of light stilled for a moment, and then began moving faster than before, advancing toward them at a quick pace. "Stan? Is that you?" a male voice called. Evie recognized it. "Who's with you?" A moment later, Chief of Police Sànchez's face appeared in front of them, illuminated by the electric lantern he held in one hand.

"My sister," Stan said, nearly in tears. "She found me."

Evie started to cry, too. They were saved.

"Well," Sànchez said, looking bewildered. "I don't know how you got down here, young lady, but I'm sure glad to see you both alive and well. C'mon, let's get you out of here. Your mom is worried sick." He stooped down to gather Stan into his arms and carry him. Evie followed him down the tunnel and back up again, toward voices, toward light, toward home.

As they saw the entrance to the mines appear in front of them, Stan turned back to look at her, a small smile on his face. "You were right, Evie," he said wonderingly.

Evie nodded, and walked back out into the world after them.

Evie saw her mother standing at the front of a crowd of police officers and EMTs, her head in her hands; Aunt Martha was beside her, looking like she'd aged fifty years overnight. The night was lit by flashing lights in red and blue, and the whole scene was wrapped in yellow caution tape. It was loud and chaotic, but all of that stopped dead the moment Chief Sànchez and Evie stepped out of the tunnel and into the light.

Aunt Martha stared at them, open-mouthed, before shaking Mom by the shoulders. Evie watched her mother raise her head from her hands, slowly, as if she were afraid of what she might see. Her face was pale, haunted, her eyes red-rimmed and smudged with black mascara. She looked at the chief in disbelief. "Is that my baby?" she stammered.

"Mom!" Stan shouted.

Hearing his voice broke her stillness. Mom ran over to Stan and threw her arms around him as he lay in Sànchez's arms. "Oh my god, I thought I'd lost you, I thought I'd lost you," she cried, touching his face. "Why are you carrying him? Is he all right? What's wrong with him?"

"He's just fine, ma'am," the chief of police said. "Just twisted his ankle, is all. We'll get him checked out by the paramedics. He'll be right as rain, just as long as he stays clear of these mines." He gave Stan a meaningful glance, and Stan had the decency to look abashed.

"I'm sorry, Mom," Stan said, teary-eyed. "I'm really sorry . . ."

"It's okay, honey," Mom said, sniffing and wiping dirt from his cheek. "I'm just so glad you're okay. I was just scared, I—"

"Evie found me, Mom. I don't know how, but she found me in the dark and got us out."

Mom blinked. "W-what?" she stammered. And then, for the first time, she noticed Evie in her tattered dress, standing just behind them. "Evie?"

"Hi, Mom," Evie said.

Mom was shaking her head, her mouth opening and closing. "But . . . how?" she finally said. Before Evie could think of how to answer, she rushed forward and pulled Evie into her arms.

"Damnedest thing," Sànchez was saying. "No idea how she got down there, but she'd led him almost to the end of the tunnel by the time I found them. We'll need to ask you a few questions later on, Miss Archer, once you're feeling strong enough."

Evie nodded but said nothing. *Even if I did answer their questions*, she thought, *they would never believe me.*

Mom pressed her cheek against Evie's, and the words began to rush out, like water from a dam. "You didn't answer my texts, and then Stan was missing, and I didn't know where you were, either, and I couldn't stop thinking about the last things we said to each other—we were so hateful and angry, and if that had been the last thing I ever said to you, then I don't think I could live with—"

"You don't have to," Evie broke in. "I'm here. We're all here."

Mom cried until Evie begged her to stop. "Mom," she said, wiping tears from her own face. "C'mon, it's okay. Calm down. Your makeup, it's all down your cheeks—"

"I don't care," Mom said. "I don't care how I look or what anyone thinks. Oh honey, I cared so much for so long, and where did it get me? All I care about is you and your brother. Forget the job. Forget the house. I never want to feel that way again. I never want to be that scared again."

"Me neither," Evie whispered.

"I hate to break up this tender moment," Chief Sànchez said, "but I've got to get this young man over to the ambulance to get checked out. How about you, Miss Archer? Do you need medical attention?"

Evie looked up from her mother's embrace and shook her head. "Nothing some coffee and a bagel couldn't fix. Thanks, Mr. Sànchez."

The chief nodded. "My Tina will be happy to know you and your brother are all right," he said, and turned away, carrying Stan toward the flashing lights.

As the personnel around them began to pack up their equipment, Evie said, "Mom, I . . . um, I haven't been entirely honest with you lately." She paused. "I haven't been entirely honest with anyone."

Mom looked at her expectantly.

"Ever since we got to Hobbie House," Evie went on, "I've been . . . seeing things, hearing things. Like before."

Her mother nodded, solemn. "I know," she said.

Evie's eyebrows furrowed. "You know?" she whispered.

"Evie, I haven't exactly been honest with you, either."

Evie stared at her mother in confusion. "What do you mean?"

Mom gave a small, humorless smile. "I believe you. I always have. But I spent years doing my best to convince myself—and you—that I was wrong. Don't forget, I grew up with Martha for a sister. She was always . . . strange. Different. She knew things she shouldn't—couldn't—know. Your grandparents and I, well . . . we did our best to ignore it. 'What would the neighbors think?' That's what they'd say when Martha wasn't there. And when you started talking about the Man in the Red Sweater . . ." She shook her head. "I just knew you were like her. But I thought . . . I thought maybe I could stop it from happening, you know? Cure you of it, like it was some kind of disease. I thought I was doing right by you, taking you to Dr. Mears. But now—" She looked down at the ground.

"You believed me?" Evie said softly.

Mom's lip curled, and she nodded. "I remember back then . . . I was out at a lunch with a friend of mine once, a year or so after everything happened, a real estate agent who worked in the city. I asked her about that house, the one you broke into with your friends. I asked her why no one had bought it all those years—a perfectly good brownstone in Lower Manhattan. She said the last owner was an older man who'd lived alone, a Mr. Peterson. Wife had passed on, no other family to speak of. He just stopped paying his bills one December, and they shut off his heat. After a week or so, the mailman realized he wasn't picking up his mail and alerted the police. They found him inside, sitting in an easy chair, with the remnants of a Christmas dinner on the kitchen table. He was frozen to death. My friend said buyers didn't like that—thought it was too sad, and always ended up not ever making an offer on the house."

"He was wearing a red sweater when they found him," Evie whispered. "Wasn't he?"

Mom looked at the ground. "I'm sorry, Evie. I just wanted you to live a normal life. I just—" She covered her mouth with one hand, shook her head, and then turned and walked away.

"Mom, wait!" Evie said.

Aunt Martha intercepted Mom, and Evie watched the two of them exchange quiet words. Aunt Martha nodded, and Evie watched her mother go lean on their little silver car, her hands on her knees. Aunt Martha walked up to Evie, her face tight with concern.

"Is she okay?" Evie asked.

"She will be," she replied. "She has a lot of guilt to work through."

"She told you?"

Aunt Martha sighed. "She was terrified, waiting here for them to find Stan. All those feelings she's been holding back for who knows how many years . . . they all came pouring out. Guilt for working too hard. Guilt for not working hard enough. Guilt about the divorce. Guilt about you." She cocked her head and looked at Evie as if for the first time. "I always knew you and I shared something special. Being with you always felt a little like being with Holly. I thought she had it, too, you know. The touch."

"She did," Evie said.

Aunt Martha looked at her strangely, a confused smile on her face. "You say that like you know for sure . . ."

"I do know," Evie replied. "I found her, Aunt Martha. I found Holly."

Aunt Martha took a step back from her, her eyes wide. "What?"

"It's a long story, but . . . I found her. Or, I guess she found me."

Aunt Martha's eyes were glassy with tears. "Did you—did she—?"

"She's not coming back," Evie said. "She's gone."

She nodded, and a single tear slipped down her face. "Did she say anything about me?" she asked softly.

"She doesn't blame you for what happened. Not at all," Evie said. She took her aunt's hand in hers. "She just misses you."

Aunt Martha sniffed and took a shuddering breath before wiping her eyes. She squeezed Evie's hand. "Thank you," she whispered. After a moment, she asked, "Is that what all this was about since you arrived in town? The way you were acting? You were so frightened . . ."

Evie nodded. "I know I should have told you, I was just—"

"Trying to protect me?" Aunt Martha broke in.

"Yeah."

Martha laughed. "We really are cut from the same cloth, aren't we? I probably would have done the same thing."

"You did stay here for forty years to watch over the house."

"I did."

"You know, you could move away if you wanted," Evie said. "I have a feeling the house won't be the same as before. I think it might be okay now."

Martha shrugged. "Why would I leave?" she asked. "Everyone in the world I want to be with is here." She put her arm around Evie's shoulders and squeezed. Together, they gazed out over the trees to the town below. It was a little after 3:00 a.m., the darkest part of night—and from up on the mountain Ravenglass was a twinkling quilt of streetlights, nestled quietly in its wooded valley. For a moment, Evie wondered at how she'd managed to travel from the root cellar to where she appeared in the tunnels there on the mountain. It hadn't felt like that far. But then again, she felt a world away from the girl who'd fallen down the rabbit hole back in Hobbie House.

"The tarot reading you gave me," Evie said.

"Yes?"

"Did you choose those cards on purpose? Did you know what was going to happen?"

Aunt Martha shook her head. "No, I never know what's going to happen. I just try to listen to what the universe is telling me, and let them guide me in the right direction. That's all anyone can do, even us. We just hear more than other people do. What happens is up to you. Your choices make your future, not the cards. The cards are just a guide."

"Well, the cards—you—were just what I needed."

Aunt Martha's face looked ethereal in the moonlight, her hair silvered and blowing in the cool breeze. She took a deep breath and sighed. "That is the greatest gift you could give me, sweetheart."

Stan's voice cut through the conversation. "Mom?"

Evie and Aunt Martha turned to see Stan standing near the car with one of the paramedics, a tall woman with brown skin and short, naturally curly hair. Stan had a thin silver blanket wrapped around his shoulders, a pair of crutches, and a bandage wrapped around his ankle. "Other than being dehydrated and a mild sprain on that ankle, your son is doing just fine, Ms. Archer," the paramedic said to Mom. "You can take him home."

"Oh, honey," Mom said, and pulled Stan into her arms again. "I'm so glad you're okay."

"Me too," Stan replied.

"I am absolutely furious at you for going into those mines, but I'm too happy to yell at you right now. So how about a rain check on the yelling?"

"Sounds good, Mom," Stan said with a wry grin.

Aunt Martha and Evie walked over to them, and the four stood together in the darkness as the emergency vehicles and police cars began to pull out of the area and make their way down the mountain. "Let's go home, kids," Mom said.

"Why don't I go with you?" Aunt Martha said suddenly. "Stay awhile."

Mom turned to her, confused. "But I thought—?"

"Things change," Aunt Martha said. "I think it's time that house and I make peace with each other. Don't you?"

Mom beamed. "I can't wait to show you what I've done with the place. I'm thinking of taking down a wall to make the living and dining area more airy—"

"As long as there's coffee in the morning, you can show me whatever you want," Aunt Martha said.

They all fell silent as the little silver car made its way down the mountain. They passed the road up to Ravenglass High School, dark and quiet now that the dancing was done. They passed Dr. Rockwell's office, the general store, the Blue River Inn—all the windows black. The neon-yellow bird still flew in space over Birdie's Diner, closed for the night. Something walked across their path as they reached the narrow lane, and Mom slowed the car to let it pass. A cat, maybe?

Hobbie House waited for them, a light shining in the kitchen. *Did I leave that on?* Evie wondered. She couldn't recall. It didn't matter. All that mattered now was that it was over.

They were home.

27

Day broke on Sunday morning—clear, cold, and blue. It was almost 9:00 a.m. by the time Evie opened her eyes, the bright sunlight shining through her bedroom window. Her body felt light and fresh. She looked at her hand where the angry rash had been and found that it was smooth and white once more. The pain had gone.

There was a warm spot at the foot of the bed where Schrödinger must have slept, but he had disappeared. *Off mole hunting*, Evie thought. She wasn't alone in the room, though. Stan dozed on the floor next to her bed in a nest of blankets, looking small and pale in his pajama pants and white undershirt. After they'd gotten home last night, he and Evie had dragged his bedding into her room and he'd settled down next to her bed, just like he used to do when he was little. He'd fallen asleep in seconds—Evie must have, too. She'd spent the whole night in blissful, dreamless sleep.

The patchwork dress was in a heap on the floor where she'd dropped it the night before. Slipping soundlessly out of bed, Evie tiptoed around Stan's nest and picked it up. It was filthy from the mines, the skirt ripped in three places—again. Evie sighed. Despite the fact that the dress had been a product of her terrifying connection with Holly—and by extension, with Sarah Flower—Evie still felt an affection for it. She'd spent weeks creating it, and it was unique and beautiful, her very own patchwork dress. She decided that once things calmed down a bit, she'd clean and repair it once more, in Holly's memory. The Lost Girl of Ravenglass was no longer her enemy—though she'd be hard pressed to call her a friend.

But she was, after all, family.

Evie opened the door to the closet and hung the dress on a hanger alongside her other handmade dresses. She was about to close the door when she remembered Holly telling her to "look in the mousehole" in her bedroom to find the notes she'd left behind about Sarah Flower. Evie hadn't had any idea what she'd meant at the time, but standing at the closet, she remembered finding Schrödinger in there that first day they arrived, with a dead mole in his mouth. She'd always wondered where the mole had come from, until she realized that perhaps there was a way inside, up through the dark old bowels of Hobbie House.

Kneeling, Evie quietly cleared away the suitcases and boxes on the floor and groped around in the dim light for an opening in the wall. When she felt around the hardwood floor, she discovered a small, round hole in one of the slats—like a missing knot in the wood. Hooking a finger into the hole, she pulled, and the short slat lifted away, revealing a hole. She reached inside, and sure enough, there was a rubber-banded packet of papers there, thick and dusty. She brought it out of the closet into the light, blew off the dust, and sat cross-legged on the floor to inspect it. There were copies of photographs, pages from old books—all accompanied in the margins by Holly's neat handwriting in blue ink. It would take hours to go through it all. As she was flipping through the pages, one slipped out of the pile. It was a photocopy of an old portrait, a blurry picture of a little girl in a bonnet. A line of text was printed underneath: SARAH ELIZABETH FLOWER, RAVENGLASS, MASSACHUSETTS, THE YEAR OF OUR LORD EIGHTEEN HUNDRED AND FIFTY-ONE.

"Mmm." A thick, sleepy voice broke her concentration. Stan was awake and blinking at her from across the room. "What are you doing?"

Evie pushed the pile of papers back into the closet and shut the door. "Nothing important," she said. "How are you feeling?"

Stan shrugged into his pillow. "Okay, I guess," he said. "Hungry."

"You should probably take a shower first. You look like a chimney sweep."

"Yeah, well . . . you don't look much better."

"I'll go after you," Evie said. She started to get up, and then paused. "Stan . . . ," she said.

Stan sat up and hugged his knees into his chest. "What?" he said.

Evie took a deep breath and said, "I'm . . . I'm sorry I didn't protect you."

His eyebrows furrowed. "From what?"

"From danger, from those stupid friends of yours, from . . . I don't know, everything. You're my little brother, I should have put you first. But I didn't. I was so caught up in my own problems that I ignored what was going on with you."

Stan stared at her for a moment and then scoffed. "There you go again, making everything about you."

"W-what?" Evie stammered.

"*You* didn't make me angry—well, sometimes you do, but still—*you* didn't make me set a house on fire, and *you* didn't make me go down into the mines. I did that. I was pissed off at everything, and I just . . . I don't know. I just didn't care anymore." He looked up at her. "It's not your job to protect me, and it's not your fault that all this happened. It's mine. So just . . . let me have it, okay? You don't need to fix everything. Especially the things you didn't break."

Evie nodded, swallowing the lump in her throat. "Just do me one favor," she said, her voice husky with emotion.

"What?"

"Stay away from Dylan Sullivan. He's bad news, Stan. Trust me."

Stan made a face. "Don't push your luck. Aren't you supposed to keep your friends close and your enemies closer?"

"Just be careful. Please."

Stan stood up and gathered his black hoodie and jeans from where they were piled next to him like a discarded snakeskin. "You've been seeing things again, haven't you?" he muttered.

Evie looked at the floor and nodded.

"Is it gone, whatever it was? Did you make it go away?"

"I think so," she replied.

Stan hugged his clothes to him and nodded back. "Good," he said. "Good." He slowly walked out of the room. A minute later, she heard the shower turn on.

The smell of coffee lured Evie downstairs. Aunt Martha was sitting at the kitchen table in Mom's lavender nightgown, the Sunday newspaper spread out in front of her. She was working on the crossword puzzle, tapping a ballpoint pen against her teeth. Without the trappings of her psychic persona, she looked weirdly normal. When Evie walked into the kitchen, Aunt Martha's eyes lit up. "Oh, Evie, you're up! 'It's under the beach umbrella.' Five letters."

Evie thought for a minute before answering. "Shade?" she said.

Aunt Martha smiled. "Ah! Yes, that's it. Of course . . . Why didn't I think of that . . ." She wrote it in with the pen and moved on to the next clue. She looked up at Evie, her eyes soft. "How are you doing today, honey?"

"Better," Evie said truthfully. "A lot better." She moved to the coffee machine and poured herself a cup. "How does it feel being back in the house?"

Aunt Martha sighed deeply, a small smile touching her lips. "It feels . . . peaceful," she said.

"Yeah," Evie agreed. "And quiet. Really quiet. Where's Mom?"

"Out on the porch," Aunt Martha replied. She took a bite of her bagel and settled back into her crossword puzzle.

Evie made her way outside to the porch, where Mom was sitting with a steaming cup of coffee, staring at her phone. She looked up with a start when the kitchen door clicked shut behind Evie. "Good morning, you," Mom said with a tight smile. She was her neat and put-together self again, but dark circles still ringed her eyes. "Get some sleep?"

"Lots," Evie said, sitting down in a rocking chair next to her. They both sipped their coffees silently for a few minutes, staring out into the naked woods. A flock of honking Canada geese passed by overhead, flying south for the winter.

"I just got off the phone with your father," Mom finally said. The words dropped into the silence like a boulder into a lake. Evie's pulse quickened.

"I told him what happened," Mom went on. "He had a right to know."

Evie nodded, staring into the black circle of her coffee mug. "So?" she asked.

"He's still in Paris, but he's making plans to fly home early. Maybe tomorrow. Then he's going to get the car from the city and drive up here. To see you. And Stan."

Evie sat up in her chair. "He's coming here? To Hobbie House?"

Mom nodded. "It'll be fine, honey. He says you haven't been answering his calls or messages, so he just wants to see that you guys are all right."

The idea of her father in the house filled Evie with a mixture of dread and anticipation. What would she say to him when he walked through that door?

"Okay," she said. "Okay." She could feel something welling up inside her. A memory kept hidden for so long, now out in the open, fresh and raw.

What is wrong with you?

"I'm sorry, Mom," she blurted suddenly.

Mom sat up and looked at her. "Sorry? For what? It's me that's sorry. I still feel so awful about—"

"It was my fault," Evie interrupted. "The divorce. If it weren't for me and my . . . problems, you and Dad might still be— We all might still b—" She stopped, unable to finish the sentence.

Mom set down her cup on the little side table and took Evie's hands in hers. "No. No, no, no. That isn't right. That isn't true. Why would you say that?"

"Because, because—" Tears welled up in Evie's eyes and began to spill over the edges and down her cheeks. "Because I broke the table," she said, feeling stupid. "That night, with the spaghetti dinner—you and Dad were fighting about me and how hard I'd made everything, and then I broke the table and . . . and nothing was ever the same after that. Everything was wrong after that."

Mom closed her eyes and hung her head, not saying anything for a moment. The silence was filled only by the sound of Evie's sniffling and the birds. "Oh, Evie," she finally whispered. "You didn't break us, honey. Your dad and me, our marriage was broken long before that night. Maybe it always was. And we weren't fighting about you that night, it was about . . . well, it was about everything. I'm so sorry you had to hear it, and I'm so sorry you've been blaming yourself all this time." She smoothed Evie's hair gently, tucking a stray lock behind her ear. "It'll be . . . awkward when your dad comes to visit, but we'll make the best of it. He and I might not agree on a lot of things, but there's something we'll always agree on, and that's you and your brother. And you two are a hell of a lot stronger than glass. Okay?"

Evie smiled back, wiping the tears away. "Okay."

"Hey," Mom said in a cheery voice that Evie didn't mind

hearing for once. "I don't know about you, but I'm tired of eating bagels for breakfast. Do you feel up to running over to Birdie's and picking us all up something?"

"Sure," Evie replied. "I'll just take a quick shower and get dressed. Any requests?"

Mom shrugged. "Surprise me," she said with a grin.

The diner was bustling with the Sunday morning after-church crowd, and Evie had to squeeze herself through three families waiting for tables to get to the register. It was loud with the chatter of patrons, the same oldies radio station playing on the sound system. Birdie stood at her station in her bright yellow apron like the captain of a ship, calling out orders to the cooks in the kitchen, and helping the waitresses run the plates filling up the pass. As always, the place smelled spicy and savory and sweet all at once, and Evie's mouth began to water.

"Ah, Evie," she said when Evie stepped up to the counter. "You look good for once. You here to eat or take away?"

"Take away," Evie replied, laughing a little to herself. "And thanks, I *feel* good for once."

"What do you want?"

"Surprise me," Evie said, echoing her mother's phrase.

"I can do that," she said, and shouted an order to the cooks. "Five minutes," she told Evie.

Evie nodded. Mama Bird was in her chair nearby, looking at

Evie with curiosity. "Hi, Mrs. Kim," Evie said with a wave. "How are you today?"

Mama Bird stared at her with cloudy eyes, and then at her daughter. "Birdie, who is this girl?" she muttered. "I've never seen her before."

Birdie scoffed. "Oh, Umma—yes, you have. That's Evie Archer. She's the girl living in Hobbie House, remember? We drove her home the other day."

Mama Bird shook her head. "No, that was someone else. Someone else." She stuck out her wizened hand and took Evie's. "Nice to meet you, Evie Archer," she said.

Birdie sighed, looked at Evie, and shrugged.

"Nice to meet you, too, Mrs. Kim," Evie said.

A voice shouted over the diner crowd's chatter. "Hey! Evie!" Evie turned toward the sound to see Tina sitting in her favorite booth with her laptop in front of her.

"Oh! Hey!" Evie nodded to Mama Bird and made her way over to where Tina was sitting. On the oldies radio, a new song began to play. "I once had a gown," a crooning voice sang. "It was almost new, oh the daintiest thing, it was sweet Alice blue . . ."

"Oh my god, I never expected to see you here," Tina said when Evie sat down. She looked at Evie as if she'd risen from the dead. "Are you okay? I heard some crazy things about what went down at homecoming last night. Kimber was acting super weird, raving about seeing a monster or something. And then your brother? My dad said they got him out, and that you were down there with him? What the heck is going on, Evie?"

Evie bit her lip. She thought about Mom, Aunt Martha, and

Stan waiting for her at home. She was finally going to have a normal day, and she didn't want to waste a single minute of it talking about the past. "I'll tell you everything—just not now. But only if you promise to believe me."

"*With little forget-me-nots placed here and there, when I had it on, oh, I walked on the air!*" the song went on.

Tina sighed, running her fingers through her sea-green curls. "After what I've heard . . . I'm willing to believe whatever you say. But listen—"

"Thanks, Tina. That means a lot to me. I'd love to chat, but I really should be getting home as soon as my food's ready, so—" Evie got up and had started to turn away when Tina grabbed her arm.

"Evie, wait," she said. "Please. I've got to ask you something."

A chill climbed Evie's spine. She swallowed. "What is it?"

Tina licked her lips. "Have you heard from Desmond today?"

"*And it wore, and it wore, and it wore, 'til it went, and it wasn't no more . . .*"

Evie blinked. "Desmond? No, not today." She pulled her phone out of her pocket and pulled up her text messages. When she'd found it in the kitchen when they got home the night before, it had worked just fine. She'd sent a message to Demond before going to bed, just to tell him that she was okay, and she really wanted to talk to him. The message was unread. "I was going to call him after breakfast, maybe meet up somewhere, but—"

"Evie." Tina's eyes were full of worry. "No one's seen him since last night. And he's not answering his phone." She shifted in her seat. "Someone . . . someone said that after you left, Desmond said he was going to go after you. That he knew you'd find a way down into the mines, and that he couldn't let you do it alone, so—"

Evie felt the blood freeze in her veins. "No," Evie murmured. "No . . ."

She remembered the voice, down in the shadow land. The voice calling her name. She'd thought it was Desmond, but nothing was real down there. It couldn't really have been him, calling out to her from the darkness, could it?

"My dad was over at the Kings' this morning," Tina was saying, though her voice seemed far away. "Everyone is looking for him . . ."

What had Holly said, right before Evie left?

"Sarah and I, we're not the only ones down here."

Desmond was lost.

But something in the shadows had found him.

The song on the radio reached a crescendo as Evie stumbled, catching herself on the edge of the table.

"'Til it wilted, I wore it, I'll always adore it, my sweet little Alice blue gown!"

ACKNOWLEDGMENTS

Writing this book was a leap of faith. It was unlike anything I'd ever written before, and it came with a legacy that this story needed to honor. The fact that it's in your hands today is thanks in no small part to a group of people without whom its existence would never have been possible. First, I would like to thank CloudCo for entrusting me with Holly and this amazing project, and Benj Dawe, for his brilliant concept and the haunting cover art that captivates anyone who looks at it. Thanks also to the entire team at Penguin Workshop and Penguin Teen, who have supported this book beyond my wildest dreams. Unending gratitude to my agent, Allison Hellegers, whose belief in me has made so many dreams come true; my editor and Holly's biggest cheerleader, Gabriela Taboas Zayas, who has put as much of her own heart into this story as I have; and my intrepid team of readers, Mania Jabès, Adam Corpora, Heather Allen, and Brittany Kozlewski, whose careful eyes pored over these pages, and who made me feel like this book was something special. People say that writing is a solitary endeavor, but I have never felt alone on this journey. And what a wonderful, surprising journey it has been. Who knows what will happen next?